THE
QUASI-CRYSTAL

THE QUASI-CRYSTAL

J. D. RASCH

LAMINA PRESS
RYE BROOK, NEW YORK

THE QUASI-CRYSTAL
© 2025, J. D. Rasch. All rights reserved.

Published by Lamina Press, Rye Brook, New York

978-1-962247-04-7 (paperback)
978-1-962247-05-4 (eBook)

Learn more at JDRasch.com

Publication managed by AuthorImprints.com

Rogi kept thinking of the teachings of the Koan and the Talum. It was the Talum that focused on finding the Tree. The Koan gave lessons on how to behave in society. Over the years the wizards had equated the two—to find the Tree, to obtain enlightenment, you needed to bring harmony. That's what the wizards thought, that's what drove them. But what if that wasn't true? What if there was no need for the Tree?

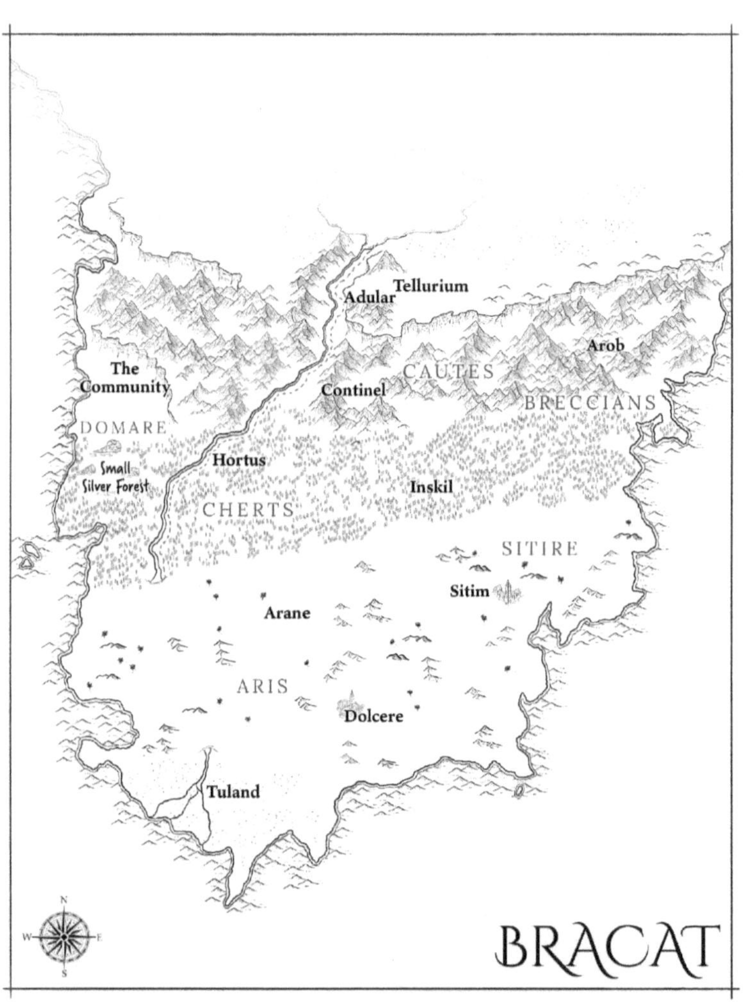

Tellurium
Adular
Arob
The Community
CAUTES
Continel
BRECCIANS
DOMARE
Hortus
Small Silver Forest
Inskil
CHERTS
SITIRE
Sitim
Arane
ARIS
Dolcere
Tuland
N
W
E
S
BRACAT

The Fog
Ran-dahl's Island
Docks
Market
Castle
Valki Institute
OGNITA CITY
Van Stronghold
N
W
E
S
OGNITA

AUTHOR'S NOTE

I TRY TO HAVE A theme for each book in The Wanderer series. Each theme is something that I'm trying to work out for myself—that's why I used the term *Koan*, a paradoxical anecdote or riddle in Zen Buddhism, for the name of the holy book. *The Quasi-Crystal* is mostly about a new place, Ognita, but also looks at Bracat to see what happens as time moves on from "The Moment," a pivotal scene at the end of *The Silver Forest, Book Two* that changed how people thought. Can such a change be maintained, or do we just revert back to our old ways?

This is how *The Quasi-Crystal* begins, but there is another theme in the story: knowledge versus ignorance. One of the main characters in the book is the fog. It is the fog of the unknown or the fog of ignorance. In fact, *The Fog* is what I originally titled this book, until one of my daughters objected, saying it needed the same number of words as the first book, so I tried to think what title would get across the message of the book.

The Quasi-Crystal title came about as a metaphor of sorts. A quasi-crystal is a real thing in science. According to the Encyclopedia Britannica: "Quasi-crystals contain an ordered structure, but the patterns are subtle and do not recur at precisely regular intervals." I took this to mean that they exist in two dimensions at once, that of a crystal and that of a solid. So, in the book, the quasi-crystal is a bridge between two worlds.

But this isn't the only element of science in the story. There are many references to physics and physicists—although names of the physicists have been altered so they wouldn't get in the way of the reading experience. I couldn't get in all my favorite scientists as some of their names would be difficult to hide, but there are many I did include. If you're up to it, see if you can find any of the hidden names! I'd love to hear from you if you do.

The Wanderer series has been quite a ride for me—I never thought the first two books would see the light of day, but they have, and here we are with book three, *The Quasi-Crystal,* with more in the works. Thank you for joining this world, and I hope you enjoy the story.

CHAPTER 1

RAN-DAHL LOOKED OUT ON THE whirlpools and eddies that surrounded the island where she was imprisoned. It was either stay on the island or be locked away in some damp cell, or maybe just disappear like so many of her colleagues, her friends. She didn't expect rescue, nor did she want it anymore. She had brought nothing with her except her thoughts. Even King Ruvbain II couldn't take that from her.

No guards hampered her, no shackles bound her. Ruvbain thought it too dangerous to leave anyone with her—anyone who could be convinced to help, to spread the word. Yet Ruvbain didn't get rid of her. He knew he still might need her knowledge of the fog. She had studied the fog long before Ruvbain II had taken over from his father. He had even been her student at the Valki Institute, and a promising one at that. She wondered what had happened to turn him against knowledge.

She had been here for so long. Sometimes she wondered what she looked like after all this time exposed to the wind and sun. She remembered being beautiful, once. All that seemed so trivial now. She had no use of beauty here, and her solitude had allowed her to develop her other capabilities.

She thought of the island not as a friend—it was too bleak for that—but as a rival that had to be mastered. She knew its secrets, where it hid its fresh water, which plants were edible. She knew its seasons and how to survive its severe weather. Her isolation allowed her the time she needed. Time to develop her mind, time to study the fog.

She still needed help. No matter how much she studied, she couldn't penetrate the fog. It was a place of uncertainty, of mystery. Her research had disturbed Ruvbain, and when his father died and he had taken over, her colleagues had started to disappear. When Gaelil no longer appeared to teach his lectures, she'd known she didn't have long, and she'd read all she could about the fog in the Institute's library. The books gave the history of the fog—they said it had been small once. But none explained what it was.

When they came for her, she'd reached out her mind to her friends and told them to hide. They would only communicate mind to mind. They called themselves the Fog. When she'd found her mentor, Gaelil, he was dying in a cold, damp cell. They exchanged ideas about the fog until, one day, she posed a question on how to penetrate the fog. He had said it was an interesting question, and then he was gone.

CHAPTER 2

HER DECISION TO TAKE THE relics from her village had not been popular. But they were hers—well, not exactly hers, but more hers than anyone else's. Besides, she felt the need, or more like a compulsion, to return them. There had been no argument, even though she knew the small assembly of villagers hadn't liked the idea of her striking off on her own to Dolcere. But she was the leader of the village, just as she had been the leader of the thieves, and the villagers deferred to her. She wanted to go to Dolcere, the city of the Prophet. She had heard the ones who had killed Gital were there. She wanted to speak with them and hoped returning the relics would give her access.

There had been thieves on the roads when she passed through the forest, but they mostly were her friends. Now she was in the desert. She should have listened to the traveler who had sold his talize to her and sworn he would never brave it again. He'd warned her about the blowing sands, the nightly howls of the wolves and the soft sands that could suck you down. She ran her hand over the soft, deep crimson fabric of the talize that protected her. But the sands found their way into any slight opening and cut every exposed part of her body. She bore the scars of her travel on her legs, and even her face was scarred.

She lost half her food when she traveled too near the soft sands. She had taken out some of her provisions for a midday meal while she rested from the burning sun. It attracted wosakes, the snake-like animals beneath the soft sands. Pom barely escaped with her life. Then came her problems with the wolves. She was more prepared for their nightly scavenging, hiding her provisions when she slept, pitching her tent on rocky outcroppings that would hide her from view. One night, however, she didn't find a protected place to sleep and the wolves found her. She heard them first—or, more exactly, sensed their presence—and that's what saved her. She managed to grab water, and the relics. There was no time to take down the tent or pack any gear. She heard the wolves ripping through her belongings. She never turned back.

She no longer had her tent to block the blowing sands and keep the frigid desert nights at bay. She rationed her water so it would last the four days left of her journey, and she felt weak from the lack of food.

Exhausted and bloodied, she entered Dolcere, the city of the wizards, scarred and hungry. Nobody welcomed her as she walked toward the Tower of the Wizards.

She put on the white robe that had been packed with the relics. She had been told the white showed that you knew nothing, that you were open to knowledge, to learning. She approached a guard at the tower.

"I have come to see the . . ." She didn't know what to call them.

"The Keepers?" the guard asked.

Pom nodded.

"So have all these other pilgrims."

Pom gazed around the courtyard. There were hundreds of white-robed supplicants.

"Are they all waiting for an audience with the Keepers?" Pom asked in a dry, croaking voice.

"Most. Some have come to see the Dark Wizard."

Pom had not heard that term before and looked quizzically at the guard.

"The wizard from the north."

Still no recognition.

"Malzus."

Pom knew this name. "What does he teach?"

"Not sure. Nobody has been let in to see him. I don't think the wizards would allow it."

"I didn't think they came here anymore."

"Sometimes. Although I hear they spend most of their time up north, looking for the Prophet."

"I met him once."

"Everyone says that."

"I suppose, but I really did. He was with the Keepers. But they weren't Keepers back then, they were soldiers."

"So you met the Prophet and the three Keepers?"

"No."

"I didn't think so."

"I mean there were four of them, plus the Prophet."

The guard looked at her as if seeing her for the first time. "Not many people know that."

"Know what?"

"That there are four Keepers."

"Why not?"

"Because there are only three here in Dolcere."

"What happened to the fourth?"

"He went home."

"To where?"

"You tell me."

"Well, one was an Aris, Areana; another a Chert, that would be Bradoc; and the third was a Caute, and his name was Wetell."

"Those are the Keepers in Dolcere."

"The last one was a funny one. He wasn't like the others. If I remember correctly, he was from Tuland. Remer was his name."

The guard nodded, as if she had passed some sort of test. "What do you want of the Keepers?"

"Nothing."

"Then why have you come?"

"I've come to return something to them. Something I had taken some time ago."

"Let me see," the guard insisted.

Reluctantly Pom opened her satchel. The guard peered in and then looked at Pom. "Come back tomorrow at first light, and I'll get you an audience with the Keepers. And make sure to bring the bag."

This surprised Pom, but she was glad she'd succeeded so easily. Now she needed to find a place to rest and maybe get some food. Her weariness was overwhelming. She turned back to the guard, but he was no longer there.

"Excuse me." She approached a group of the white-clad pilgrims. They opened their ranks to admit her. "I've just come off the desert and am in desperate need of food and shelter."

A woman came over to Pom and rested a comforting hand on her shoulder. "You may join us at the hostel. It's where most of the pilgrims stay." She smiled at Pom, a warm, welcoming smile. "My name is Calb."

"I'm Pom."

Other introductions were made. Calb was a Sitire; a man in the group, Tarn, was from Domare; and there was a woman, Anter, who was Aris.

As the group made their way to the hostel, Calb explained who they were. "We came to see the Keepers, but that rarely occurs. Mostly we come for the other Seekers."

"Why are you called that? I thought you were pilgrims," Pom asked.

"Pilgrims travel to worship. We look to understand."

"Understand what?"

Calb let out a warm laugh. "You've just uncovered our biggest controversy. Understand what, indeed? The simplest answer is, everything and anything."

"Some seek to understand how Asmar connected us. They want to recreate the Moment," Anter offered.

"You called him Asmar."

"Yes. The Seekers—or I should say the real Seekers—don't call him the Prophet. He was—I mean *is*—a great man, a great thinker. But a prophet? There is no evidence of that. Many here"—Calb looked around at other white-robed figures they were passing—"maybe even most, have turned Asmar into a prophet. But based on the writings of his disciples, this was not a categorization Asmar would have accepted."

"What writings?"

"Well, the three Keepers have written some. And then there are those who met Asmar during his quest. Many of them are Seekers. I'll introduce you to some at the hostel tonight. But the most prolific writer about Asmar's life and philosophy has to be the great scholar of Tuland, Remer."

"And he's not in Dolcere," Pom stated, confirming what the guard had indicated.

"He visits occasionally, but he spends most of his time in Tuland, studying, teaching, and thinking."

"I met him." Pom was not sure she should have said that. She needed Calb's help and wasn't sure if this might spark some jealousy.

"Excellent! This is certainly a stroke of good fortune."

"How so?"

"We are trying to put together the puzzle of Asmar's life and his conversion. The more we know about the period before, the more we understand. When we get to the hostel, and after you have eaten and rested, we will make good use of you."

The sun was setting, turning the desert sky a fiery red. The air cooled the city, but the deep chill was moderated by the waters of the oasis. Pom was glad to be away from the naked expanse of the desert.

"This is where we live." Calb put her arm around Pom's waist and led her into the one-story building that was the color of the desert. Pom felt safer now than she had in some time.

Dinner was simple, but tasty. Her hide shoes had been taken from her and replaced by comfortable ones made of a desert plant.

"If you're going to see the Keepers, wear the cloth shoes," Calb advised her.

"Why?"

"You know very little of the Teachings for one who has met him."

"I met him early in his quest. But even then, I could tell there was something special about him."

"Very well, let me explain some of the basics. The core tenet is to cause no suffering. We try to keep to that as much as possible. Of course, different people have different interpretations of just how far that goes. But mostly we agree on a few key actions, including not eating or wearing animals. We also reach out to our fellows to help reduce suffering. What that means is even more open to argument."

After dinner she was introduced to the other Seekers.

"This is Nomey, a Domarian. She is one of the High Seekers because of her close relationship with Asmar."

"How did you know him?" Pom asked.

"When I was a child . . ." Nomey began.

Pom was surprised that this young girl would speak of her childhood, when she was barely removed from it.

Nomey started again. "When I was a small child, Asmar came to our village and healed me. My mother was enlisted to help him heal others in our village until the High Priest, out of jealousy, chased Asmar away. Asmar left my mother with *The Book of Healing*, which was an odd thing to do."

"Why so?"

"Because my mother couldn't read. But from the day he left the book in our care, my mother gave me two jobs. The first was to keep the book safe, and the second was to learn to read the book. I am glad to say that I have accomplished both." Nomey smiled warmly.

"And your mother?"

Nomey's smile disappeared and she involuntarily looked to the sky. "She's no longer with us, I'm afraid. I couldn't help her when she became ill, the cure for her sickness wasn't in the book." Nomey paused. "But now it is." She smiled.

"I don't understand?"

"Now it's in the book." Pom still looked confused, so Nomey explained, "The cure to my mother's disease, it's now in the book."

"How did it get there?"

"Why, I wrote it."

"Yes, but where did you find it?"

"I didn't find it, I figured it out. And when I got it right, I put it in the book."

Calb explained further, "You asked before what we seek, and this is your answer. Nomey seeks cures. She studies plants and how people become sick. She has set up clinics to treat people who need help, and she teaches others to do what she does."

"And they teach me as well," Nomey added.

"Of course. Others study their own minds. They go deep into meditation and reach out."

"Like wizards?" Pom asked.

"Kind of like that. We have learned that wizards are not as special as we once thought, although they are more learned. As Seekers we want to reclaim what we had forgotten, like how to build the great castle of the Sitire or the fortress at Tellurium. We want to know how the roads were built to last so long. We want to understand the land and even the stars."

"And how are you doing?" Pom asked.

Calb laughed. "We're just starting. It's all so new and we have so much to learn."

Pom then told the Seekers her story. How she had stopped Asmar and his party in the forest, intending to rob them. But Pom had found something special in Asmar and brought them to the encampment, against the objections of Gital. She told of what happened to Gital, how the Cherts had killed him. How after Gital's murder, she had stripped the travelers of their weapons.

"This is excellent," Calb exclaimed. "We had heard about the Keepers being disarmed, but we never thought we would meet the one who disarmed them. This was one of the pivotal moments of the Transformation."

Pom could barely keep her eyes open. All this information was intriguing, but she couldn't concentrate. Calb saw her weariness and showed her to a small but comfortable room in the hostel.

In the morning, new robes had been laid out for her, along with fabric foot coverings and finely woven undergarments. Everything clean and fresh, a new beginning. When she entered the common room, breakfast was ready. She was served her food as a sign of respect for her status. Pom was not sure she liked being catered to like this.

Pom got to the courtyard early. The previous night at the hostel had been strange. She hadn't thought about learning before. Sure, everyone learned the basics, depending on what you did. She had learned farming and hunting from her parents, before they were killed, and Gital had taught her how to be a thief, before he was killed. But to learn new things, things that you didn't need right away—that was new.

Pom shivered in the cold air of the early morning. The guard had not yet arrived, and only a few Seekers had assembled. She recognized some from the hostel. Calb explained that they called themselves the Followers of the Prophet. When they prayed, they faced Tuland, in the south. Another group, Calb explained with a disdain she tried to hide, called themselves the New Followers of the Prophet. The main difference, at least as far as Calb had found, was that they faced north, toward the Silver Forest and the Golden Tree, when they prayed.

The air warmed, and finally Pom's patience was rewarded as the guard appeared. He seemed surprised to see her.

"Well, the Keepers have agreed to see you." There was something odd in the way the guard spoke.

She realized what it was and said, "You weren't going to bring me to the Keepers, were you?"

The guard stood silently at this accusation.

"But why?" Then the pieces started to come together. "You wanted what's in the bag. You were going to take them and sell them." As a former thief, she shouldn't have been surprised by this, but she was. She went on, "You do this often, don't you? Take things from Seekers, promise them an audience. What do you tell them when they're turned away?" Pom knew she was right. It was as if she could read the guard's emotions. Right now it was pretty plain that he was exceedingly uncomfortable.

"Nothing. We let them hang around, and eventually they get tired and leave."

"Do the Keepers see any of them?"

"The Keepers tell us who they want to see. They know who is here and they tell us who to bring."

"And what do they say about what you do to the others?"

"They don't care."

"So you do what you want?"

"Look, I don't know why I'm tellin' you all this. If the Keepers don't care, why should you? If you want to see them, follow me. If not, go home." The guard turned and walked into the tower.

Pom froze at first, thinking this was a trap, but her instincts told her it was safe.

She was led into a small, unadorned room that had a dirty window overlooking an inner square. She stared out at the paved yard and saw a funny-looking wooden machine with arms protruding from it, some high and others low. The wood was rotting and some of the arms were falling off.

A door opened, but nobody entered. Pom waited, but still nobody appeared. Finally, she decided to see where the door led and entered a large, crystal-lined chamber that gave off a golden light. Seated at one end were three robed figures, one woman and two men.

"Why have you come?" the woman asked.

Pom was startled by the comment.

"Forgive me." The woman began again, somewhat more kindly. "We accept few visitors these days and my manners are suffering. I remember you." She continued, "You are the thief."

"I was."

"Was?"

"I was a thief. Ever since . . ." Pom struggled to remember the word people used.

"The Moment," the woman added.

"Yes, the Moment. Since then, I've settled down."

The woman nodded. "Why have you come?"

Pom paused before asking, "Why did you agree to see me?"

One of the men, the larger of the two, answered, "We thought you had something important for us. We can sense your mind."

"Like the wizards?"

The third of the Keepers answered, "No, not like them. They can invade your mind. We do not."

Pom was struck by the careful wording. "Do not? Or cannot?"

"That is an interesting question," he responded. "I don't know how to answer. We have never tried, so there is no way to tell."

"Now, as for you"—the woman closed her eyes as if trying to recall something—"Pom, I believe, is your name."

"Yes," Pom said. "And you are Areana, Bradoc, and Prince Wetell."

Wetell replied, "I prefer not using the honorific."

"The what?"

"The title 'prince.' I don't want to use that."

"Why not?"

Wetell sighed. "I have learned things since the Moment, and one is that I don't want to be a prince."

"But someone needs to lead."

"Possibly, at least for now. I leave that task to my father and brother."

"But—" Pom began to argue.

Bradoc raised a hand to silence her. "We can debate Wetell's philosophy some other time. We have explained why we brought you here. Now, why did you want to see us?"

"To return something to you."

"What do you have of ours?" Bradoc asked with some trepidation.

Pom took the burden off her shoulder and removed three parcels. She unwrapped each slowly. The first was a crystal sword forged by the Aris. As it was freed from its covering, small rainbows glistened on its surface. Areana gripped the arms of her chair, willing herself to remain immovable. The second package was a gem-encrusted sword made of a blood-red crystal mined and carved by the Cautes. But this sword belonged not to the former prince but to Bradoc, given to him by Wetell's father, Lord Montan. Bradoc rose to his feet, attempting to speak. No sound emerged. The final package contained a simple bow of finely crafted wood. Wetell, the calmest of the Keepers, sat straighter at its appearance.

Pom didn't understand. She had thought the Keepers would be pleased at the return of what had been their prized possessions. Bradoc approached the blood-red sword. Pom felt a coldness enter her and backed away. But the coldness was not coming from Bradoc, who stared at the sword, then knelt slowly, grasped the hilt, and raised it with the practiced grip of a soldier.

"If you have a weapon, you will use it," he whispered. Bradoc waved the sword overhead.

Use it! The command was meant for Bradoc, but Pom sensed it as well.

Put it down! This thought emanated from Wetell, who sat with his eyes closed, concentrating.

Areana echoed Wetell's command. *Put it down.*

Bradoc approached Pom, sword raised. She had nowhere to go. In their last encounter, she'd had her band of outlaws to protect her, but now it was just her and Bradoc, and she was no match for the Chert general. She felt the cold stone pressing against her back as the sword descended.

"Don't!" Pom yelled. She felt a dark force pushing Bradoc on. He and the other Keepers were trying to fight this force, but it wasn't enough. Pom pushed back against the darkness. A loud crash came from her right side. She waited for the pain, she waited to collapse. Nothing happened. Opening her eyes, she saw Bradoc returning to his seat, the sword embedded in the wooden floor at her side. The voice pushing Bradoc on had ceased.

"We don't allow weapons in here," Bradoc said simply. He stared icily, his head in his hands.

Areana approached her rainbow sword, her eyes unfocused. The mysterious voice pushed her forward. *Pick up the sword*, it commanded. She grasped the sword, and as she raised it, the colors flowed out.

Pom's hands shook. There was some force in this room, a dark force she had to stop. Rather than yelling out loud, she closed her eyes and thought, *Leave them alone!* The dark force withdrew.

Areana's eyes cleared. "I was hoping never to see this again, particularly here." She ran her hand lovingly down the blade, slicing it open. Pom felt the darkness creep back, but she let it pass through her and it dissipated. Areana's hand dripped with the dark red of her blood. Instinctively, Pom rushed to the wounded Keeper.

Areana held up her bloodied hand. "Stop! Do not approach." Then, grabbing the hilt with one hand and the blade with the other, she brought the weapon across her knee. The sword shattered into two parts. Areana repeated this again and again until the sword was no more. Tiny prisms lay scattered about the floor. When she was done, the sword's power over her was broken.

"That must hurt terribly," Pom said in amazement.

"In ways you probably can't imagine," Areana said as she limped back to her seat.

Pom stared at the prince, at Wetell, who rose and stood straight backed, trying not to move toward his bow.

I can't. The icy voice had softened. *I'm sorry . . .* the voice communicated, and then withdrew.

The darkness lifted, and Wetell calmly walked to the bow. He picked up a shard of the rainbow sword. This small piece of the whole gave off a beautiful and full spectrum of light. Wetell used it to slice the string of the bow, rendering it useless.

"I never liked swords very much—bows are much easier." He looked at Pom. "Perhaps I should explain."

"There's no need." Pom bowed her head deeply, hoping that showing deference would placate the Keepers.

"You've done us a great favor once again," Wetell went on.

"Again?"

"Yes. Last time you relieved us of our weapons. Without that, we could not have continued on our quest. You freed us from our past. For that we are grateful."

"I had no idea."

"You showed us kindness," Areana said, holding back her pain.

"I sent you out into the wilderness unarmed."

"If we had been armed, we would have been killed by the Domare."

"I didn't know that at the time."

"True," Bradoc continued. "But after what we did . . . letting us go free showed mercy."

"You were not at fault." Pom fought back tears at the memory of Gital's death.

"That's a point we need not debate," Bradoc replied. "You have done us another favor by bringing our past back. In helping us overcome."

"Overcome what?"

Areana looked surprised. She glanced at her fellow Keepers and then back at Pom. "You don't know?"

"Know what?"

"Why do you think we're called Keepers?"

"Because you keep the teachings of Asmar."

Bradoc nodded. "That's part of the reason."

"There's another part," Wetell explained. "We keep Asmar's father."

"The Dark Wizard?"

"Yes," Areana said. "He's here in Dolcere."

"You hold him prisoner?"

Bradoc chuckled. "We couldn't imprison him, he's stronger than we are."

"He wanders free, then?"

"No."

"He imprisons himself," Wetell explained.

"He struggles in his mind over what he was," Areana added.

"The weapons you brought were too much of a temptation for him," Bradoc said.

Areana continued, "He tried to enter our minds, control our actions."

"But he didn't. We kept our minds protected," Wetell said, then added, "with your help."

"What do you mean, with my help?" She thought again of the icy presence. "I shouldn't have come."

"Quite the contrary. If you hadn't come, we wouldn't have grown stronger."

CHAPTER 3

"IT'S JUST AN ORDINARY ROCK. It's of no interest." Melis was dismissive. He didn't want to encourage Theb, his former apprentice. Besides, Melis still felt betrayed by Theb, who had cut the Peace Gem for their enemy. "It's . . . I don't know . . . pre-crystalline, if anything."

"It's not pre-crystalline," Theb insisted. "It's something else. I can't describe it. I've never felt anything like it before. When I saw it in the mine, it seemed to glow. It was beautiful." He sighed, "It's not pre-anything. Maybe it's . . . I don't know . . . *post*-crystalline."

Melis laughed. "I've never heard of a post-crystal, and I've been cutting gems for longer than you've been alive."

"Post-crystal is a bad term, I admit, but there is something about it that's different. It's hard to describe. I don't know, maybe *quasi*-crystal."

Melis looked skeptical.

"It seems to extend in directions we can't see," Theb said. Then added, "It just *feels* different."

Melis took the stone from the young gem cutter. "It's just a stone," he concluded, and tossed it back as he walked away.

Theb was protective of the gem, even though nobody else wanted it. He had seen it glow; it had been a golden crystal, even if just for a moment. And there was something else that troubled him. It was the weight. It was heavier than it should be. He spent much of the day just gazing at the gem, trying to figure it out. He studied it under the lenses that magnified the structure. He immersed it in water to determine the density. He performed every test he could think of, short of doing anything that might physically harm the gem. Still, it would not reveal its secrets.

It was soon after the discovery of the gem that the dreams started. A woman was calling to him. She was very tall and dark, dressed in flowing robes of pale blue fringed with gold. She wanted the gem, and somehow he needed to bring it to her.

"How?" he asked her. She pointed into a fog, from which a ghostly image emerged. He knew this image. It was one of death—a Saeren! As the image came clearer, it changed, looked more familiar. It was someone he knew. Lefi. What did the dream mean?

CHAPTER 4

ADULAR WAS BUSIER THAN LEFI ever remembered it being. Since the Moment, it had become a hive of activity, as it was the last place Asmar had been seen before his ascent into the Silver Forest. The wizards were staying nearby, at the fortress at Tellurium, while they continued their search for the Golden Tree. They allowed Lefi, the former owner of the fortress, free rein, although Lefi hated how Malzus had destroyed it. The wizards traveled north, where Asmar was reported to have gone, searching for some sign of the Tree. Even though they made no progress, still they kept trying. Sometimes they traveled together and other times their travel was solitary, but the results were always the same.

The wizards had other obligations that eventually brought them back to Tellurium, one of which was the care of the former Saeren, the men the Dark Wizard had stripped of their minds. Trying to heal the damage he had caused, Malzus reached out to the other former Saeren. He had become a familiar presence in their minds, and for some reason, they trusted him more than they did the other wizards. Lefi, however, rejected him. He wouldn't let Malzus back into his mind. Even with Malzus's help, three of the former Saeren had died by their own hand, not able to reconcile what they had done under the control of the Dark Wizard. Two others had just given up, showed no will for life, and gently passed from this world. That left five who were under the care of the wizards, but even after all this time, they were little more than shadows.

Lefi alone had recovered, if his life of pain and grief could be called a recovery. From his tower at Tellurium, he could see into the town of Adular, where his family had ruled for generations. That rule had ended. The townspeople no longer wanted him—most hated him. Not that he blamed them. He had been forced to commit many unspeakable acts while under the control of the Dark Wizard.

"You blame yourself," Rogi said as he entered the throne room, the room the Dark Wizard had ruled from when he fled to the north.

Somehow, Lefi found comfort in this room. Well, not comfort, exactly, but a sense of connectedness. It linked the three parts of his life: before the Dark Wizard, the time of Malzus, and now. Malzus had changed the throne room, which stood at the top of the fortress. He'd had the floors removed from the top of the tower to the bottom, except for a narrow path that rimmed the circumference of the room, and a slightly larger one through the center. This was Malzus's attempt to protect himself from attack, but, of course, his defeat had come from within, where no amount of protection could help. Lefi sat on the path in the center of the room, feet dangling off the side, surrounded by a sheer drop.

"Malzus was strong. It took many of us to defeat him. There was little you could have done," Rogi said.

"It took one to defeat him. Just one," Lefi countered.

"Asmar certainly had much to do with it, but he didn't do it alone."

"And how is my former master?"

"Recovering in Dolcere. He is trying to make amends for his past. He knows he has done wrong and repents daily."

Lefi was silent for a while. He was silent much these days. He used to be quite talkative, but now he had little to say, or little that seemed important. "He has been restored to your council?"

"Yes."

"Yet you say he repents. If you let him back into your council how does he repent?"

"He tries to restore the former Saeren."

"Not very successfully," Lefi replied.

Rogi nodded. "He is holed up in the wizards' tower, deep in contemplation."

Lefi shook his head. "How is that making amends?"

"I know," Rogi replied, "but there is little else we can do."

"You mean there is little else you choose to do."

Rogi sighed. "What is it you would have us do? He is still powerful. And at least he no longer seeks to control minds."

Lefi stared at Rogi, "So you will do nothing that threatens your council now that you're complete." He knew that the holy book of the wizards, the Koan, mandated there be nine wizards.

"We're not sure."

"But you number nine once again."

"Asmar," Rogi began, "is in the Silver Forest. We know he still lives, so he cannot be replaced on the council. Yet we have no contact with him, we can't touch his mind. So we don't know if we are complete."

Lefi turned away. He didn't care; he saw no point in these silly rituals. Eight or nine was not important. What was important was that one of their number had destroyed his mind, ruined his peace.

Rogi was anxious to change the subject. "Preadus should return soon."

"Is that good?"

"No, it means they have failed again."

"Why do they keep trying? They know they'll fail."

"That isn't necessarily true—they do try different things."

Lefi was dismissive. "Do you really believe that, Rogi?"

"No."

Lefi didn't care about the wizards' return, but he was anxiously awaiting another's. "Is the Wanderer back?" The Wanderer had worked with Lefi to prevent the former prince of Adular from going the way of the other former

Saeren. They'd worked together on his mind control, help-ing him to heal, at least partially.

You're lost in thought. Lefi felt the familiar touch of the Wanderer.

I was thinking about how much has changed since the Moment.

"And how much hasn't changed," she answered as she entered the room.

"I suppose. But things have gotten better."

"And for you? Are things better?"

Lefi considered this. Were things better for him, after all he had done? After all he had to live with? With his former tormentor still free? "No."

The Wanderer placed a comforting hand on his shoul-der. "What of your dreams?"

Lefi looked at the Wanderer in her sand-colored robes. "There's a new one now."

The Wanderer waited.

"This dream isn't bad like the others. It's just disturb-ing, or confusing, really." Lefi shook his head. "There's a woman. It's hard to see her—she seems out of focus. She wants me to bring her something, something from here, from a mine. I don't know why she wants it, but it appears to be very important to her."

"Where is she?"

Lefi squinted as if trying to peer into the darkness. "On an island somewhere, I think. I can sense water—not calm lakes or rivers, but turbulent waters. I believe she is alone and has been there for a long time."

"What will you do?"

"There is nothing to do. It is just a dream."

CHAPTER 5

POM WENT TO THE SQUARE daily with the other Seekers. She had not been called by the Keepers since that first time, but it didn't matter. Exchanging ideas with other Seekers was what interested her. She spoke with those who believed as Calb did, but also to the Followers of the Prophet and the New Followers of the Prophet. Calb's glib response to the differences between the two groups, Pom decided, was an oversimplification. Even the difference in which way they faced to pray was not as silly as she'd first thought.

One of the New Followers, a young and attractive Aris youth named Zart, had explained that they did not pray but meditated. Their orientation to the Golden Tree was to get them to focus on the future—on what the Prophet had shown was possible. He admitted it didn't really matter which way one faced, but it did eliminate unnecessary decisions.

Pom spoke with another Aris boy, Moty, who subscribed to the philosophy of the Followers of the Prophet. He explained that their orientation symbolized where the Prophet had come from.

Zart pointed out that until Asmar had come to Dolcere, he had not been the Prophet. Moty argued that the Prophet had been born in Tuland, and further, there was no evidence that the Prophet had ended up in the north, where the New Followers claimed. The only thing certain was he'd started in Tuland.

By the end of the argument, Pom discovered that she really didn't care and that Calb's group, particularly Nomey, appealed to her more. Pom spent much of her time helping Nomey at her clinic. She found she was good at dressing wounds and diagnosing diseases. She began the difficult task of reading *The Book of Healing*. She even hoped to add a cure of her own someday.

In the evenings at the hostel, the Seekers would exchange ideas. Different Seekers would start sessions on a topic they had a special knowledge in or in which they just had an interest. A Chert miner taught a session on how the crystal's bonds were formed. He was assisted by a Sitire woman who had been studying how the Aris made their crystal swords.

History classes were held, but beyond a certain point, they became quite speculative as no one had a good explanation as to who the builders of the roads and ancient buildings were. A group had been organized to explore the library of Dolcere, and that was leading to remarkable discoveries. Plans had been found on how to make building materials that were stronger than what was currently in use. There were descriptions of how crystals could be used to power new types of machines. All this was quite exciting to Pom, who attended as many of these presentations as she could, although many she did not understand all that well.

One evening Pom, taking her usual scattered approach to learning, wandered into a room with just a few in attendance. An older woman sitting at the front smiled as Pom entered.

"Welcome. My name is Yau. Thank you for joining us."

"I am Pom."

"Yes, I know. You are quite famous among the Seekers. I am pleased you can join us."

Pom blushed. She had not gotten used to being so well known. Looking around the room, she saw three others. Yau, it turned out, was from the people of the High Rock—the Community—where Asmar had met Ning. Yau explained that Ning had gone with Asmar to the Silver Forest.

A woman in the room, who Pom knew was from the Domare, asked her, "Did you know Ning?"

"No, that was well after Asmar had left my company." Pom found these types of questions common. People asked about things that had occurred well before or well after her encounter with Asmar. It wasn't until her arrival in Dolcere that she had even heard most of the stories.

Yau began the session. "I am going to teach you the song of my people."

The Domare woman looked upset. "That is where the Prophet was almost lost. Your song nearly imprisoned him."

Yau met the critique directly. "You're correct. We were afraid and stagnating. Our song was not one of hope but of fear and despair. Since the Moment, that has changed."

This time a Chert woman asked, "How has that happened?"

"We have opened our Community and our song to others. We are stronger with these new harmonies. Rather than closing ourselves to the outside, we now embrace it."

The third student, a young Tulander, said, "I have heard that your people are our best hope to recreate the Moment."

Yau nodded. "I have heard that as well. And while I would like to believe that my people could do this, I think that no one people and no one person, save Asmar himself, will be able to accomplish what you say. However, we might as well try."

"Do we need to do something?" Pom asked.

"Like what?" Yau responded.

"Like sit in a circle, join hands, something like that."

Yau looked quizzical.

The Tulander cut in, "You haven't had any training, have you?"

"What type of training?" Pom asked.

"Meditation, contemplation. The basic training that Seekers undergo in order to reach out their minds and join together in the song."

"No."

The Domare woman spoke. "I had assumed, because you were such a high-ranking Seeker, you would already be accomplished at these things."

"My rank, as you call it, is accidental. It comes from a chance encounter with the Keepers and Asmar. And all that happened long ago."

"But the Keepers called you," the Chert stated. "What did they want?"

Pom considered this. "I'm not sure."

"I don't see how you'll be able to participate in our song," the Domare woman said with regret.

"Unfortunately, I must agree," said the Chert.

Pom turned to the Tulander, who gave her a lost look, as if resigned to losing her.

"I guess you're right. I won't be of much use." Pom rose and started making her way to the door.

Stay. This came as more of a request than command, and it had a musical quality to it. Pom turned and faced the others.

Stay, she heard again. This time she was looking at the four in the room, and nobody had spoken. The request, the song, had come from Yau—not spoken but sent directly to Pom.

I will, Pom communicated back, but no words passed her lips.

She could hear the music. It was a simple melody. Pom knew that was for her benefit. Nothing too complex at first. The song of Yau washed over her, then those of the others, simpler than Yau's but still beautiful in their simplicity. Pom wanted to join the orchestration but didn't know how. Her frustration caused a discordance in the music.

Yau communicated through the music, *Yes, you are with us. You have been since we started.*

How? Pom communicated back.

The answer came in song, as if the sequence of strings being played created meaning, created their own reality.

You don't need to try. You are a natural. Your song is pure and clear. We suspected that, we thought you were special.

The others agreed. *Do not try,* they sang. *Let it come naturally. Your song is beautiful, let it grow. We will help.*

The stronger songs of the others receded, and Pom's became more prominent. It was simpler, but perfectly pitched. The song seemed to create thought, rather than thought creating the song. Ideas flowed into Pom's mind, carrying images and feeling. She began to understand the music. It contained the fears and desires of her fellow singers, Yau's strength and her amazement at Pom. Other songs played in the background.

Some of my people are joining us, Yau explained.

Pom explored these new entrants, trying to learn something from each. She heard a faint addition, soft yet beautiful. More so, she thought, than her own song. *What is that?*

I hear nothing, Yau sang back.

Pom listened harder, wanting to bring the song forward but not knowing how. The small voice became stronger.

Beautiful came Yau's comment.

Come to me, help me, the small voice seemed to call out.

Who are you? Pom asked.

Ran-dahl. And the song stopped.

CHAPTER 6

FOR FORTY DAYS THE WIZARDS were away, searching for what they couldn't find. They came back from their search with what they'd left with—their blue talizes and their silver pulcher staffs. Silently they strode through the fortress. Lefi avoided the wizards as best he could. Their mere presence disturbed what little peace he had obtained.

Rogi no longer traveled with them but stayed to looked after the former Saeren. The returning wizards made their way to the council room. A line of people waited for Preadus, as always—they had disputes only he could mediate. These were the cases that involved the leaders of the communities. Either they had a dispute with another leader, or their subjects had a dispute with them.

Will you be able to hear disputes today? Rogi asked of the Great Wizard. *Many have been waiting for your return.*

Let them wait one more day. Preadus's frustration came through in his thoughts. Then he was back in control. *I am sorry, Rogi. If you can ask the supplicants for one day for rest and meditation on what has happened, then I will hear their disputes.*

Rogi nodded. It was their mission to help others. It was written in the Koan as the way to enlightenment. Yet it did not always come easily to the wizards. Mediating merchants' disputes might be necessary according to the Koan, but Preadus would rather spend time in meditation or studying the old books.

Preadus communicated to Rogi what had occurred over the last forty days. The wizards had seen silver glimmerings in the distance, just like the other times. It was encouraging and tantalizing. It drew them on, and they'd hoped that this time they would see the forest. It enticed them forward, farther and farther north, farther into the cold. As they chased the ever-receding glimmers of the Silver Forest, they'd grown discouraged and after forty days turned back. It had ceased to surprise them that the journey back had taken less than a day. They had been away forty days, but had only traveled one.

Preadus ordered the other wizards to their chambers for rest and contemplation. *We will discuss our journey once we have had time to reflect,* the Great Wizard commanded.

When they reconvened, the sun had set and the crystals in the council chamber glowed with a golden light.

The discussion began abruptly with a statement by the wizard, Wellum. *We know the forest is there.*

We have been searching ever since Asmar disappeared, and yet, after all this time, we have been unable to find the Silver Forest, let alone the Golden Tree, Thurmore added.

Preadus let the others go on to release their frustrations. Finally, he interrupted. *Why is this so? Why have we not been allowed to enter the Silver Forest?* He kept his mind calm, fighting his increasing irritation. Why had Asmar, with his slight training, been allowed to find the Tree when he, the Great Wizard, was denied? Where was the fairness in this? He needed an answer, but that had proved as elusive as the Tree.

Possibly it isn't there. Dragorn expressed a concern that was growing among the other wizards.

It is there, Wellum stated flatly. *We have seen it glimmering in the distance. Doubt will only make our task more difficult.*

If the forest is there and we can't find it, the fault must lie in ourselves, Dragorn stated.

But we have tried everything, Thurmore commented. *We have reached out to the people and helped them on their road to peace. We have cloistered ourselves and studied the lessons of the holy books. We have done our fasts, our meditations. What else can we do?*

Have patience. Preadus sensed the growing frustration of the wizards that echoed his own. The forest was there—he knew it. But it remained hidden. He'd had dreams of running faster and faster but never being able to reach it. The forest was hidden from them, but why? By whom?

Might it be because we're not complete? asked Wellum. *Asmar can't be found, and if he isn't with the council, then we are only eight. The Koan mandates the council must be nine.*

Or maybe— Karal began, but was interrupted.

Or maybe it's me? came a voice, not from within the council room but from far away, from the city of Dolcere. *You blame me.*

The truth of these words silenced the others. The truth as spoken by Malzus.

You are wrong, however. Said not with malice but as a simple fact. Malzus went on, *It is not because of me or my son that you fail in your quest. It is because of what you seek.*

We seek the Tree, Dragorn said simply.

Yes, you seek the Tree. That is the problem, Malzus answered.

Isn't that what we all seek? Isn't that what Asmar sought?

I don't seek it—at least, not anymore—and my son never sought it.

Why, then, did he find the Tree, and you don't?

My son sought something and the Tree sought him. I seek nothing and have yet to find that peace.

Enough, Preadus interrupted. He knew Malzus was right, and he wanted to try something different, something that would help them find the Tree. But he didn't know what. He had nothing to offer Thurmore or the others.

Since his son's rehabilitation, Malzus's ambition, his desire to find the Tree, had waned. This introspection had been needed at first. But now? Malzus was still the most powerful of the wizards, but he did not use this power to help in the quest.

Let us all repair to our chambers for contemplation and fasting. When we are ready, we will meet again and determine what we will do next.

As Thurmore's mind disengaged, Preadus felt something. Frustration? Sure, they all felt that. It was something else. Hatred. He hated Preadus, hated not finding the Tree, hated the uselessness of the quest. A shiver went up Preadus's back. He would need to watch Thurmore.

CHAPTER 7

"IT DOES SOUND STRANGE." TIOX held the stone in his hand and considered it carefully.

"But it all kind of makes sense," Theb countered. "It's connected to the gem, I know it is."

Tiox tossed the stone up in the air, as if that would reveal something of its basic nature. "I know I'm no expert on gems, but this just seems like an ordinary rock."

"Don't trust your eyes, trust your feelings."

Tiox closed his eyes and held the stone gently cupped in his hands. Did he feel something? Maybe—or was it just in his mind, just the power of suggestion? "I don't know. What makes you think there's something special about this rock?"

"It's a gem."

"Alright, fine, about the gem."

Theb's mind wandered back to when he'd first met Tiox—General Tiox then—a commander in the Breccian army. A commander of the enemy. The Breccians had been sent to overrun the mine, which had yielded one of the greatest gem finds ever. It was only the intervention of Asmar that had prevented Tiox from killing everyone. Since the Moment, the Cherts and Breccians had forged a peace of sorts. Slowly at first, but now more lasting. It was because of Asmar, when he'd connected the minds of all people, that the peace began. Tiox had gone from enemy, and potential murderer, to friend.

"There are many small things," Theb went on, "such as where I found the gem."

"And where was that?"

"In the Cave."

There was no need to explain which cave. The Cave always meant the mine where Theb and Tiox had first met—the one that held the most incredible gems ever discovered.

"In the gem pocket?"

"Not in the one you saw. It was in a pocket much farther down, discovered very recently. We expected to find gems like we did in the pocket you saw, but there was only one gem."

"The one you're holding?"

"No. Or I should say, there was only one traditional gem. It was about your height and a deep crimson. Around it was just sand."

"Is that unusual?"

"Very. We would expect more than one gem in a pocket like that. Either that, or no gems at all. Finding one—with no evidence that others might have been created, even if they were subsequently destroyed—is quite unusual."

"But there was something else?"

"The structure of the gem is quite different. A stone or rock would have no crystalline structures, or very small ones. This gem seems to have an incomplete structure; it seems a *quasi*-crystal."

"I've never heard of a quasi-crystal. How do you know it didn't just stop growing?"

"I think it did the opposite."

"What's the opposite?"

"It grew past what it should."

"That makes no sense. If it did that, shouldn't it be just as large as the red crystal?"

"Unless it grew differently."

"What does that mean?"

"I'm not sure."

Tiox shrugged, not knowing what else to say. "What do you want me to do?"

"I know this sounds strange, but somehow that former Saeren, Lefi, is connected to this."

"How do you know that?"

"In a dream I was told to go to him," Theb responded. "I know it sounds crazy, but I want you to go with me to see him."

"Your mysterious gem intrigues me," Tiox replied. "I believe Lefi is at the castle in Tellurium."

Theb nodded.

"I'll go if we stop in Harot on the way. It has been so long since I was home."

Theb agreed, and three days later they left for Harot, the mountain city of the Breccians. The city had prospered since the Moment. Trade flourished as the Breccians became more adept at mining and gem cutting. There were now lights, powered by cut crystals, lining the major streets, and stones laid to make the streets more passable. The Cautes were still on average the better gem cutters, but there were a growing number of Breccians whose skill rivaled those of the better Caute cutters. Theb had taught classes in Harot, and one of his students in particular was coming along very well. He hoped he would have the chance to see her.

"Will you visit any of your former students while we're here?" Tiox smiled knowingly.

"Maybe a couple," Theb replied defensively, and then added, "I am anxious to move on to Tellurium. But I would like to see Teyer."

Tiox grinned, but Theb added, "She was one of my best students. She is better than many of the Caute masters."

Tiox nodded. "I'm sure she would never forgive you if you didn't stop by."

As Theb and Tiox made their way through the city, people stared. Partly because they couldn't escape their fame—they both had been close to the Prophet—but also because they were so different in appearance. Theb was small and slight. His days studying every detail of gem cutting, bending over his fine tools, and perfecting his craft left little time to venture out. Tiox, by contrast, was a massive man, about three times Theb's size. His time as a soldier had given him a well-muscled physique and, even though he had given up his calling as a man of war, he still maintained his strength.

After entering Harot, the first stop the two travelers made was to pay their respects to King Ramez. Ever since the Moment, Ramez had become a friend of the Seekers. He provided a haven for them, establishing hostels for shelter and supplying food. This explained the mass of white-robed figures the two passed as they made their way to the castle. Tiox could see shops closed as Seekers clogged the street, crowding out their customers.

They approached the castle of Harot, the towers soaring high above the city. It was a relic from a long-ago era—the skills to build something so tall and grand had long been forgotten. It was all the Breccians could do to keep the castle in good repair, and that had been accomplished only recently, with the assistance of the wizards. The wizards alone seemed to understand the complex nature of the structures.

When they finally reached the castle, they were escorted through the vaulted corridors to the throne room by an unarmed guard. This was one of the changes Tiox noticed, and he was not sure it was welcome. Another noticeable difference: The walls of the castle were lined with paintings and tapestries about the Moment.

"Why are there gold halos around Prince Wetell and the other Keepers?" Tiox asked, recognizing one of the images that included the prince.

"That is to show he is a Keeper," Theb answered.

"Those must be Bradoc and Areana, then?"

"Yes."

"But there are others with halos—smaller, but still there."

"They are all people who have touched Asmar in some way. The closer they were, the larger the halo."

"You mean I have a halo?" Tiox laughed.

"If you allowed one of the artisans to capture your image, I'm sure you would have a large gold halo. Like this." Theb stopped short in front of one of the images. It was titled *The Gem*, and it depicted Theb preparing to cut the Peace Gem, with Tiox standing beside him.

Tiox blushed, but Theb was not sure if it was from anger or embarrassment.

"This is outrageous," Tiox started. "I never... who could allow such a thing?"

Before Theb could answer, a door opened and they were escorted in to see King Ramez, who was dressed in the white robes of the Seekers. Above the king's throne, Tiox noticed, was an image of the king himself, twice his actual size, surrounded by an intricately embellished golden halo. Tiox was so stunned that he almost forgot to bow.

"Rise, Tiox. We no longer bow to the king," Ramez said.

Another change. "But Your Majesty, it is a sign of respect."

"I realize now, Tiox, that all this bowing never really garnered any respect. That is achieved in a very different way."

"Of course, Your Majesty," Tiox began, "but if I may..."

"Please."

"Some of the changes you've made are dangerous."

"Such as?"

"You're no longer armed. The guard that escorted us here was likewise unarmed. How are you being protected?"

"That is an interesting paradox you pose. The more I hand out weapons, you claim, the less danger I am in. And the fewer weapons, the more danger."

"It isn't a paradox, it's just common sense. I remember the days when any number of your commanders would have come in here and tried to kill you, just to sit on that throne."

"Were you among them, Tiox?"

Tiox went silent. There had been a time when he would have killed his king—but not to take the throne. It had been when Ramez had been under the Dark Wizard's control, and Tiox had felt that the king's destruction was the only way to save the Breccian people.

"That was an unfair question, and you need not answer. I know there was a time when my death would have been best for my people. But not anymore. Now I wear the robes of a Seeker, and I am interested in their philosophy. But I am not a Seeker. I have not renounced this world, nor am I naive enough to leave myself defenseless."

Ramez mechanically moved his hand toward his hip, and Tiox realized Ramez had a dagger under his white robe.

"But things needed to change," Ramez went on. "I was touched by the Prophet—even the slight touch of his mind revealed a new way to see. The way things were could not last. So I changed, as have things in my realm."

"You must be hungry after your travels," the king said. "I'm afraid you'll find the food one of the things that has changed."

Tiox knew the Seekers had adapted to the diet that Asmar and the Tulanders followed. They ate no animals. Asmar's ability to reach out to the minds of the animals and sense their feelings, desires, and intelligence made it difficult to slaughter them.

"That is expected," Tiox answered.

CHAPTER 8

THEIR TIME IN HAROT HAD been disturbing to Tiox. Change was taking place too quickly.

"Teyer seems to be doing well," Theb said of his former student.

Tiox smiled. He knew Theb was fond of Teyer, and now that she was a young woman, Tiox wondered where it might lead.

"Yes, she does."

"You spent quite a lot of time with her."

Theb blushed. "We discussed gems and gem cutting."

"Really?" Tiox teased.

Recovering a bit Theb, replied "Teyer is doing well."

Tiox smiled.

"Anyway," Theb went on, "a strange thing happened with the gem when I showed it to her."

"Which gem?"

"The one everyone has been making fun of—the rock." Theb said, exasperated.

"Sorry, tell me what happened."

"I showed it to her."

"What was her reaction?"

"At first, it was like everyone else. But I explained the more subtle aspects of the gem."

"Did that convince her?"

"A bit, but then the strange thing happened." Theb stopped.

Tiox urged, "Go on."

"I'm not sure how to describe it. At first I thought it just a trick of the lighting, it was so fleeting. But Teyer saw it too. It seemed like the crystal glowed." Theb shook his head. "That's not a good explanation. It seemed, for a brief moment, the crystal became whole."

"What do you mean?"

"I'm not sure. It's like seeing something in one place that was really in another place, or in that place and another place at the same time."

"That doesn't make sense. How can something be in two places at once?"

"It was more like it wasn't really in either place. Or you couldn't be certain which place it was in."

Tiox was tempted to dismiss what Theb had said, but he had seen strange things before, and Theb wasn't one to make things up. "We will have to keep an eye on that gem to see if it happens again. Then maybe we can figure out why."

Theb and Tiox rode on to Adular. When they arrived, Tiox noticed all the changes in the town that had happened since the Moment. The city flourished with pilgrims and Seekers, who used this as their staging point to search for the Golden Tree. There were many, also, who came to make their fortunes off the pilgrims. Some sold food or other supplies, and others sold hope, both real and false.

Stands were set up along the main road, offering all types of salvation. One that particularly caught Tiox's attention was a small table with a sign draped above it that read KEY TO CONTEMPLATION. It claimed to be the first step on the path to enlightenment. The man behind the table was doing a brisk business.

"I want to speak with him." Tiox pointed toward the man as he dismounted.

"What in the name of the Tree for? He is obviously a charlatan."

"I'm curious as to how things work here."

Tiox walked over to the stall while Theb held his mount. When the former general reached the back of the line, the old man who sat behind the table was animatedly explaining something to a client. The others saw the massive man and stood aside.

"I'll wait my turn," Tiox insisted, but to no avail. He soon found himself behind the customer who was receiving a lecture from the old man.

"Please stand back until it's your turn," the seller croaked at him. The man he was assisting looked up at Tiox, and at the sight of the massive Breccian, he stepped back and let Tiox approach.

"You see what you have done to my business," the old man complained.

"What is your business?"

"Are you from the elder council? Have you come to check my permits?"

"I didn't know you needed a permit."

"You don't, so what do you want?" The man was agitated.

"I want to know"—Tiox read from the man's sign—"the 'Key to Contemplation.'"

"I can't help you."

"So you are a fraud, like I thought."

The other customers looked at each other and began to back away. The man calmly answered, "It is just you I cannot help."

"Why not?"

"You don't want help."

"That's not so."

The man stared intently at Tiox. Then he made a short bow to the Breccian. "I stand corrected," he said. "Deep inside, you do want help. But on the surface you mock it. You are too proud, too much in control, to achieve what you want." At this he turned to a new customer, but she was not interested in being helped.

"That's not true," Tiox retorted weakly. Had the man really seen this in him?

"If it is untrue, then your opinion of me is correct."

Tiox was going to let the remark pass—the man's assessment was just a guess—but something stopped him. "You have assessed me fairly."

The old man turned back to Tiox, a glint in his eye. "Then maybe I can be of assistance, after all." He looked around at the people in line. "I am closed for the day. Come back another time." He indicated Tiox. "Follow me. Your friend too, if he cares to."

Theb wasn't pleased at this development. "What about the horses?"

The man waved a hand, and a young girl came to take the horses from Theb, who looked at Tiox for guidance. When Tiox nodded, Theb shrugged and dismounted.

The man grabbed two sticks and walked out from behind his stall. His legs moved stiffly as he used the sticks to propel himself forward. Despite the impediment, he moved quickly.

"Where are we going?" Theb asked.

"Just follow me."

Theb said, "This might be a trap." Instinctively he felt for his gem, hidden under his cloak.

Tiox chuckled. "Let them try," he said to Theb.

Then he turned to the old man. "What happened to your legs?"

"Saeren."

"You survived an encounter with the Saeren?" Theb was impressed.

"Not *the* Saeren, *a* Saeren. And it was not after me. I was in its way when it struck out. Still, even that slight touch left me paralyzed."

"Was the Saeren . . ." Theb began, but was not sure how to finish. Finally, he just blurted out what he wanted to know. "Was it Lefi?" Theb knew Lefi had been a Saeren, but he had never considered how much harm Lefi had done.

The man nodded. "I don't blame him. At least, not anymore."

"He wasn't responsible for what he was made to do?" Theb prompted.

"That is not what I said," the man replied.

They had been led down a winding crowded alleyway. Children ran around the streets, and women were washing clothes and hanging them in front of their cramped living spaces. White-robed Seekers were talking to the men sitting idly in the streets and to the women, sometimes assisting in their chores.

"Here we are." The man tucked his sticks under one arm and started to ascend a steep set of stairs, using the railing for support.

Theb was next, followed by Tiox. The flimsy stairs creaked under the Breccian's weight. When they reached the top of the stairs, they were led into a small living area. A makeshift stove occupied one corner and a sleeping mat the other. Those, and a low table and a few sitting pillows, were all that could be seen. Having been in the army, Tiox was used to having little, but even he was surprised by the poverty of the surroundings.

The man seated himself on one of the cushions and motioned for his guests to sit. "I am Sevas."

"Is it like this throughout Adular?" Theb asked, indicating the poverty of the room.

Sevas smiled. "There are quite a few that have much, much more, and I would suspect few that have less. It was different when the Dark Wizard was here. Then, what you see here would have been considered the norm."

"Won't someone help you? Family? Doesn't the city help?" asked Tiox.

"I thank you for your concern, but it is unnecessary. As for family, I have none—at least, none anymore."

"What happened?" Theb blurted.

"I mentioned the Saeren was not trying to get me, that I was in the way," Sevas replied.

"Yes."

"It was my family he was after. My wife and daughter, and my mother." He paused, fighting to keep his composure. "They saw the danger of the Dark Wizard. They had the strength to fight him."

"I'm sorry." Tiox's voice was soft. The Saeren were his former allies, the Dark Wizard their leader. Now things were different. Foes had become friends, the past had been buried—but not completely. "I'm sorry," he repeated.

Sevas waved his hand. "That does nothing. They are gone. I do what can be done. For them I will help you achieve what has eluded you."

"And what is that?"

"Understanding."

"Will that take long?" Theb asked.

Sevas shrugged. "It will take as long as it needs to."

"Come on, then," Theb said to Tiox. "We need to get to Lefi." He rose and looked at his friend.

Tiox's gaze was locked with Sevas's. "You go ahead. I'm going to stay here. At least for a while."

"You can't—"

Tiox turned to Theb and said, "Go." His tone reminded Theb that Tiox had once been a general.

Theb's mount covered the distance to Tellurium quickly, and he arrived at the gates of the great fortress. He marveled at the way it was hewn out of the stones of the cliff. He wondered why they'd built a fortress in the first place. To have a fortress, one must have enemies. And this was a great fortress, so that implied great enemies.

Theb was met at the gates by the Wanderer. "Good, you have come. Please follow me. You are expected." She led Theb to the fortress.

"I've come to see Lefi."

"Yes, I know."

"A woman in my dream told me to come."

"Lefi has had similar dreams, as have I."

"But it's not a dream. The woman is real."

"I agree."

"We have to find her."

"That would be very difficult, as we don't know where she is."

"She's on an island in the ocean."

"But which one? The ocean is vast."

"I don't know," Theb admitted. "But I know how to find out."

The Wanderer stopped and studied Theb. This was the first time in a long while anyone had said something that surprised her. She stared expectantly.

"My gem. It will show us where she is."

CHAPTER 9

RAN-DAHL HAD BEEN GIVEN NO supplies, no tablets for writing, nothing to help with her computing, so she used cave walls and burnt wood to write her equations and diagrams about the fog. But now her mind was growing stronger, and her memory had become her tablet. It was not enough. She needed to create the song. The right vibrations, the right chords, at just the right pitch, would penetrate the fog. For that she needed others—and the crystal that existed half in this world and half beyond the fog.

She rose from meditation, her long legs stiff from days of inactivity. Today she would seek nourishment once again. Thirty days of nothing but water and meditation, of reaching and planning. Thirty days of trying to look through the fog. Now that Gaelil was gone, she reached out to others from the Valki Institute. Some shied from her touch, afraid she might bring ruin to them. But a few warmed to her.

Eot, who used the equipment at the Institute to measure forces in the fog, relished the connection. Before Ran-dahl's exile, Eot had been one of her most promising students. With the help of K'ren—Ruvbain's wife and a former Valki student—she had managed to avoid detection. She had conducted her experiments on the fog in secret and was thrilled when her former teacher had touched her mind. Ran-dahl's mind conducted the same experiments, and Eot eagerly pumped her for information.

There is an attractive force in the fog. Eot reached out to Ran-dahl.

The strength of the fog depends on your distance from it. So it was weak at first, and now it is slowly getting stronger, Ran-dahl replied.

That's strange, Eot replied.

Yes, but I believe that to be only the beginning of the weirdness of the fog.

We must explore more, Eot said.

There is little more we can understand from this side of it.

No one has been able to penetrate the fog, Eot replied. *I could reach out to K'ren. She was the expert on its attractive force.*

No. Who knows what she might reveal to her husband? Ran-dahl replied.

She wouldn't betray us.

Not knowingly. But we can't risk it, at least not now. We may need her help later, but for now I will wait for the others to arrive. Then we will enter the fog.

These others know nothing about the fog, Eot said.

But they know of the Golden Tree—that's what drives them.

And are they connected?

Maybe, Ran-dahl replied. *But until they arrive, tell no one else about them, not even the members of the Fog.* She felt a small glimmer of excitement. Eot was right, the "others" knew very little and were untrained. But she would guide them. The members of the Fog feared Ruvbain. They wished her luck, of course, but did little else. She was not angry, not even disappointed. She understood that this was her mission, her quest. She had given up everything to find out about the fog. Now others were bringing the key, and she allowed herself a little hope.

CHAPTER 10

SHE WAS CALLING TO HIM. No, it wasn't a call—it was a song. What did she want of him? She reached out from her island, beckoned for him to come. It seemed so real. Lefi was half convinced she did exist.

The wizards had left once again on their quest, and the Wanderer had returned. It was clear that the wizards wanted nothing to do with the Wanderer, and she obliged them by being in the same place as the wizards as little as possible. The Wanderer spent her time teaching the former Saeren how to regain control of their minds.

"You are progressing well," the Wanderer said.

"It doesn't seem so," Lefi replied. "I am still haunted by dreams of the woman calling to me from an island."

"It's not a dream."

"It must be."

The Wanderer shook her head. "I've had the same dream."

"And so have I!" Theb stepped from behind the Wanderer.

"I forgot to mention, you have a visitor."

Lefi nodded and rose.

Theb reached out his hand, but Lefi just stared at him. "The woman is real?"

"I believe so," Theb replied.

"Where is she? Who is she?"

"I don't know exactly where she is, other than on an island a long way off. Who she is, is not much clearer," Theb said. "But I believe she is a scholar of some sort, and we need to find her."

"We would need to cross the ocean to get to her," Lefi replied.

"And that would be very dangerous," the Wanderer said.

"But the wizards traveled here by ship," Theb replied.

"Their craft was superior to anything in Bracat, and even they barely survived."

"Wasn't their ship wrecked on our shores?" Lefi asked.

The Wanderer nodded. "It was, but not by the waters."

"Then it is still intact?" Theb said.

"It was wrecked by the wizards' own hands," responded the Wanderer.

"Why would they do that? They cut off their only way to return to their home," said Theb.

"That's exactly their point. They came on a quest. The end of the quest was to find the Golden Tree. If they couldn't, there would be no point in returning. And if they succeeded, there would be no need."

"So this woman in our dreams—she comes from the lands of the wizards?"

"I don't think so. She comes from farther off."

"Then there is no way to find her. And even if we could, there is no way to reach her," Lefi said.

"We need to find her," Theb insisted. "We must rescue her."

Lefi shook his head. "That's not what she wants."

"What do you think she wants?" Theb asked.

"To go into the fog."

"The fog?" Theb had never seen the woman clearly but had figured it was the nature of the dream. "What fog?"

Lefi stared at the gem cutter. "It's what isn't real."

"That makes no sense. You said it wasn't a dream."

"It's not a dream. It's something else."

All at once, the pieces fell into place. Theb looked at the Wanderer, eyes wide, "The Golden Tree lies within the fog!"

Lefi sank into his chair and muttered, "Yes. This one I will find."

CHAPTER 11

"FOOLS, ALL OF THEM! THEY'LL never find it!" Malzus wasn't sure if he'd actually spoken those words or thought them. It didn't matter, there was no one to hear. He had isolated himself from others so that he could not touch the minds of those he had harmed.

He had stopped the thing they called the Moment. He had been joined by a few others, but without him the Moment would have lasted longer—maybe even become permanent. But he couldn't let that happen. The other wizards had shielded themselves from the Moment, so they'd felt only its fringes and had not recognized its importance. But he had been forced to see others, feel others, understand others. It had hurt too much. So he'd destroyed it.

Now, Malzus feared he would never find the Tree. He had to come to peace with that. Before he could embark on a quest for further understanding, he would need to accept responsibility for the enormity of his actions, and that he couldn't do—not yet.

Occasionally the old feelings of his own significance returned. When that woman had brought the weapons to the Keepers, it had sparked rage and frustration. It had been a struggle to bring his emotions under control. The Keepers had done well to resist. But the woman, Pom—she had a surprising strength, an understanding. If not for her, his rage might have gone unabated. She had unknowingly calmed his mind. There was a peace about her that he coveted.

Then there were his worshipers. Hearing them call out to him was the hardest for him. The worshipers of the Dark Wizard feared what the Prophet, his son, taught, and they yearned for him to take control once again. Their adoration was unwanted, but difficult to deny.

And there was the promise he had made to his former Saeren. He had pledged to help them, to heal them. But that wasn't going well. It fed his own anxieties. Still, it was what he needed to do to get the other wizards to accept him back into the council.

Malzus tried to clear his mind. It was time for him to reach out to one of his former Saeren.

Lazis. He waited for the former Breccian ruler to reply.

I'm here. The voice was weak.

You need to forgive yourself, Malzus began.

For what? Lazis replied. *We almost won. If it hadn't been for Asmar—*

Malzus cut him off. *You need to accept responsibility if you want to heal.* He had to get Lazis to understand what they had done was wrong.

But Lazis didn't believe that. *No! We need a better plan. We can still defeat them. With your power we can rise again.*

It was difficult working with the former Saeren. Other than Lefi, they wouldn't admit to being wrong. They had been defeated but hoped to rise once more. This was Malzus's test. The former Saeren called to him, his followers called to him. He still had the power to take over the council, now that Asmar was in the Silver Forest. He could do it! He could resurrect his plan.

That is not the way, Malzus finally responded. *I tried and failed.*

We could try again.

It won't work. Malzus knew the old way wouldn't succeed. He had learned from the past, from the Moment. He needed a new way. He needed the Tree to forgive him.

He couldn't keep the connection to Lazis—it was too painful. The Breccian wouldn't listen. Malzus could enter Lazis's mind and make him change, but that wasn't who Malzus was anymore—at least, he hoped not. He entered Lazis's mind to soothe him, but that was all. He couldn't make any real progress to heal him or any of the other former Saeren. They were passive and wanted him to control them once again. It was tempting, but he fought the urge.

He needed another way—and the woman, Pom, intrigued him. She was strong but untrained, like he had been once. If he could gain her trust and help her, maybe she could redeem him. If not, perhaps he could use her to find the Tree. They could find it together.

It was all very confusing. But he knew he needed her—and she needed him.

CHAPTER 12

THE WANDERER FELT A LIGHT tug at her mind. It was almost like a child pulling on her clothes. Someone was trying to get her attention. No, not someone—it was a wizard. She turned as the wizard Rogi entered, clad in flowing blue robes.

"I want to go."

The Wanderer could have feigned ignorance of what Rogi meant, but she knew. He wanted to travel on the quest for the Golden Tree.

"Is that wise?" she responded.

Rogi gave a slight laugh. "Probably not. But nonetheless, I want to go."

The Wanderer nodded, surprised for a second time in as many days. "It is not my decision."

Now Rogi looked surprised.

The Wanderer explained, "It is not my quest."

Still Rogi did not understand.

"I'm not going," the Wanderer stated simply.

"I understand."

"Do you?"

"Yes, I believe I do. You've already found your Tree."

"But aren't there three trees?"

"That's what is taught." Rogi glanced around as if to check for eavesdroppers. "But I'm not so sure."

"About what?"

"If there are three trees." These words came out slowly, as if he was afraid to utter them.

The Wanderer waited for him to go on.

"I'm not the most powerful or the most learned wizard," he began tentatively. "But I have studied the writings of the Koan and the interpretations in the Talum." He paused before uttering his heresy. "I no longer believe the Talum is always correct." He hung his head, as if a great weight had been lifted. As he looked up again, tears welled in his eyes and they held a lost expression.

The Wanderer waited for the enormity of Rogi's words to settle. Then she asked, "What do you believe?"

"I don't know. But I no longer believe we will find what we seek along our current path."

"So you believe there are other paths?"

Rogi nodded.

"And the other wizards?"

"They believe differently. The trees for them are physical. You find the Tree, you obtain understanding. You follow the classical teachings in the Talum and you find the trees."

"What's your view now?"

"That first you find understanding, then you find the Tree."

"But you believe the Koan has the key to understanding," countered the Wanderer.

"The Koan is a key to understanding." Rogi was trying to be clear. "It is the Talum that is imperfect."

"In what way?"

"It explains things well, but not well enough." Rogi ran his hand through his hair. "It's hard to explain, it is all very new to me. After the Moment, things seemed odd. The Talum could not explain the Moment. The others kept looking for the Tree along the old path. But there has to be a deeper truth, a new path."

"What makes you believe in other paths?"

Rogi sighed. "Asmar found the Tree, we can assume that. He didn't return, and we would know if he was in this world, in our dimension. Since we followed the same physical path he did, we should have found the Tree. So I concluded he found a different path. One we don't know, one we can't find. The other wizards keep looking along the same path for something they missed." Rogi shook his head. "That's why I stay behind and think."

"And what do you think?

"I think we must rethink."

CHAPTER 13

TIOX HAD KNOWN DEPRIVATION BEFORE, but this time it was different. At first he had fought it. It was against his nature to trust. Trust was not really the right word—it was more an openness. The former general had been suspicious when his new teacher told him to give everything away. This was a scam, he told himself. But the coins, the food, the clothes—all went to others. Sevas kept nothing. Tiox looked for the angles, signs of kickbacks, but none of that occurred. He was stripped down to the fundamentals, but no further. After this, nothing happened. Sevas went out about his business as he always had, sometimes coming back with a minimal amount of food for himself and his guest. He never asked for help or volunteered information.

After five days of confinement, Tiox asked, "Am I allowed to go out?"

"Why not?"

"I didn't know if this was part of my training."

"Oh."

"Can I go out?" Tiox felt odd asking this shriveled creature permission, yet he felt compelled to do so.

"Your choice."

"Then I will." Tiox rose, but didn't advance. "I may not return."

Sevas shrugged. "Your choice," he repeated.

Tiox sighed. "You said you would teach me."

"I said no such thing."

"You did. You said you would teach me how to obtain understanding."

"No. I promised to help you achieve what has eluded you."

"It's the same thing."

Sevas shrugged again.

"So what am I to do?"

"What is it you want to do?"

"Understand."

"Understand what?"

Tiox paused. He hadn't really thought about that. Did he really want to understand? Did he want Sevas to make him understand?

"What I want"—Tiox altered his demand—"is to talk."

"That I can do. What is it you want to discuss?"

This again was not an easy question. What did he want to talk about? What would give him insight into the world?

What would help him expand his mind, help him emulate Asmar?

"I would like to talk about . . ."

Sevas waited expectantly.

". . . you."

Sevas smiled. "We shall talk about me. But first I need to go out and raise money for food."

"I should go with you," Tiox offered.

Sevas nodded to his guest. "Come along, then."

"After all, it's because of me that you no longer attend your stand and have to resort to begging."

"Don't give yourself too much importance. I do what I want. Come with me, or not, because it's what you want to do."

It would have been easier to follow Sevas if Tiox had felt he was doing the old man a favor. But that excuse had been taken from him.

"What did you do before?"

"Before what?"

"Before you were injured."

"I was a merchant."

"What did you sell?"

"Anything. Sometimes food, sometimes land, sometimes even people."

"People?"

"I would find work for them. I was a middleman. Someone had land to sell, and I would find a buyer. A farmer wanted to sell his food, I would broker a deal with the stall sellers."

"Did you make anything yourself?"

"No."

"That must have been a difficult business."

"Yes."

"And is that why you live like this?" Tiox swept his hand around the cramped quarters.

"The work was difficult, but very profitable. Before my injury, as you call it, I had a large home and land. Things became more difficult with Malzus—but that actually increased my wealth."

"How can that be?" Tiox was ignorant of the workings of towns. He was more comfortable with the way an army was supplied.

"Things were hard to come by. People paid more if someone could find what they wanted."

"That someone was you?"

"And others. But I was one of the better ones."

"Didn't that bring you to the attention of Malzus?"

"Yes," Sevas admitted.

"And he destroyed you?"

"No. Malzus is a smart wizard. He knew better. He didn't want to destroy me, he wanted my help."

"For what?"

"He had armies that needed supplies, towns that needed to be run. He needed people like me to do this. And we did, we helped him."

"Willingly?"

"At first. Then some of us began to have doubts. We tried to pull away."

"And he killed them?" Tiox was beginning to understand.

"Some. But he was usually more subtle. We would be hard to replace, so he did other things."

"What?"

Sevas pointed to his legs. "Taking away our will."

"He entered your minds?"

"There were simpler ways to break us. He didn't take away our minds, he took away what was most dear. In my case"—Sevas paused—"it was my family."

"You gave up your business, then? That's when things went wrong?" Tiox was drawn to this man's story. What had happened to make him the way he was?

"Things went wrong, in a way, but still I became richer."

"Why did you go on?"

"I thought I had to. Or, more accurately, I was too weak to stop."

"He would have killed you?"

"If only he would have done so! I tried myself, but the Dark Wizard prevented me. I was more afraid of what he would do to others. Our prince, Lefi, was already under his control. The Dark Wizard had his armies close at hand. I know Prince Lefi doesn't recall what he did during that time—or chooses not to. But I remember what he did, and what I did. We can say we had no control, but still, we did it."

Tiox thought of his own actions. He had not been under the control of the Dark Wizard, yet his actions had helped the Dark One.

"When did you become poor?"

"When I gained wealth."

Tiox gave him a quizzical look.

"It's not really confusing. The Moment freed me from Malzus, but it did more than that. I touched, even if it was ever so slightly, the minds of others. I understood them and they understood me. I had no need for so much wealth, so I decided to pare down to what I needed. The rest I gave away."

"This is what you need?"

Sevas smiled at the general. "No, but I decided to keep a few luxuries."

Tiox shook his head. "I understand you had more than you needed, but now, it seems, you have barely enough to survive."

"Then you are beginning to understand. Since I gave away my possessions, I have been steadily acquiring wealth."

"In what way?"

"I observe, I talk with people. When possible, I read what others write."

"To what end?"

"To the only end possible—to understand."

CHAPTER 14

"I WISH TIOX COULD HAVE seen this." Theb gazed at the crystal. There could be no doubt now that it was a crystal, although a strange one. For a short while, the crystal had glowed. It had turned from a dull, half-formed rock into one of the most perfectly formed, beautiful structures he had seen, and then back again into a rock. It seemed oddly out of focus, though. As if it were constantly moving or not really in any one place. If asked the color, Lefi would have said a deep red or violet. But on closer examination it had blues, greens, and yellows. A whole spectrum of color, depending on how one observed the stone.

"I'm afraid the other wizards will want the crystal," Rogi warned. "We should leave Tellurium,"

"We can't just leave, we have no plan. We don't know where we are going," Lefi said half-heartedly.

"We need to start out. Tomorrow at the latest, or I fear our quest will be lost before it can start," Rogi said.

"If it's the wizards you fear," the Wanderer interjected, "I'm afraid you're too late."

Preadus and the other wizards entered the room where Theb, Rogi, Lefi, and the Wanderer waited.

Preadus looked at Rogi and then at the Wanderer. Finally, his stare came to rest on Theb. *You must surrender the crystal*, he demanded.

Theb shook his head, and Rogi took a step forward.

Preadus reached out to Rogi. *You must not defect from us.*

He approached Theb, avoiding gazing at the crystal. "We were concerned. We sensed a strong force being emitted from Tellurium."

"It must be from the crystal," Theb replied, and he produced the stone.

Preadus took a tentative step forward, and Theb pulled the crystal back.

Preadus said, "I have heard of crystals like this one. They are quite rare."

"Do you know why it glows?" Theb asked.

"I know something about it," Preadus replied. "Certain vibrational patterns match the structure of your crystal. Those vibrations complete its structure for as long as the vibrations continue."

"Where do these vibrations come from?"

"They can be from anywhere. The most powerful come from our own minds. When we communicate mind to mind, it creates powerful vibrations. If they have the right frequency, that could power your stone."

"Can this power reach around our world?"

"Theoretically, I suppose so. But it would be very difficult."

"Why?"

"As the power travels, it dissipates. So the farther away someone is, the exponentially stronger the power needs to be and . . ." Preadus trailed off.

"And?"

And we would have sensed someone that strong. The answer came not from the Great Wizard, but from his son. Malzus went on, *I am the most powerful of the wizards.* This was said as a fact, without boast or pride. *I would have sensed this power if it existed. Your friend, the Wanderer, may be as powerful as me, maybe a bit more or less. And if I missed this power, surely she would have sensed something. Ask her if she has.*

Theb looked at the Wanderer, who stood motionless. "What if this power is new?"

"Highly unlikely. A power that strong does not just emerge. It takes much study and contemplation."

"Unless"—Lefi had a sudden realization—"they didn't care about us until now."

"That's true," Preadus replied, "but why direct it toward us now? If you would allow us to study the crystal, we could give you more answers."

"It was not directed at us, but at Theb and Lefi," Rogi corrected the Great Wizard.

"Yes, of course. Rogi, you are correct. Still, we must study the crystal. Theb and Lefi may join in this. Even"—he paused, and then forced out this offer—"the Wanderer may join. But the crystal must be studied."

No! The response was from Malzus. *The crystal is theirs. It will do us no good. You can study it, but it will not lead us to the Tree.*

You can't know that, Preadus responded.

Malzus went on, *I do know, as do you. Your past quest for the Tree has failed. Your next quest will fail as well.*

Impossible! Preadus's rage finally bubbled up. *We will be reunited with the Tree. It will happen. It must happen!*

The possibility of finding out more about the crystal intrigued Theb. He moved toward Preadus, and Rogi's hands slipped from his shoulders. Theb offered the crystal to the Great Wizard, but he didn't take it. His hands were reaching out, but they couldn't seem to travel the distance to retrieve the stone. Sweat beaded up on the Great Wizard's brow at the effort.

Finally, his arms dropped to his sides. "Okay, he can keep the stone," said Preadus, and he turned and strode from the room. The other wizards followed.

"We are free," Rogi explained. "We won't be pursued. He has freed us."

"Preadus?" Theb asked.

Rogi shook his head. "Malzus."

CHAPTER 15

THEY GATHERED IN THE COURTYARD each morning, the New Followers of the Prophet facing north and the Followers south. Pom continued to meet new people and share ideas. Her friendship with Nomey grew, and Pom decided that she also wanted to be a healer.

"I will never have the skill you possess, Nomey," she confided in her young mentor.

Nomey considered this and replied, "That may be true, but you possess an empathy I don't. You make people want to be healed."

"But people want that already."

"This goes deeper. Your strength is getting them to heal themselves."

Pom was about to argue, but then realized Nomey was right. She seemed to sense the causes of illnesses in people.

Not the broken bones and cuts, but the deeper wounds—the ones caused by the body not working like it was meant to. She seemed to be able to alter the songs of some of the people and allow them to heal themselves.

"My mother told me Asmar had that same ability," Nomey said.

The two circulated among the Seekers. Many came up to them to talk about their ills. Nomey might give some powdered herbs or tell them to come to the clinic. Pom would look into their suffering, and many were better just from her touch. As the news spread, the number who sought her grew.

One early morning, Pom was once again in the courtyard. She felt a tap on her shoulder.

"I've been looking for you."

Pom suspected a Seeker looking for relief from some ailment. But when she turned, she saw a tower guard—the guard who had taken her to see the Keepers—waiting anxiously.

"What for?"

"You've been summoned," he replied.

Pom had wondered if she would see the Keepers again, so the news was not unexpected. But something about the guard's manner and the way the invitation was delivered made her suspicious.

"I have nothing of value," Pom said to ward off any attempt at robbery.

"We don't do that anymore," the guard replied tersely. "Ever since your visit, the Keepers have forbidden the taking of tributes from supplicants."

"Is that what you call it? Tribute?"

"Never mind. All I meant is that you are safe from us. Are you coming?"

Pom looked to Nomey, who was listening in on the conversation. She shrugged at Pom.

"Why not? Lead on."

Pom fell in behind the guard. He led her to the tower, and they entered through the same door as before. Once inside, however, they took a different turn.

"This isn't the way we went last time," she said.

"No, we're going to a different place," the guard replied uncomfortably.

Pom shouldn't have found that unusual—there was no reason to assume the Keepers only met in one place. Still, she felt some deception.

She said bluntly, "What are you hiding?"

"I'm not allowed to say."

They climbed up the narrow, winding stairs, passing occasional slits in the wall that let in the light from outside. As they climbed higher, the guard became noticeably winded and moved more slowly.

"Up there." He pointed at the summit of the tower.

"What's there?"

He shrugged.

Knowing she would get no additional information, Pom climbed the remaining distance. Even in the morning sun, the steps were dark. The last slit that had let in the brightness was far below them.

She entered a small, dark room. As her eyes adjusted to the dim light, she made out the back of a seated figure. He was dark—it wasn't just his hair and the black robes he wore, but a darkness about the man himself. Books were strewn open on the floor. A bronze pulcher bowl and various powders and colored crystals were also spread out. There was a logic to the placement of the objects. Pom studied the man in more detail. His hair was unkempt, his robes clean but wrinkled. He sat on a low stool with his legs crossed.

There was something odd about the way he sat. She realized he was not actually seated on the stool but hovering above it, his arms grasping its edges. She marveled at the tremendous strength it must take to balance himself for so long, without seeming to tire. She stood transfixed by his effort.

A voice made its way into her mind. *You are Pom*, it stated.

"And you are Malzus." She knew she should be afraid of the Dark Wizard, the one who had led the rebellion against the council of wizards. The one who had killed her friends, her family. She should be afraid. But she wasn't.

"What do you want of me?" she asked.

Nothing.

"Then why am I here?"

I want to help you.

Pom laughed at the oddness of the reply, then caught herself. "Sorry," she said, "but that is a strange offer, coming from you."

"Not so strange." He spoke in a calm voice that seemed to come from far away. His back still toward her, he slowly lowered himself to rest on the stool, uncrossed his legs, and stretched. He placed his feet firmly on the floor and effortlessly extended to his full height. Then he turned to face Pom.

She didn't see what she had expected—the face of a crazed killer. The Dark Wizard was tall and gaunt. His eyes looked weary—not tired, but as if they had seen too much. His features were soft.

"How do you want to help me?" she asked.

"I want to teach you."

She reminded herself not to trust her own instincts. This man was a wizard, able to control her thoughts.

"I'm not doing that," he said.

She realized he was reading her thoughts. *How do I know?* Her words were not spoken but sent from her mind to his. Even this smallest of touches, mind to mind, had a profound effect on Pom. She sensed a great sadness, deeper than any she had ever felt. He didn't answer her, but she knew he wouldn't risk doing something as obvious as influencing her—that would jeopardize his goals. But she also knew it was not beyond him to do this. That he struggled to control his urge to take over not just her mind, but that of many others.

That's what happened with the Keepers. Even though this was unspoken, she knew Malzus understood.

Yes, he replied.

Why did you stop?

Malzus paced the room, trying to quiet his mind. When he spoke, he was calm. "Because I needed to. Because they asked me to. Because of you."

"I had nothing to do with it. It was the Keepers who pushed you away."

Malzus shook his head. "Impossible. What they did was a minor slap, a gentle nudge. They cannot control me."

Said not with any sense of arrogance, but as a simple fact. "I must control myself, but you—"

"I can control you?"

"Of course not."

"So what about me, then?"

"It was your song. You reached out and it calmed me. It allowed me to gain control again."

"How did I do that?"

"It is just part of you. It is a gift—or burden—you'll have to bear."

"Others seem more interested in my ability than I am."

"That's unfortunate."

"Why? Why should others care? Why do you?"

Malzus reflected. "As to why I care, it's complicated. I know many consider me evil, but my error was not in my desire but in my execution."

The choice of the word "execution" startled Pom.

Malzus continued, "What I wanted was not that different from what my son wanted. I had his strength, his power, but not his wisdom. As a result, I did many things that I should not have."

"It was not his wisdom you lacked, but his compassion."

The Dark Wizard considered this. "I believe you are correct."

"You still do." Pom didn't know why she knew this, but she was sure it was true.

"Probably," Malzus admitted.

"Tell me," Pom continued. She was unsure why she was pressing the most powerful of wizards. "Do you feel regret?"

"Yes." Malzus closed his eyes.

"Remorse?"

The answer came slowly. "No."

"Why not?" Pom persisted, wondering why he kept answering her.

"In any great quest, things happen. Some benefit, but at a cost. Even with my son, there were losses. Your friend Gital lost his life. If Asmar had not come, he would still be alive."

This memory stung Pom.

"I did too much. It was painful to have others suffer, but some suffering is inevitable. I regret that I caused too much suffering for what I accomplished, however…"

Pom waited.

"If it hadn't been for me and the perceived evil of my ways, Asmar would not have accomplished what he did. How can I feel remorse at the result?" The effort of explaining had tired him. He lowered himself to the stool.

His arguments made sense to Pom. "You're wrong."

"No, I am correct."

"You believe so, but deep within, you know you're wrong. That's the cause of your conflict. You feel guilt, but you can't mourn. You do feel remorse, but you can't admit to it."

"You're wrong!" Malzus shot back.

Pom went on, "You're not like your son—you understand that. He harmed no one, others learned from him. I used to blame him for Gital, but no longer. He was the ray of light. He showed us the way. You were the cloud that tried to block his light."

Malzus raised his voice. "Without me, he would not have been possible!" Standing again, he approached Pom.

Pom backed away. She felt him reach out to her mind, trying to silence her but at the same time trying to stop himself. She went on, "Without you he would still exist. If not your son, then someone else's. It would have happened."

Malzus pushed into her mind. *He needed me to exist.*

"You wanted to be him!" Pom yelled back.

Malzus collapsed on the floor. The intrusion into her mind stopped. She waited.

The Dark Wizard looked up at her, once again in control. In an eerily calm voice, he admitted, "There is truth to what you say."

"Do you still want to teach me?"

"And to learn from you. But no more for today."

Pom left the tower, tired and drained.

When she made it back to the hostel, Nomey looked at her with concern. "Why do you want to deal with a creature like him?" she asked her friend.

"He can teach me things."

"Others can teach you," Nomey replied.

Pom shook her head. "They can't teach what he can."

Nomey started to object, but Pom stopped her. "I need to rest," she said, and went off to her rooms.

The next day she once again went to the tower and was escorted by the guard almost to the top. The final flight she ascended on her own.

She entered the room to find Malzus once again hovering over his stool. He slowly unfolded his legs and stood to his full height, and Pom involuntarily took a step back. But she wouldn't let herself be intimidated by the wizard, so she deliberately stepped forward again.

"What is it you want to teach me?" she demanded.

We have no need to speak. Just think and I will hear you.

What is it you have to teach me?

To reach out your mind and connect. You have talent, but you are untrained.

Pom considered. *How do we start?*

You must open your mind to me, Malzus replied.

Pom's pulse quickened. What would Nomey say? That it was a crazy idea. That it wasn't worth the risk. She was probably right. Still, this was her chance. *How do I do that?*

Relax your thoughts and let me into your mind.

Pom complied, but at the first touch of Malzus's thoughts, she recoiled and reflexively pushed him out. His mind was angry; he was cold, yet also sad. She felt the iciness of his barely suppressed rage.

This is what I need you for, Malzus said. *I need more control over my thoughts. I need your strength to push them back.*

No, Pom replied. *Just pushing them back will not give you what you want. You need to let them go. You need to replace them with other thoughts and feelings.*

Shall we try again? Malzus asked.

Pom once again relaxed her mind and let Malzus enter. As the iciness washed over her, she tried to ignore the fear and hate that coursed through her. She remembered the song she had sung with Yau and began the tune. It was a great effort to calm the Dark Wizard, as he kept on trying to reassert his feelings. But slowly, as she linked her mind to Malzus, she felt the iciness recede and a calmness enter. Finally, he had enough control to continue.

I will show you how to reach out your mind, Malzus told her. With their minds still linked, together they left the stuffiness of the tower room and went out into the openness of the desert. She felt free traveling this way. Malzus directed the two of them out of the desert into the forest that was so familiar to her. They went to her village, and she saw the life she had left. Disdain washed over her. This was a petty existence. The drudgery of everyday life. How had she stood it for all those years?

These are your thoughts, not mine, she said to Malzus.

They should be yours as well, he replied.

No, Pom pushed back. *You need to accept these people as they are.*

Never came the reply.

The disdain reasserted itself, the anger came back, and Pom pushed Malzus from her thoughts. Relief, then disappointment, washed over her as she looked around. They were back in the tower. The euphoria of leaving her body, of traveling through the world, was gone.

"You can't do that."

There is no need to speak.

"You can't just dismiss people like that," she said aloud. Pom felt Malzus pushing back, but then the pressure subsided.

This is why I need you.

But we are done for today, Pom stated, and turned to start her trek back to the hostel.

You will come back tomorrow? Malzus asked.

Pom paused before replying, *I will.*

Pom returned the next day and for many days after that. Each morning the guard opened the gate for Pom, but he no longer accompanied her. Malzus was gaining control over himself, and Pom was now able to reach out on her own. She felt her song getting stronger, but her body was weakening from the exertion.

They had been together for sixty days when Pom finally felt strong enough to ask Malzus, *Why are you doing this?*

I am preparing you for when you will be needed.

For what?

Soon a quest will begin, and you will be part of it.

A quest for what?

For the Golden Tree.

But the Tree has already been discovered.

Malzus shook his head. *Have you seen it?*

No.

So what does its discovery mean to you?

I have been touched by it, through Asmar.

That is not enough! Malzus shouted. *That is not enough,* he repeated more calmly. *My son accomplished much, but there is still much left to do. He discovered one path to the Tree. There are more ways to the Tree, more levels to understanding.*

Will you go?

Malzus reacted as if he'd been stung, but his voice displayed no sign of pain. *No. If I go, the quest will fail.*

Pom didn't press. She understood Malzus was too unstable. He would be a liability on the quest.

You need to go, Malzus explained. *If I can teach you what you need, I will feel part of the quest. I can help by helping you.*

Pom narrowed her eyes. She knew the real reason he wanted her to go, and so did he. *You want the knowledge, and you want to get that through me.*

Yes.

How will you do that without controlling my mind?

That was my original plan. But it would not work. I need to be able to connect with you when you touch the Tree. The only way that can happen is if you agree.

And the only way to get me to agree is if I trust you.

He nodded.

Pom was glad for the honesty. She wanted his knowledge—but not at any cost. *There is very little chance it will work as you suppose.*

Yes, I know.

Then why do it?

It is my only chance.

CHAPTER 16

THE WANDERER REACHED OUT. *YOU need to leave her alone.*

You've avoided me for all these years, and now you reach out to scold me? Malzus replied.

You're pushing her too far.

She needs to learn how the world is.

You risk taking away her purity.

You abandoned her in favor of Lefi. She needs guidance, and she is not getting that from you. You only have time for Lefi.

She doesn't need my help. The Wanderer paused. *And your help is destroying her.*

Yet she keeps coming back of her own will.

Is it?

I haven't compelled her to return to me. She does that because she wants to learn from me.

You're like a drug to her. It isn't good, but she can't help herself.

So you say. I give her what she needs.

And you take what you want from her.

And what is wrong with that?

Everything.

NO! Malzus shot back. *It is easy for you to lecture me. You've obtained everything you wanted. You found the Tree. You wander the land doing what you want. What do I have? Years of failure, years of regret. Pom gives me hope. And I can help her.*

And she doesn't seek the Tree, the Wanderer replied, *whereas you do.*

I can't help that. I know what the Tree is. I long to touch it. What is it like?

There is no way to describe it.

There must be. I need to know. I need to see the Tree!

It isn't up to me. My own brother can't find the Tree either. It has driven him mad.

I'm not mad. At least, not anymore.

Then be careful with Pom.

I will protect her, Malzus replied.

And I will protect her as well, the Wanderer said, *from you.*

CHAPTER 17

"YOU NEED TO STOP," NOMEY said to her friend.

"I can't," Pom replied.

"He's ruining your mind. You need to leave him."

"No! Without me he is worse. He's gaining control, gaining insight."

"To what end?"

"He helps me as well."

"He's destroying you. When you return from the tower, you're tired and drained. The guards almost have to carry you back here. Yet the next day you return to him. Days go by and we don't see you. Please, at least stay with me a few days. Get better before you return."

The idea appealed to Pom. A few days' rest without the stress of learning or teaching, without touching his mind. That was what she both feared and craved. The mind of

Malzus was complex. He allowed her to explore the labyrinth of his thoughts. Some corridors she wouldn't enter—they were too dark. Others gave great insight. The ones that contained the most suffering, that drained her the most, were the ones that contained his regrets. The sorrow he felt, drawn not only from himself but those whose minds he touched. And then there were the voices from deep within his mind. Malzus wouldn't let her explore there, but she had felt them. They contained great wisdom, but she was afraid of them as well.

"He needs me," Pom replied.

"And what about you?"

"And I need him." Then Pom added, "At least for now."

"Very well. I'll keep putting you back together as best as I can."

Pom smiled at her friend, and the next morning returned to the tower, and for ten more days after that. The last day, Pom could barely make it back to the hostel.

"You're going to rest, that's all there is to it!" Nomey insisted.

Pom was too weak to argue. She needed a break, not just to recover physically, but to think about what had been happening to her. Her exhaustion was only partially due to the Dark Wizard. After her sessions with him, she would reach out on her own, searching for the voice she'd heard with Yau. She thought she could hear it, but faintly. Once she had recovered enough, she resolved to pick up again with Yau to find the voice.

"Drink this," Nomey demanded.

Pom took a sip of the offered liquid and almost spit it out. "This is awful! What poison are you giving me?"

"It'll give you strength."

"It'll kill me," Pom countered.

"It's a new formula I'm working on."

"I think it needs a bit more work."

Nomey shrugged and sniffed the mixture. "Do you think you can drink just a bit? It really is good for you."

Pom took the cup back and raised it to her lips. Could she overcome her senses and drink the vile, smelly concoction her friend had prepared? As the liquid passed her lips, she attempted to turn off her sense of smell. She stifled the impulse to gag. As she emptied the cup, her mind took over and she was no longer overwhelmed by the vile odor. She was able to concentrate on the individual scents, each pleasant on its own—it was the combination that caused problems. Pom realized she could identify all the herbs and plants Nomey had used. There were a few she didn't know the names of, but she could picture them. Nothing in the potion would cause harm, and she knew they would help her.

Nomey looked surprised. "I guess it wasn't as bad as I thought."

"It was worse." Pom smiled. She then suggested some alterations in the formula that would have the dual impact of increasing the effectiveness and making it more palatable.

Nomey nodded and wrote in a small book. "I think that will work, but how did you know?"

"I'm not sure," Pom admitted.

After Pom had recovered for a few more days, Yau paid her former student a visit. "Will you have time to join us before you go back to Malzus?"

"I'm not going back." Pom had not realized this until she spoke the words.

Yau looked relieved. "We will await your return, then."

"Yes, I would like that."

A few more days passed before Pom rejoined Yau and her group. In that time of recovery, Pom roamed the streets of Dolcere, something she had not done since her arrival. She had been so concerned with the Keepers, the Seekers, and the Dark Wizard, and the rest of her time had been spent at the hostel. Now she roamed freely, feeling no pull from her former obligations. She traveled to different parts of the city, where people from different lands had made a home. Even the Sitire and Domare had small but growing enclaves. She wandered the streets without any plan. When she was hungry, she bought food from a stall or shop. One in particular that she enjoyed was a small, nondescript shop from which a wonderful aroma emanated. The owner was a kind elderly man. He recommended a pastry called a scion. She purchased the sweet-smelling delicacy and wandered until she came to a secluded park, where she sat to enjoy her treat.

As she finished her scion, she noticed a movement in the trees. She looked around, but the park was deserted and she saw no one. She felt a presence, though—more than one. They were hiding from her. Pom stood and started to walk, picking up her pace as she went.

Wait! A voice echoed in her head. *Wait!* Another voice, and then two more.

Pom twirled around, looking for the people connected to the voices. "Where are you?" she shouted.

No need for words. We hear you. The four figures appeared from behind the trees. They wore black robes.

"Who sent you?" Pom asked.

You have seen him, one of the four stated.

Pom knew who they were talking about. "You still follow him?"

He is the only one who can lead us to salvation, said the third black-clad figure.

And he has chosen you to help him, said the final one.

"We help each other." Pom sensed the anger in the four followers of Malzus.

He refuses to see us, yet he called to you.

Why? asked another.

"You want him to go back to what he was. I help him move forward," Pom responded.

It's not fair. The four communicated at once, and they started after Pom.

She turned to run, but each path was blocked by a black-clad figure. They were closing on her. She reached out her mind to show them she wasn't against them and they had no reason to hurt her. But their minds were closed. Should she reach into their thoughts and control them, make them stop against their will? She stood frozen, not knowing what to do. The first of the black-clad figures raised his arm, a dark rock held in his fist. He was going to strike her down. Pom put up her hands to protect herself and waited for the blow, her eyes closing automatically.

Then an icy wind swept over her. The blow didn't come. She opened her eyes and saw all four figures lying on the path. She sensed their breath leaving them—they were dying.

Leave them be! Pom shot out to Malzus. She reached into the minds of the four to pull them back to life.

Malzus replied, *I won't let them harm you.*

I'm safe now, Pom reassured him. *You can let them be.*

The four started to stir. One crawled to his knees and looked at Pom. "You let us live." His voice was dry and cracked.

Pom nodded.

"Go," he said. "Go now, before we ..." He didn't finish but just motioned with his hand.

Pom straightened and walked out of the park, back to the safety of the hostel, and collapsed on her bed.

The next morning, Nomey gave her more of her restorative drink. Pom reflected on what Malzus had done the previous day. His mind was in deep conflict. She felt his despair. He had wanted his followers to worship him, but he also knew it was only by suppressing his own desire, his own ego, that he could obtain what he sought. He knew despite his strength, or maybe because of it, he would never accomplish his goal.

Pom went to Yau's classroom. The two women, one Chert and one Domare, and the Tuland man were with Yau. They were seated on the bare floor, deep in meditation. She heard their song and slowly reintroduced herself. She realized she had not known their names before, but now they came to her. The Domare woman was named Arkani; the Chert, Nima; and the Tulander, Sen. They greeted each other with their song. They accepted Pom, and she, them.

Something happened, Yau said. *It has made you stronger.*

But sadder, Sen added.

Both true, Pom admitted as she directed their song, closing off the part of her mind that held the memory of the other day.

The five were joined by others; some were Yau's people, others she didn't know by name. Some were strong, others not, but each added their own strains to the music. Pom realized she was supposed to direct the song, to give it purpose and meaning.

No, she sang to the others. *I won't tell you what to do.* Instead she reached out on her own. Some followed, but they traveled with her of their own choice. Yau was there, but so were others who came from beyond the small room. They gave their strength out of their own desire to understand.

With their aid she felt whole again. She sought the voice. She knew the name that belonged to the voice: Ran-dahl.

Here I am came the response to the unasked question.

How can I find you?

Follow the crystal.

Pom almost understood, but the meaning seemed just out of her reach.

Ran-dahl sensed this. *The crystal has a field that pulls on you.*

What crystal? Where is this crystal?

That I can't see clearly. It's in your land, held by one whose mind is deeply conflicted. Seek him out and come to me.

The song grew weaker and faded away—it had taken much effort for Ran-dahl to reach out so far. Pom thought about the crystal. When Malzus had first called her, she had seen his crystals, and Malzus was certainly deeply conflicted. Maybe one of them was the crystal Ran-dahl described. Despite her previous resolve, she knew she must visit the Dark Wizard at least one more time.

Pom abruptly left Yau and hurried back to the hostel. She didn't sleep much that night. She kept thinking of Randahl, the fog, and having to see Malzus again after what he'd done to his followers.

She woke early the next day and went to the tower. Now the guards just let her in, and she hurried up to the top.

Malzus was waiting for her, seated on his small, low stool. *You've returned to me.*

Yes, Pom replied. *I didn't want to. Not after what you did.*

And what did I do, other than save your life?

You still don't understand.

Malzus rose easily from his seated position. He walked over to Pom and laid a hand on her shoulder. She didn't pull away.

Neither do you, he said.

Pom started to object, but Malzus put up a hand to quiet her. *Why have you come? I assume it's not to learn from me.*

Pom shook her head.

You have learned all I can teach you, then?

I have learned all I care to from you.

Malzus breathed deeply. Pom felt his anger at her, but he controlled it. He nodded.

I've come to you on a different matter.

The woman?

You were there, then?

No. This admission was difficult for him, but Malzus forced himself to explain. *I started with you. I followed at first as you ventured forth, but then I realized . . .* His voice trailed off.

Pom waited.

I realized I didn't belong there. His voice cracked slightly. *I was not pure enough, I wasn't focused.* He struggled for the words. *I didn't belong.* Malzus sat on the small stool, deflated. *I need you,* he went on with an air of desperation, *to hear for me, see for me, sing for me!*

I can't, Pom replied reluctantly. Now she realized why she had resolved not to work with the Dark Wizard again. It was not what he would do to her, but what he wanted from her. *Even if I wanted to, I can't give you what you ask. I'm not one of your Saeren that you can use as a tool.*

The mention of the Saeren, the ones he had almost stripped of their will, the former men over whom he had obtained absolute control, sent a pang of regret through him. But, she realized, his regret was not for what he had done but for the loss of their abilities. Through them he had extended his reach, his power, his understanding.

Pom looked at him. *You understand?*

Yes, you're right, of course, he admitted. *I wanted to use you as I did the Saeren. I know it was wrong. But it doesn't feel wrong.*

Until it does, Pom stated.

Until it does, there is no hope for me. There is no way for me to understand.

Pom nodded and turned to leave. She hadn't asked about the crystal. She knew he didn't have it. It had been her excuse to come one last time to see him, to help him understand, to help herself. She would find Ran-dahl's crystal, but it was not here.

A few days later, she was summoned to the tower once again. At first she thought Malzus wanted her, but there was nothing more he needed from her, at least for now. The call from the Keepers had been a surprise.

"They are coming for you," Areana explained to Pom. "Are you prepared?"

"Prepared for what?" Pom countered.

"For your quest—the search for the Tree," Bradoc filled in.

"Probably not," Pom admitted. "But it's not like I have a choice."

"You always have a choice," Wetell stated calmly.

Pom considered this. "I don't think I could ever be totally ready for a quest such as this. Yet I feel I must go."

Wetell looked at her kindly.

"I want to go," she admitted. "Not just for Ran-dahl, but for me. I want to know what's beyond the fog. I want to know the truth."

CHAPTER 18

HE FELT THE SONG AND joined. The core of the song came from a distance, but it was still strong. The purity of one voice drew him. Its beauty and simplicity helped make things clear. The singer was reaching out, seeking someone far away. She needed help. He lent his strength to her and was drawn along with her, farther than he had ever gone. As her mind opened more, things that had troubled him became clear. And then he heard the far-off voice, asking them to come. Them? No, he was not the one being asked; he was just helping. This was not for him, but for her—the one with the pure voice.

The faraway voice spoke of a crystal that would direct them, that could find her through the fog. And then it was gone, the connection broken.

"Are you okay?"

Sevas opened his eyes to see the hulking figure of Tiox bending over him.

"Were you there?" Sevas asked.

"At first," Tiox admitted. "But I couldn't follow."

"Your friend has a crystal, I believe?"

Tiox nodded. "He believes it is one."

"I think he's right. We must go to Tellurium." The old man had hoped he would never have to visit that place of so many evil memories. "Let us go, now."

CHAPTER 19

THEB RUSHED TO HIS FRIEND to embrace him but stopped short. "You seem different," he said.

Tiox smiled. "I feel different as well. I feel more . . . open."

Theb looked at him quizzically.

"It's hard to explain. When we have more time . . ."

Theb nodded. The others in the room—Sevas, Lefi, Rogi, and the Wanderer—were deep in conversation.

"We are to leave tomorrow," Lefi explained.

Sevas nodded. "Where will you go?"

"Tuland, eventually," Rogi said. "Ran-dahl is across the ocean, and Tuland has the easiest access to the waters."

"And then?"

Rogi considered, and then went on, "I have some maps of the ocean that we brought from our homeland. That will help. But the real problem is, we don't know which way to go."

"But you do," Sevas corrected.

The rest turned to him. "Which way, then?" asked Lefi.

"Follow the crystal," Sevas explained. "It'll get stronger as you approach Ran-dahl."

"Maybe," Rogi conceded, "but there has been no change in the crystal since it was brought here."

"There is one who can help," the Wanderer said.

"Who?" Rogi asked.

Sevas suddenly understood. "The woman in Dolcere. You must go there."

"Aren't you coming as well?" Tiox wasn't about to leave Sevas behind.

"No. I can't travel with this." He pointed at his broken body.

"I'll carry you, if need be," Tiox declared.

Sevas replied, "It's time for you to go out on your own."

"I'm not sure I'm ready," Tiox answered.

"You probably aren't," Sevas replied, and raised a hand to forestall any response from Tiox. "In any event, you will go and I'm staying."

Tiox sighed, then nodded his assent.

They set out early the next morning. Tiox took the lead on his stout brown-and-white horse. Lefi and Theb fell in behind him, and Rogi, traveling in the white robe of a Seeker and leaving his silver staff behind, rode a pure-white mount. The Wanderer had disappeared, so Sevas alone was there to see them off.

"I will be with you," he said to Tiox.

As the troop started out going south, Lefi announced, "We must go to the Domare before heading to Tuland."

"We should get to Tuland quickly. We need to prepare for our journey," Rogi argued.

"You go there if you want. I need to return to the Domare."

"I don't understand why," Rogi replied. "But we will stay together."

Tiox was uncomfortable with Lefi's decision. Even though they had been allies of the Breccians, their strange beliefs made him uneasy.

"We will go not only there," Lefi continued, "but also to the Community. Only then will we go to Dolcere and Tuland."

"It's a waste of time," Rogi said.

Lefi pulled up and turned his horse to face the others. "Let's not forget," he said simply.

Tiox and Rogi looked confused. Theb looked up from his crystal and blurted, "That's it, of course!"

"What's it?" Rogi asked.

"The key to finding her."

"Ran-dahl?" Tiox asked.

"Of course," Theb repeated, but didn't see a need to go on.

Tiox finally broke the silence. "It is not so clear to me, so if you wouldn't mind . . ."

"Sorry," Theb said. "I think we've almost forgotten."

When it seemed as if he wouldn't say more, Rogi prodded him. "Forgotten what?"

"The Moment, of course."

"What's that got to do with the quest?" Tiox asked.

"We are retracing Asmar's route," Theb said.

Rogi eyes widened, "This is where the wizards have gone wrong. They seek the Tree without seeking understanding." He turned to Lefi. "We'll follow you, wherever that may lead."

CHAPTER 20

"YOU MUST NOT INTERFERE," THE Wanderer stated flatly.

"They're strong, they'll be able to overcome any petty interference from me."

"You underestimate yourself, Brother," the Wanderer went on. "You almost ended Asmar's quest."

"I did no such thing. In fact, I helped him. At least in the end."

"You taught him about evil."

"And you taught him about good?"

"I helped him find his way, that's all."

"As did I, in my own way."

"Poisoning him is hardly helping, Old Man."

"So you use the name that has been forced upon me, rather than the one given to me by our mother."

"You refused that name after she died."

"You mean after I killed her?"

"You had no choice."

"There is always a choice. Isn't that what you say?"

"We've been over this many times. Unless you are able to move beyond what happened, you will be doomed to eternal torment."

"I *should* suffer eternal torment for what I did, to both our parents. They died because of me."

"If you insist, we can have the same argument once again. You knew they were using me and my power to help them reach out. They had discovered the techniques of Malzus long before he and his kind came to these shores."

"That doesn't excuse a thing. There were choices, there must have been. I just couldn't find them at the time."

"They were destroying my mind, sapping my strength. I was no better than a Saeren until you intervened. It was my fault as much as yours. I was stronger than them. I could have resisted, I should have fought back."

"Maybe so, but you trusted them—as did I, at least at first. But they sought knowledge, not understanding, and their quest for knowing drove them beyond reason. You were stronger than me—you had such promise, such understanding—but you wouldn't fight. I needed to get them out of your mind. I needed you back."

"So you pushed them out, without my help. What a massive effort it must have been for you! The struggle went on for three cycles of the moon. You tried to save them, but they wouldn't listen. They fought back with all their strength, but you managed to protect yourself—and me."

"I managed ultimately to kill them both. What haunts me still is at the end, the very end, they seemed to understand what they'd done. I think they let go of you just before they died. It wasn't so much that I beat them—they just wanted death, by the end."

"I was left like those former Saeren up in Tellurium. It was you who nursed me back and gave me your strength. But who was there for you? Who was there to heal your mind? You live with the scars of your life, as I live with mine."

"I swore that when I recovered, I would not let anything like what our parents did ever happen again, if it was in my power to help."

"So you wander and find those you wish to help."

"As you won't let me help you, I help others as best I can."

"You do help me, more than you know. Without you, I would be like our parents, with no light, no matter how foggy, to look to."

At the mention of fog, the Old Man looked at his sister. "I will try and do what you ask. I will try not to interfere."

CHAPTER 21

IT WAS HIS FATHER'S FAULT, Ruvbain thought as he stared at the portrait of his predecessor. He had established the Valki Institute and called all the scholars together. He had wanted them to find out about the fog; but the scholars studied much more than the fog. They studied the power of crystals and the flowing of the pulcher trees. Then their research spread to the best way to govern, and they talked of things like liberty and freedom. Had they forgotten who had given them their freedom? Who had set up and funded the Institute? It was enough that they questioned the meaning of the fog given by the priests. The impenetrable field sent by the creator. Something unknowable, it represented the mystery of life, the mystery of the creator.

But Ruvbain had been brought up believing the fog was knowable. He had studied with the scholars; understood, at least partially, their theories. He'd even met his wife, K'ren, while studying the fog. The more he understood, however, the more concerned he became. Not just because the more they studied the fog, the more dangerous it seemed, but because studying what the priests said was knowable only to the creator was raising discontent.

To protect himself and Ognita, he'd had to quell those ideas. So those who strayed into these areas of thought tended to disappear. He had also learned that from his father. Some never returned, but others, like the troublesome Ran-dahl, he still might need.

Ruvbain wandered the upper floors of his castle, looking for K'ren and his son, Nipio. It was good his son was born only six months ago—K'ren was busy caring for him instead of causing trouble studying the fog. She had been one of the smartest at the Valki Institute and wouldn't listen to reason when he had asked her to stop.

Ruvbain reached the nursery and gently pushed the door open. K'ren sat with her back to the door, holding Nipio, who was latched onto her breast. Ruvbain had suggested a wet nurse for their son, telling K'ren it was beneath her to feed their child. She'd laughed at him. But when it came to finding a nursemaid, K'ren was all for that. She said it would give her time to keep up with her studies.

Ruvbain watched in silence for a while before he cleared his throat.

"Just wait," his wife said, not even turning around. "I'm almost done."

She finally handed Nipio to the nurse and covered her breast. She smiled at him. "I haven't seen you for a while. You've been so busy."

"I missed Nipio."

K'ren frowned.

He added hastily, "And you, of course."

Ruvbain walked over to the nurse and stared at his son. This would be the next ruler of Ognita, and it was his job to preserve it until Nipio was ready to take over.

"How is Ran-dahl?" K'ren asked.

Ruvbain turned sharply. "You know better than to ask that. She's an enemy of the state."

K'ren rose and went to her husband. "It's just us."

Ruvbain glanced over at the nurse.

"Don't worry about Ntan. She's loyal."

"To whom?"

K'ren let out a short laugh. "To Nipio, of course."

"And to you," Ntan broke in.

Ruvbain sighed. "We need to be very careful. The religious factions are gaining power, and any sign of sympathy to the scientists could be . . ." He trailed off.

"Surely, you're not giving in to them?"

"I'm just trying to preserve the peace," Ruvbain replied. "I want there to be a kingdom for Nipio to take over." He turned and left the chamber. He didn't want to worry his wife too much, but he was afraid for what might come.

CHAPTER 22

"I WILL TAKE YOU TO my people," Yau said to Pom. "The others you need to meet are going there as well."

Pom didn't relish traveling into the desert once again, but she knew it was necessary. She would be needed to reach out to Ran-dahl and find a path to her. Under Yau's tutelage, Pom had gained control over the powers Malzus had taught her. She still was not strong enough to travel far on her own, but with the help of Yau and the others, she could reach out and draw people together. It was not like the Moment; it was more like the song of Yau's people. Individuals harmonizing together, but not sharing one mind.

"Will Nomey come as well?"

Yau shook her head. "She's needed here."

Pom found her friend to say farewell. Nomey handed her a sheaf of papers. "If you can get to the Domare town, please give this to Wen. I want them to have these new cures for ailments."

"I will," Pom replied.

They left the safety of Dolcere and traveled out into the desert. The heat and the cold were as severe as Pom remembered, but Yau knew the desert, and while they were not comfortable, it was more bearable.

"You need to wrap your talize like this." Yau demonstrated the proper way of wearing the protection from the desert. "Otherwise, sand will make its way in and scar you."

Pom nodded and followed the instructions. "I wish you had been with me the first time I ventured into the desert. It would have saved me much pain."

"Yes, but then you would've learned less. Now you know to respect the desert."

Pom gazed out at the vast expanse of sand that stretched from horizon to horizon. These golden grains, seemingly so innocent, had almost killed her. "And how did you get to know the desert so well?"

"It was after the Moment. My people knew we needed to reach out and reconnect with the world. We did so first with our minds, but that was not enough. It couldn't replace actual contact with others. So a few of us ventured away from the high rocks. I was very nervous—it was the first time any of us had journeyed from home. Except for Ning, of course. I went alone, as an individual. The Community was still with me, but it was different. I'm still not totally comfortable with the feeling, and I'm looking forward to being back, even if only for a short time.

"I was one of the first to leave. Others traveled to different places—Tellurium, Continel, even Tuland. The first time I traveled to Dolcere, I was escorted by a band of Aris, who taught me what to do and how to travel. It was a very easy trip." Yau shook her head as if she wanted to say more. Pom waited, and eventually she continued, "The first time I left Dolcere and returned home, I did so by myself. Remembering, of course, all that I had been taught."

"And was that as easy as your first trip?"

"Hardly. My journey was much worse than yours. I lost most of my food and water after only a few days. I was attacked by the wolves and managed to crawl into a small hole in the rocks, where they couldn't reach me. I stayed there for two days, afraid to come out, wanting desperately to get back to my people and never venture out again."

"What happened?"

"A traveler found me and healed me, and taught me what to do in the desert. I spent ten days with her, and it was one of the most fascinating experiences of my life. She spoke little but seemed to say much. I remember a gray wolf that used to follow her from time to time."

The two pitched their tent for the evening and lit a small fire. They ate dried fruits and vegetables.

"How is it that you have such a beautiful song?" Yau asked.

Pom shook her head. "I don't really know. It's almost like the song was always in me, but I didn't realize it until you brought it out." This didn't really explain how she felt, so she went on, "It's as if you have a feeling deep down that you know something is the right thing to do, yet you don't do it because no one else is doing it. Then something happens to make you realize the others are wrong. This is what happened to me when I met Asmar. He didn't change my mind about anything, but he made me realize what I already knew."

Yau nodded. "It was similar in the Community. We hid ourselves away for too long. We knew it was wrong, but it had become so ingrained that nobody questioned it. Asmar planted the questions—although we didn't listen, at least not at first. In fact, we almost destroyed him. Something we regret deeply."

"When did you realize things were different?"

"It started when Asmar was freed from the Community. Something deep in our past told us to let him go, a voice not heard in many generations. We believe it was the voice of the Founder, but we can't be sure. In any event, we let Asmar go. And we also began to think as individuals. Before that, individual thought was subjugated to the thought of the Community. It was the Community that did everything. It was always 'we' or 'us' and never 'me' or 'I.'" Yau couldn't help flinching at those last two words. "You see, I'm still not comfortable referring to myself as an individual. But I'm working on it."

Pom nodded sleepily to her companion. She had developed a deep affection for Yau, and she believed the feeling was mutual. The two gently fell asleep in the chill of the desert.

CHAPTER 23

IT WAS SIMPLE TO FIND the Community, unlike in the past, because this time they were not hiding. Still, when the travelers arrived in the valley surrounded by the high cliffs, they did not find what they expected.

"I would have thought there would be encampments of pilgrims," Tiox said to his companions. The valley was empty, devoid of the plethora of white-robed Seekers they had encountered elsewhere.

Lefi replied, "They let in who they want. It was simple for us to find them because they wanted us to come. But for others it would not be possible."

Rogi nodded. "I felt their presence, but I would not have been able to find them without their consent. They are very powerful together. So much so that the wizard's council never detected them until they revealed themselves."

The lack of other visitors made Theb nervous. "They trapped Asmar when he came here. How do we know what they intend for us?"

Rogi replied, "They relented and let Asmar go. The wizards have had contact with the Community since the Moment, and while they are still not the most open society, I wouldn't worry about them abducting us."

"What would you worry about, then?" Theb asked.

Rogi laughed. "There is plenty else to worry about. You can worry about how we plan to travel the seas to find Ran-dahl, you can worry about navigating rough seas, you can worry—"

"Okay, I get it." Theb cut the wizard short.

A flimsy rope ladder was flung down from one of the cave openings in the high rock.

"It seems like we've been invited in," Tiox commented.

Before they ascended, they saw to their mounts. The horses had carried them far, patiently navigating the long trek, but it was unfair to ask them to wait. So they unsaddled them and set them free.

If we need you, we will call, Rogi communicated to them. He was sure they understood—if not the exact words, then the feeling.

As they climbed, they heard the song. Theb realized he had been hearing it for some time, but somewhere beneath his consciousness, guiding them toward the Community. The voices guided him up the rope ladder, steadying him. As he approached the cave entrance, the song grew stronger. Theb heard many individual voices making up the song. He even heard slight undertones of discordance in the music that were embraced and made part of the whole. It was a beautiful song.

They were greeted by a woman. "Welcome to our Community." Her name, Contin, came into Theb's mind through her song. The man by her side was Arlin.

"You are Ning's parents," Rogi commented.

Contin nodded. "Our daughter accompanied Asmar when he left the Community. She is in the Silver Forest with him."

"Have you been able to reach her there?" Rogi asked. "We have tried to contact the wizard Asmar, but to no avail."

Arlin replied, "We have had no contact with Ning since she left the Community, but we know she is there. Her song has left us, but its shadow still remains."

"You must be tired and hungry after your journey," Contin said. "Please take some time to rest and eat. When you are ready, we can take you to see the Forty." She pointed to the fresh fruits and vegetable dishes that had been laid out on the rough wooden table.

Theb realized he was quite hungry; travel rations weren't enough for him. "Thank you," he said, as he piled a plate with various treats. Then he saw that he was the only one sitting and eating.

Tiox broke the uncomfortable silence with a warm laugh. "I think I'll join you, my friend, although I'm probably not as famished as you seem to be." Then, turning to their hosts, he said, "We thank you for your generosity." He added a slight bow.

Contin and Arlin returned the bow and withdrew from the room, leaving behind their song, which seemed somewhat lighter than before.

Theb turned to Lefi. "Why are we here?"

"The same reason as before. To learn, just as Asmar did. And don't ask 'to learn what?'—if I knew that, we wouldn't have needed to come."

Theb was busy stuffing himself. Tiox also ate heartily, but not as much as he used to, while Rogi and Lefi ate little, just enough to replace the energy they had lost on their travels.

When they finished, they discovered they had been provided water to wash with and clean robes. The robes were earth tones, the same type and color worn by the residents of the Community, although Theb had noticed Contin had added a fringe of deep purple to her robe.

As they relaxed in the small room, Lefi explained a bit more about why they had come. "We need to understand more of their song," he began. "If we are to find Ran-dahl, I believe the Community can help us."

"How?" Theb asked.

"In different ways, depending on our needs. But we won't know exactly how until we speak with the Forty."

"I've heard of them, but what are they exactly?" Tiox asked.

Rogi replied, "They are the leaders of the Community. They control the song."

"How can they do that?" asked Theb.

"Control is probably not the best word. It's more like they channel the songs of the Community through them. Rather than controlling the songs, they meld them together—they are the conductors of the song."

"But doesn't that give them the ability to control the song as well? To keep out unwanted strains?" Tiox inquired.

"I suppose so. And they used to do that, until Asmar came."

"You mean, until Asmar left. When he came, they used that technique to try to keep him here," Theb corrected.

Rogi nodded. "Yes, you're right, my friend. Asmar and Ning were the ones to put an end to the control."

"But it could happen again." Lefi broke into the conversation. "For now, they have taken a more passive role in the song."

"It's like the Moment, melding all the songs together," Theb commented.

"No!" Lefi said, more forcefully than the others had heard him before. "It is not like the Moment. In the Moment, there was no gatekeeper, no conductor, no controls. The Moment was much purer than anything the Community can do."

Arlin and Contin reentered. "The Forty await you," Contin said.

They followed the couple through the maze of caves that made up the Community. Theb tried to keep track of all the twists and turns, but he quickly became lost. He didn't like the idea of being at the mercy of the Community and hoped the others could find their way out.

They stood at a simply carved entrance, smoothed over the ages by people's light touches gently wearing down the hard stone. Contin silently signaled for them to enter, but she and her husband stayed behind.

Rogi led them into the chamber. It took Theb's eyes a while to adjust to the gray light that permeated the chamber. He made out forty ghostly shapes in niches in the wall. Their song reached out to him, calming him, welcoming him. Theirs was a gentle touch on his mind, allaying any fears he had of being overwhelmed by their song.

We welcome you to the Community, the chorus of voices communicated. *You have nothing to fear from us. We have changed from what you knew. We only want to help you.*

Help us with what? Lefi asked suspiciously.

The song came back to them without offense. *We seek to help in your quest. We can help you find your way.*

How can you help? Rogi asked.

We can help prepare your minds and make you stronger the chorus came back.

We can also help you find the direction you need to travel came another strain of the music. *We can help the crystal come to life.*

It's my crystal! Theb found his voice, adding discordance to the otherwise polished sound.

The Forty took the discordance in stride. *It is your crystal and shall stay with you. We do not need to possess it to help.*

Theb found his mind calmed by this song.

There is another way we can help, the song continued. *There is another coming to us who will be needed for you to succeed in your quest.*

Theb felt the rightness of the song. Despite his distrust of the Community, he knew they must meet this person. Without consulting the others, he replied, *We will stay with you until she arrives.*

The Community sang to them, *You can seat yourselves in the inner circle and open your mind. We will instruct you according to your needs.*

The four found there was an inner circle on the floor of the cave, with the stone smoothed in places, worn away by past occupants. As he lowered himself, Theb looked around at the others. The general song faded into the background and a new melody appeared. This one was more focused, with ten voices communicating with him—ten of the Forty who were to be his teacher. Slowly he felt their song wash over him, then through him, simple and mild. At first, he couldn't tell what was happening. Then Theb's body relaxed—he hadn't realized how tense he had been, how the burden of the crystal weighed on him. His mind began to wander, and he thought of the extraordinary events that had brought him to this place, high up on a hill, looking for a woman who was far away. Why was he doing this? What was the point? He didn't have answers to these questions, but it didn't seem to matter. He was in search of knowledge, and that was all that seemed important.

As he thought this, he felt the encouragement of the song. The Community was helping him to see more clearly. It was not like his encounters with the wizards. There was no bending of his will, no subversion. The Community knew his mind better than he did—they felt his song before Theb understood what he himself felt. But the Community let him discover his song for himself.

As Tiox tried to get comfortable on the small patch of smooth stone, he felt the song wash over him, settling his mind, relaxing his body. When he'd been with Sevas, getting his mind settled had always been the most diffi-cult part. Now the song showed him what he had been doing wrong. It seemed simple—he just needed to let go. Sevas had explained all this to him, but he hadn't really understood.

Rogi was uncomfortable in the tan robes of the Com-munity. He missed the blue he'd worn as a wizard. It had been hard for him to separate himself from the council. It was all he knew. When he was a child, he had been identi-fied as one with the power and mental capacity to become a wizard. He had left his home, his parents, at a very young age. He thought he might have a brother, or maybe a sister, back home, but he wasn't sure. He'd been cloistered away from the world, his contact with his family cut off. The other wizards were all Rogi had. When they'd come to this land on their quest, it had seemed exciting. But then it had all gone wrong. First, the quest was more difficult than he had expected. Then there was Malzus. He had destroyed everything the council had tried to build. Rogi thought about those words: "the council tried to build." Had they been successful? He wasn't sure. Maybe things needed to be broken down, old patterns lost, new ones built. But the cost. The lives lost or ruined. Did it have to be that way? Rogi felt caught between the world of the wizards and a new world, one that he had yet to understand. The song of the Community began to work with him.

Reluctantly, Lefi assumed his place in the inner cir-cle. After Malzus's intrusions, he found it difficult to open his mind to others and feared the touch of the Forty. He felt a light touch, not of the Forty but a smaller group—a barely perceptible song, reaching out to him. Instinctively he drew away. The song did not follow but opened up to him, allowing him to enter but not entering his mind. He could explore the song, wander through it. Cautiously, he approached the song, gently probing, adding some questioning notes.

We understand you, they sang. *We were like you before. We were afraid, too. We couldn't trust.*

And now you do?

More than before came the reply.

Lefi sensed their unease. He was an outsider they were letting in. He had been part of an entity that, if given a chance, would have destroyed the Community. Yet they still allowed him to probe their song.

Why do you open up to me? he sang. *I sense you fear me, as I fear you. Yet still you allow me into your song.*

We are learning, as you learn. We are learning to trust again. It is the only way we can grow. It is the only way we can avoid the mistakes of the past.

Lefi tried to open up to the song and let his mind wander, but it wouldn't work. He couldn't trust. But if he couldn't open his mind, he would be of no use in the quest. He tried again and again, but the song of the others remained outside. Sensing his discomfort, the song withdrew, the music fading into the distance. Lefi was both relieved and saddened. He wanted to let them in, to share his mind, but his past prevented him. Still, the song was beautiful and he wanted to be part of it. He was tired of being on the outside.

The sound was fading into nothing. The music was so faint that he was left in virtual silence, trapped in his own mind, alone once again with his nightmares. Thoughts long buried started coming back to him. People he had destroyed when he was a Saeren. He'd heard their pleading, but Malzus had hardened him. It wasn't him who had done those things—it was Malzus who had compelled him—yet it had been his body, his hands, that had committed the atrocities. It might have been the mind of Malzus that had ordered him, but he had acted. Shame washed over him, disgust at himself drew him down. He was lost, and he yearned for redemption.

The song came back. Lefi eagerly reached out, as if to a friend. He needed to be rescued, even though he didn't deserve it. This song was different. There weren't as many parts as before. It wasn't the Forty or even the ten that approached. It was one.

I am the one they call Founder came the song, emerging from the darkness. The song was deep, but Lefi couldn't place it as masculine or feminine; it had qualities of both.

What do you want of me? Lefi sang back, both wanting the song to approach and fearing it.

I want nothing of you, and everything, the Founder sang. *It is the same as what you want from me. We are both lost and need each other's help.*

Yes, that is true. Lefi understood that the Founder was not trying to calm him or help him. The Founder seemed almost as lost as Lefi. *What has caused your grief?*

I exist in a gray world of half-life. I am neither real nor unreal, I am neither alive nor dead. It is a terrible state to exist in, yet I feel I cannot let go or the Community will falter. They don't yet understand. They are making progress, but I can't go on and I can't end.

You have guided their change, then? You have brought them from the fear they felt to where they are now?

And where are they now? the Founder sang back. *They have some knowledge, but they still lack understanding. They play at knowing what to do, but if I were to disappear, they would likely fall back to their old ways. Not at once, of course—it would be slow but inevitable.*

You are pessimistic about your people. Lefi's song became more relaxed.

My people? The notes sung by the Founder seemed unfocused and confused. *How are these my people, any more than the Sitire or the Aris? They are people. That is all.*

But you have an obligation to them, more than to others.

There came a sharpness to the song. *I have the ability to help the Community more than the others, but that is just by circumstance. My obligation, as you put it, is to all people.* The song hit a rest and then went on, *Or to none.*

Lefi began to understand. He had thought of the people of Adular as *his* people, but the Founder was right. How were they any more his people than Tiox or Theb?

The Founder began the song once again. *Why do you go on this quest?*

You don't think it a worthy one? Lefi sang.

That I can't say. I don't know what a worthy quest would be, or why one would partake of a quest to begin with. My memory goes back very far, through many quests.

Were there none that were worthy? Lefi sang, but the song came out confused.

There is no meaning to that concept. I can't judge what quest is worthy or why we call it a quest. You seek to travel, but why?

Lefi's doubts reemerged. He had become caught up in this idea of a quest—a noble mission to rescue Ran-dahl. But why? There were plenty nearer who also needed his help, and Ran-dahl did not seem to need rescue. *It is not a quest, Lefi sang, realizing. I want to understand the nature of things, and the song from over the waters promises this understanding.*

Why do you seek to understand the nature of things? What possible value can that have?

It is the only thing of value.

What will you do with the understanding once you acquire it?

This again was a question Lefi had not considered. What would he do? Why was it so important?

I will act on it. I will understand the truth. I will no longer live blindly in the world.

And others live blindly, then?

Lefi considered all the people he knew. The ones who were kind, the ones who were cruel. Did any of them see the truth? *There are only a few I know who see the truth. Many others act as if they see but do not, and many more don't look for the truth.*

The song came back, agreeing with Lefi. *The Community thinks they understand, and maybe one day they will. But until then, I will stay in my grayness and help.*

The Founder's song began to fade away and the song of the ten reemerged. Lefi realized the ten didn't know the Founder had visited. As the song of the Community grew louder, Lefi listened for the faint strains he had heard. If he listened carefully enough, he thought he could just make out the song of the Founder.

CHAPTER 24

THEY HAD LEFT THE HEAT and cold of the desert behind them. The sands no longer cut them, the wolves no longer haunted their sleep. They were safe from the soft sands and the pull of the wosake. But now they faced the perils of the forest.

"This is more natural for me," Pom said to Yau. "I know how to live in the forest, and I enjoy it far more than the desert."

Yau nodded to her companion. "There is something strange here, something unnatural. Do you feel it?"

"I do." Pom shivered. "We must go carefully."

"I'm not sure that will do much good."

"We'll make it through." Pom tried to smile.

Yau folded her arms. "Let's sit and build a fire."

It was too early in the day to stop, but Pom sensed something pulling at them. Pom took off her pack and started collecting wood while Yau sat in a clearing and opened her mind. She reached out to the Community—she needed their comfort, their support. Pom started the fire and took her place next to Yau.

"They're not there." Yau couldn't make contact with the Community. Her song was being blocked. "Why would someone deliberately block our song?"

There are some who would do this, Pom communicated.

Malzus? Yau sang with despair.

"He might do such a thing, but this is not his doing. I know his mind, and this is not him."

At this, Yau became even more concerned. "There is another like him?"

"There are many like him, but there are few as strong as him."

"So there is another that destroys for no reason."

"Malzus didn't destroy for no reason." Pom was surprised at her defense of the Dark Wizard. "His reasons were misguided and self-serving, but he did have reasons."

"I have never felt so alone," Yau whimpered as she moved closer to Pom.

Pom felt Yau's panic and tried to comfort her. She opened her mind to Yau, but instead of Yau, she felt another presence, dark and cold, the intrusion totally absent of song. Yau was already enveloped by the stranger.

Who are you?

There was no answer from the stranger. Pom felt its despair and hopelessness. She tried to push the alien presence out of Yau's mind, but to no avail. Her own panic rose. They were cut off, utterly alone, and they were under attack. But why, and from whom?

I will not fight you. Pom reached out her mind to the stranger. *Say what you want of us.*

There was a silence that seemed to extend to the edges of the forest. Finally, the stranger said, *You threaten me.*

Pom replied, *Surely you are more powerful than me. We mean no threat to you.*

What you mean is irrelevant. You are a threat. Your ideas are a threat. Your very being is a threat to me, to my solitude.

We will respect your solitude. We have no desire to disturb you.

The stranger gave a cold laugh. *Whether you desire it or not, that is what you have done. I have hated your song since I first heard it. I have waited for you to come to me. I guided you here.*

Pom looked over at Yau, who sat staring straight ahead. Pom reached out to calm her. It seemed to help a little, but Pom was on her own to deal with the stranger. She tried to steel her mind against the intruder. Her experience with Malzus helped, but this mind was colder and crueler than Malzus's.

What is it you plan to do to us?

I only care about you. Your companion is irrelevant.

So let her go, then, and we can discuss what troubles you.

Again the cold laugh. *What troubles me is you. I have sought complete solitude for myself, and you have made that impossible. Your song travels everywhere, you can't help it. It invades my mind and it must stop!*

His explanation confused Pom. *I do not have that kind of power. It surely is your own mind that reaches out. It is you who seeks me. It is you who seeks redemption, who seeks com-panionship.* Pom all of a sudden realized what the stranger sought. *It is you who seeks forgiveness.*

NO!

Pom was unprepared for the violence of the reaction. She looked up past the fire, and there, in the half light, was a small man dressed in pure-white robes and clutching a wooden staff.

You are just an old man, Pom found herself thinking.

That's what they call me: Old Man. But you are wrong about me. I don't seek forgiveness. I seek destruction!

With those last words, Pom felt herself under attack. Her mind was filled with memories she had long blocked from her consciousness. The death of Gital, her parents being killed by raiders, all the pains and fears of her life came flooding back all at once. Tears welled in her eyes and the figure of the Old Man blurred. This must be what was happening to Yau, why her friend was frozen. Instinctively Pom pushed back, trying to get the images out of her mind. As she pushed, she made contact with the mind of the Old Man. Either he hadn't expect this or he'd allowed her entry, for there was no resistance. She probed his mind, looking for a weakness, some way she could stop his attack. His mind was like a labyrinth with portions cut off from one another. She felt his emptiness, his loneliness.

Pom reached out to him. *Let me help you.* She felt his hesitation. He both wanted her help and rejected it.

Leave me be, the Old Man insisted. He reached under the folds of his white robe and moved forward. He removed something and raised it to his lips.

Pom stared at the Old Man, her mind open to him, feeling his despair. Then she saw movement and heard a whoosh of air as something cut in front of her. The Old Man was standing frozen at the edge of the fire. He held a straight pipe in his left hand. It looked familiar to Pom—a blow pipe, like those used by some of the thieves in the forest to shoot poison darts.

The Old Man's hold on her weakened and her mind began to clear. "Yau!" Pom cried. Her friend lay on the ground, the dart firmly planted in her arm. Quickly, Pom removed the dart and sliced open the entry point with her knife. She sucked the blood from the wound, hoping to stop the spread of the poison.

It won't work, the Old Man said in a dead voice. *You might have been able to tolerate the drug, but I doubt she can.*

Pom wanted to rush at the intruder and strike him. She didn't care about his despair. She cared about Yau. Yau, who, despite her own fears, had managed to save her from the poison. Yau, who lay limp in her arms.

Pom reached out her mind to try to bring her friend back, to touch her, to give her strength. *Are you there, Yau?* she called.

Is that you, Pom? I'm so glad you're okay. Yau responded weakly.

You must hold on. You can survive this poison if you hold on.

But there was no reply. Pom banged on Yau's chest and tried to breathe life back into her lungs.

It is no use, the Old Man stated flatly. *There is nothing you can do.*

Pom realized he was right, but she didn't stop until long after she knew nothing more could be done. Finally, she looked up at the Old Man, tears streaking her face. *Why? Why do this? What have you gained?*

It was not my intention to destroy your friend, but sometimes these things happen.

"These things happen? What does that mean? It is not a thing that happened—it is a life that's gone for no reason. You are an empty shell, and Yau was full of life. Now she's gone, but you're still here!" Anger welled up in her. Her band of thieves would have cut this man down. They would have evened the score. Pom wanted to even the score. She wanted revenge for Yau, she wanted revenge for Gital, she wanted revenge for her parents. She wanted revenge!

Yes! said the Old Man. *Follow your instincts. Don't let your friend die in vain! Strike back! Strike back, or you will be next!*

The Old Man was ready to strike at her, Pom knew, but he also hoped she would destroy him first. Her anger drained away, and only the sadness remained. "I can't do what you want. I can't forgive you or release you. I can't do anything for you."

The Old Man raised the blow pipe. Pom felt immobilized—he was holding her—but she fought him and eventually found herself able to move. But where to? Away from him, and let him destroy more lives? She watched as he slowly crumpled by the fire. What had happened? She didn't remember reaching out or attacking him. No, she was sure it hadn't been her. She reached out her mind to the Old Man. There was nothing there—he was gone.

Then she felt another presence withdrawing from the Old Man's mind. One she knew well. *Malzus, what have you done?*

I saved you came the reply. *You weren't going to save yourself, so I saved you.*

Why?

I still need you. You are my link to understanding.

How did you do such a thing? He was strong.

As am I, Malzus replied. But that's not why. He wanted to die, he wanted release. Surely you sensed that?

Pom nodded. *You shouldn't have done what you did.*

No, you shouldn't have done what I did. There was amusement in Malzus's voice.

No one should have done that. It wasn't right.

The Old Man was going to destroy you. I was needed to do what you wouldn't.

Pom shook her head, but Malzus withdrew back to Dolcere, and she was alone with her thoughts—and the bodies of her friend and her friend's killer. She slowly walked over to the body of the Old Man. He looked so peaceful now, like an old man, asleep.

Pom was lost. She didn't know where the Community was, and she had lost her guide. The world seemed sadder. She collapsed by the fire, and as it died down, Pom felt the cold and dampness setting around her. Still, she couldn't move. Nothing mattered.

She must have fallen asleep, because a noise suddenly jolted her awake. It was late in the night; the fire was gone and darkness blanketed the forest.

"Who's there?" she called out.

"A friend" came the soft voice.

In the darkness Pom could see movement. As her eyes adjusted, she realized this stranger had removed the bodies of the Old Man and Yau.

"What have you done with them?" she asked.

They are in the ground. She didn't approach. The touch of her mind was comforting, but there was a sadness to it as well.

"You knew the Old Man," Pom stated.

"He was my brother. He was my responsibility."

"I don't think there was anything you could have done. He wanted to leave this world. You couldn't have prevented that."

"Perhaps not. But he didn't need to take your friend. I sensed the danger too late."

"He was a powerful man, your brother. I didn't sense the danger either. Otherwise, I could have saved my friend."

"If you want, I can accompany you to the Community."

Pom nodded and said, "I would be happy for the company. What should I call you?"

"People call me the Wanderer."

CHAPTER 25

THEB WAS BEGINNING TO TRUST the Community. He knew they had entered his mind, but he had let them. It would have been easy for them to control him, but they didn't. They could have taken his crystal, but they didn't. They helped him become better at opening his mind. It reminded him of his days as an apprentice gem cutter. Days of intensive study, nights of practice. His joints ached with the effort. Just remembering those days, a chill went through him. Still, he had a similar sense of accomplishment now, as he had when he had successfully cut his first gem.

Tiox, too, was learning to trust the Community. They were teaching him to let go, to let his mind wander. He no longer heeded the stiffness in his legs as he sat in the inner circle.

Rogi felt the disquiet in the Community. Something was wrong. The Community was searching for someone, one of their own.

She has disappeared, they sang, the fear coming through in their song.

Rogi melded his song with theirs. He understood now—he felt the blankness, the place she should have been. *What can I do?*

There is little we can do but search and continue to reach out.

Just moments later, the Community felt a disturbance, and Lefi broke out of the song. *This is too familiar,* he communicated. *I know this feeling. It is something Malzus would do to hide from the others.*

The mention of Malzus sent a discordance through the entire Community. This was their greatest fear: a power that could enter their song and destroy their peace. This was the reason they'd hidden themselves for so long. Their newly founded openness was fragile, and there were those in the Community who wanted to go back to the way things were. They had been stale and uninspired, but they had been safe. Wasn't that better than this fear?

One of the Community is missing, they sang to Lefi.

Lefi tried to push his mind forward into the walled-off area, but he was pushed back. The Community tried to help, but they were powerless.

She is in trouble, the Forty sang in distress. *We need to help.*

Sensing the Community's urgency, Lefi pushed harder, but to no avail. He felt another arrive, a familiar but unwelcome mind.

You will accomplish nothing. You are too gentle. This requires my skills, not yours. It was Malzus, his former tormentor.

Fear coursed through Lefi. He withdrew, hiding from Malzus.

Yes, hide. That is the safest thing to do. I will do what needs to be done. Then maybe you'll understand more. Malzus rushed past his former Saeren and pushed aside the veil that had blocked them, revealing a scene of an old man and a young woman. Another lay motionless by the fire—the one the Community was searching for. But they were too late.

The Old Man was about to do something to the other woman, but Malzus was determined to prevent it. The two minds collided. Lefi could feel no music, no song, in the confrontation. The struggle was short, and the Old Man gave in to the Dark Wizard.

Lefi felt pity for the Old Man, even after what he had done. He sensed that what had happened to the woman lying motionless was a mistake—no one was supposed to have died. But now that she had, the mistake could not be reversed, and the Old Man was resigned to his fate. With Malzus's urging, he slowly turned the poison he carried on himself. Lefi tried to stop him but was not fast enough. It was over. Tears welled up in Lefi's eyes.

I did what needed to be done, Malzus said. *He might have destroyed my best hope for redemption.*

So you were protecting yourself, not the woman?

It's all the same. Our interests coincided.

No. You don't know what her interests were. You acted for yourself.

What was I to do? Malzus's disapproval was clear. Discuss whether the Old Man might want to reconsider his decision to kill? If I had done that, the wrong person would have died.

This struck Lefi as odd. Was there a right and wrong person to live and to die? But Malzus had gone back to his fortress, back to his solitude in Dolcere.

CHAPTER 26

IT WAS HARD FOR POM to grasp that Yau was gone. It had taken so little to take away so much. Her teacher, her mentor, was gone, and all that was left was an emptiness.

"Why did he do it? Why did he take Yau from me?" Pom asked the Wanderer.

"I can't give you the answers you are looking for. At one time it would have been impossible for me to think he could have done what he did. But he changed over time, and he focused that change inward until he could not see what he had known before."

"And what is it he forgot?"

"How to be human."

"That's no answer," Pom replied. "What does it mean to be human? Humans kill each other all the time. Maybe he remembered what it meant to be human." She fell silent.

The Wanderer looked at her with compassion and sadness. "Maybe we all need to forget what it means to be human, until we remember our humanity," she replied.

The two walked on in silence for a while, not feeling the need to speak.

"You were a thief before," the Wanderer stated.

"Yes," Pom replied.

"You robbed people?"

"When we had to. It was a matter of survival." These words sounded hollow to Pom.

"Did you ever beat someone?"

This seemed an odd question given her recent loss. Why was the Wanderer bringing up a painful past? "Yes. Well, not me, exactly, but some of my band." They had surprised a wealthy merchant traveling the forest road. He had a guard with him, just one guard—a very stupid thing to do. They'd been hopelessly outnumbered, and the guard saw the pointlessness in resisting. That's how Pom liked it— if their targets were outnumbered, they didn't fight back. Pom would get what she wanted and nobody was hurt. But in this case, the merchant had hit the guard, who'd been about to surrender. In fear of his master, maybe to keep his position, the guard raised his bow and was about to load an arrow when one of Pom's troop—actually, she remembered now, it had been Gital—hurled a stone from his sling and hit the merchant squarely in the head. He'd toppled off his horse and fallen to the ground, landing with a harsh thud. Blood oozed from his skull. The guard put his bow away, and her band had taken whatever was of value. The haul was a rich one.

The merchant was still alive, and Pom had dressed his wounds. The guard had made a plea to be allowed to keep their horses so he could get his wounded employer home. Gital was against it, but Pom had let them keep the mounts. It was funny—Pom sometimes wondered what became of the guard, but she never thought about the injured man.

"Have you ever killed?" was the next question the Wanderer asked.

"No," Pom said simply. "Gital had, before we teamed up, but I never had to. What about you? Have you had to kill?"

At this the Wanderer stopped and looked intently at Pom. "That is an interesting way to put it."

"What is interesting?"

"Asking if I 'had to kill.' You could have asked if I had ever chosen to kill. But the answer is no. I chose to avoid situations where that might have been a possibility. There was a time when I could have become a soldier."

"So why didn't you choose that?"

"Because I would have been an invincible soldier."

"Then you don't believe there is ever a reason to kill?"

"No, I believe there are many reasons to kill."

"But no good reasons?"

The Wanderer shook her head. "Unfortunately, there are many 'good' reasons to kill. My brother felt he had a good reason. The Sitire and Aris feel they have good reasons. I'm sure your friend Gital felt he had a good reason, and the man who killed him probably felt the same. The problem is, there are too many good reasons."

"If someone is going to kill you, don't you have the right to defend yourself?"

"Yes, you have the right to defend yourself. You have the right to do what you please, and others have the right to do the same. And that's what's wrong." The Wanderer picked up her pace and strode ahead.

"I don't understand."

The Wanderer stopped and sighed. "Explaining rarely helps."

"One thing that confuses me," Pom said, "is that in many ways you seem different than your brother, or even Malzus. But in other ways you seem the same."

"In many ways, I am the same."

Pom shook her head. "I still don't understand."

The Wanderer sighed. "No, I suppose you don't."

Pom waited for her to explain more, but she just turned and walked on.

CHAPTER 27

THERE ARE NO OTHERS, EOT explained calmly. *He has scared off any others who have studied the fog.*

Except for you.

Yes, except for me, and K'ren.

Why do you stay with me? Aren't you afraid of what Ruvbain will do? Ran-dahl reached out to her student.

Very much so, Eot replied. But first he must discover me. As long as I only communicate with you through the mind, I should be safe.

That's true. Assuming, of course, that Ruvbain or his ministers don't practice the arts they forbid, Ran-dahl said. *What have your measurements shown you?*

It's been hard to measure the fog. I can see where it is, measure it and get a location. But when I try to confirm the location with my next measurement, it seems to be somewhere else.

This didn't surprise Ran-dahl. *My own observations confirm what you've said. That must be why it is so difficult to enter the fog.*

Eot replied. *This strangeness can't be true. There must be some error in our measurement.*

I think we have discovered something fundamental about the fog. No matter how we measure it, there is always uncertainty. What that means, I don't know—at least, not yet. But soon, when the others arrive, we may be able to find out more.

You still plan to enter the fog?

I do.

Then I'll join you. When the others come, I will take them to you.

CHAPTER 28

THEB, TIOX, ROGI, AND LEFI sat at the communal table the four shared. Food was laid out before them, but none seemed hungry. Theb had the biggest appetite, despite his small stature, but even he ate little.

Theb's experiences with the Forty had calmed him. "It is a beautiful song. And I believe it has helped me understand the crystal better."

"What does that mean?" Tiox asked. "The crystal is just a stone. How can the song help you understand it?"

"It has certain characteristics that were hidden from me before. Now I think I understand better."

Tiox didn't pursue the conversation. He was too wrapped up in his own thoughts. "I finally understand what Sevas was trying to teach me. My mind is calmer now. The Community has helped me see more clearly."

"I understand why Asmar was so attracted to the Community. Their song is quite beautiful," Rogi said.

"What of it?" Lefi cut in.

"What do you mean, 'What of it'? The beauty of the song speaks to some underlying beauty, some underlying truth," Rogi replied.

"Or to some underlying deceit," Lefi replied.

"How can such beauty be deceitful?" Tiox asked. "They have helped us, and I sense no deceit in them."

"And there is none. They don't deceive you, but they do deceive themselves."

"Yes, you're right," Theb exclaimed. "Their song is beautiful, but deceptive at the same time. They believe they know something fundamental, but they are only seeing slightly below the surface. There is a whole other level they don't know."

"How do you know that?" Tiox asked.

"It's not me. It's the crystal, the way it resonates. With the Community I feel the resonance, but it is slightly off. It's like what Lefi said."

"It doesn't matter," Tiox said dismissively. "Their understanding is greater than mine, and they've been able to help me."

"I agree," Rogi said. "Their understanding is helpful for now. But it doesn't explain everything."

"Their message is of understanding, of compassion. What is not fundamental about that?" Tiox said.

Lefi replied, "You are correct, Tiox. What they preach is fundamental. But the problem is that they preach."

"I don't understand. What is wrong with that?"

Lefi didn't answer. Instead he broke off a small piece of the crusty bread that sat at the center of the table.

CHAPTER 29

A GRAY WOLF APPEARED FROM behind the trees as twilight settled on the forest.

Pom stared at the creature. "Doesn't she live in the desert?"

"This is an unusual animal," the Wanderer replied. "She has been a good friend to me for quite some time."

The wolf didn't seem particularly afraid of them but kept her distance.

"Will she come closer?" Pom wasn't sure if she wanted this or not.

"Probably not. She seems to like our company, but she is still a wild creature and is not always so comfortable in our presence. She has been following us for a while, but stayed in the shadows. I think she came by to warn us of something."

Pom stopped and looked around as if drinking in her surroundings. She listened intently and tried to reach out to sense the forest. "Yes, there is someone out there. I can't believe I didn't recognize the signs."

"They are very clever. It was hard to detect them."

"But you knew they were there?"

"Yes. They've been tracking us since daybreak. They don't know what to make of us. They see us as easy prey, but they don't see the profit in it. One of them seems to think he recognizes you." As the Wanderer finished her comments, a brown-clad figure emerged from behind a tree. Two more similarly clad figures appeared in back of the two women and two more on either side of the road.

The one in front stepped closer, keeping one eye on the pair and the other on the wolf. He had a sword at his side and a bow and quiver slung to his back. The others were similarly armed, but none moved to draw a weapon. "You have an interesting guardian," he said, nodding his head slightly toward the wolf.

"It is her!" came a young voice from behind them.

"Do I know you?" Pom asked him.

He came forward. There was no threat in his movements. "No, how could you? I was just a young boy. But I remember you! I was there when you met that wizard and those others in the forest. The ones you let go."

"You mean Asmar and the Keepers," she replied.

"I don't know who they were. I just remember my parents saying how stupid it was, after they got Gital killed. We left that evening and joined up with another band."

Pom nodded. There were many who'd disagreed with her decision to let the Keepers go. "So you have kept up the life of the thief since the Moment?"

"What moment?" the boy asked.

The leader took a step toward them. "He doesn't know about the event you refer to. It didn't reach everywhere. We were deep in the forest at the time and have chosen to stay there. This Moment you speak of never reached us."

"That isn't true," the Wanderer replied calmly.

The leader looked at her. "I sense something strange in you. You are not like the rest." He walked closer to Pom. "And neither are you. I am curious about the two of you. I couldn't sense your presence, we just happened to see you."

"Is that strange for you?" the Wanderer asked.

"Yes, very. I can sense most people who come our way in the forest. I know who is here, who is worthwhile to approach, and who is more trouble than they're worth. But the two of you I couldn't sense at all. We followed you until this one recognized her," he said as he nodded toward the boy.

"And how is it you know nothing about the Moment?" Pom was curious.

"I didn't say I know nothing about the Moment. In fact, I know quite a bit about it. I chose not to participate in it, that's all."

"Why not?"

"This is not a time for your interrogation. I just prefer to be on my own."

"And the rest of your band?" Pom began to sense the power of the leader, but the others didn't seem to possess the same abilities. "Did you choose to exclude them from the Moment, as well, or was that their choice?"

The four companions seemed baffled by the conversation. The leader looked at them, clearly uncomfortable at the way the conversation was going. To prevent the discussion from going further, he said, "What do you have of any value? We live by sharing with others passing through the forest."

Pom laughed. "So that's what you call it? Sharing? When I was a thief, at least we were honest enough to call it what it was." She expected the leader to get upset, but instead he laughed.

"Yes, we should be honest with ourselves, at least. We take what we need—the sharing is one way only."

"Well, we have very little," Pom explained. "Some travel rations, some equipment to make camp, and that's about all. I'm afraid this is a very meager haul for you."

"You disturb me." The leader carefully examined Pom. "And I don't like being disturbed."

Pom was still recovering from Yau's death. She was unarmed, but not without resources. She could use her mind to control the thieves—maybe not the leader, but the others. She was sure the Wanderer could handle the leader, although he was very strong. Pom began to reach out her mind, to explore the minds of the others. Yes, it would be easy enough.

As she reached out, she felt another presence in the minds of the thieves. It was the leader. He was gently controlling his followers. It was subtle, almost undetectable, but it was there. Then she felt anger coming from the leader—he hated her, hated the Wanderer. But there was no reason for this. The thieves could gain nothing by robbing them, and Pom and the Wanderer were no threat to them. This hatred was irrational—but very real.

"What do you intend to do with us?" Pom asked to bide her time, trying to think of a way out.

The leader drew his sword, his anger taking control over him. "All of your type try to control us. You manipulate our minds and our feelings; you won't let us alone."

He seemed almost surprised that he had drawn his sword, but now that he had, the others followed him unthinkingly. Pom felt the connection—the leader was controlling the actions of the others. They were following, not because they understood but because it was easier to follow. She reached out her mind to the others. She could control them, turn them against their leader. The leader was strong, but the power of his mind could not compare to hers. He was more experienced in changing the thoughts of his companions, but Pom could see what he had done, could copy his actions and turn their minds against him. She could do that—but she didn't. Instead, she used her power to break the hold the leader had on the others, to free up their minds, to let them decide on their own.

The boy was the first to speak, pointing his short sword, which had been trained on Pom, at the leader. "What was this Moment they spoke of?"

"Nothing you need to be concerned over. It was just a way for people like these two to take control of us and make us do things that we wouldn't do otherwise."

"That's not what it sounds like to me," another of the band replied, lowering his sword.

"Can't you see what's happening? The two of them are controlling you again. It's just like I've been saying. We need to stay together, fight their control. I can protect you from them."

"How do we know you're not controlling us?" asked another. "How do we know who to believe?"

"You see what they're doing. Don't believe them."

"They haven't said anything," yet another said. "You're the only one talking."

"But their control is more subtle. They are controlling your minds."

"This makes no sense," the boy replied. "They have nothing we want, they pose no threat to us. Why are we bothering with them?"

Pom had done it, broken the control. They were trying to figure things out on their own now.

The leader grew more agitated. He took a step toward the Wanderer. Before Pom could move, he ran at the Wanderer, sword raised, ready to attack. The others of his troop, used to obeying, at first moved to join him but then stopped. The leader's blade slashed through empty air— the Wanderer had sidestepped the blow. He raised his sword once again as the Wanderer stared at her attacker.

But it was the young boy who spoke. "Stop!" he commanded.

The leader yelled "Traitor!" as he changed his target from the Wanderer to the boy.

The boy was unprepared, and Pom knew he would not be able to defend himself. She raced to intercept the attacker. It all happened so slowly: the leader's sword descending, the boy's blade rising in defense, her own sluggish movements toward the two. She reached for the leader's arm and grabbed the fabric of his sleeve. It slowed him enough for the boy to partially deflect the blow, but the sword struck him on the arm. And then it was over. The leader stood in front of his former follower, blade at his side. Pom positioned herself between the two.

"Attack them," the leader yelled. "We must free ourselves from their control."

But the others now moved to their former leader. Gently, they removed the blood-stained sword from his grasp and looked to the Wanderer. "What do we do with him?" they asked.

"Help him," she answered simply.

"But we don't know how. If we let him free, he'll harm others again."

Pom glanced at the boy. He had sunk to the ground, his left arm hanging limply at his side, blood caked to his sleeve.

"I need to help your friend," she said.

"We need to do something about him." One of the thieves indicated their former leader.

"I say we do to him what he was about to do to Yoney," said another, pointing to the boy.

They mean to kill him, Pom realized. "No!" she protested. "You can't."

"Then what else?" the thief asked. "What other choice is there?"

"I will speak with your leader," Pom replied. The Wanderer took over the treatment of Yoney, and Pom said to the two thieves who were restraining him, "Release him."

Their leader was unarmed, but the two were still reluctant to let him go. Pom waited silently until they complied.

"Why are you so angry with me?" she asked.

"You try to control me."

"How have I done that? I think it is you who want control, not me."

He laughed quietly. "I will admit to that. But don't you try to feign innocence with me. You and your friend try to control minds as well."

Pom shook her head in denial. "We seek only to give others understanding and let them decide for themselves."

"And if they decide something you don't like? If they decide you must die? What do you do then? Do you let them go, or do you kill them, like they want to do to me?" he said, indicating the others.

"You resist the control of others, so how can you seek to control them?"

"Because I know better than they do. I protect them from others. They need me to lead them."

"They don't seem to think that now that their minds are free."

"Are they truly free, or have they just switched to a different master?"

Pom shook her head. "I don't control their minds. I just freed them from your control. Now they follow their own minds."

"And what does that mean? Their minds are influenced by what they see. You control what they see now, rather than me—that is all that has changed. And now you will kill me so I can't influence them again."

"I have no intention of killing you. With the power you have, surely you can sense my intent?"

"Yes, I can sense your intent. You will not kill me; at least, it won't happen by your hand. But what of the others? They have no other choice."

"They have many choices."

"If they freed me, I would hunt them down and kill them. I have others in my band, and I couldn't let these three get away with this treason," the leader replied.

Pom shook her head. "I could take you with me." She didn't like this alternative, but she was at a loss to figure out another.

"And what would you do with me? Tie me up? Let me walk freely?"

"If you were allowed your freedom, would you try to kill me? But why? What have I done to you?"

He waved dismissively at her. "You don't understand, do you? You have taken away our freedom. You want everything to be open, you want everyone to understand."

Pom was confused. "What's wrong with that?"

The man laughed. "Everything. It takes away our individuality, our freedoms. You saw how the others in my band followed me when there was no interference from you. They believed in me, they trusted me. And now they want to kill me. That's what your 'understanding' brings. It is the weak that take over, and that will destroy us all."

Pom was speechless. He believed what he said. But what should she do with him? Should she turn him over to his companions and let them kill him?

"You are weak," he said, watching her struggle. " We cannot survive such weakness. If it were my decision, I would act, but you sit there not knowing what to do."

"I know what to do," Pom replied.

"Let me go?" he asked.

"No."

He shook his head. "Then you will kill me."

Pom raised her voice. "Enough of this killing! I've had enough of this, enough of death, enough of it all!" Yau's death, Gital's death, came flooding back. Tears stained her face as frustration washed over her. "Why must everything end in death? Is that what we've come to?"

And then it happened. There was no warning, no signal Pom was aware of. Just a swoosh. Then the man was staring at her, a knife blade through his neck. There was little blood. Slowly he smiled at her, as if he had been proven right. She looked up to see Yoney, a second dagger ready in case his first missed its mark.

As the leader fell into her arms, bloodying her talize, Pom stared at the boy. "What have you done?"

"What needed to be done," he replied.

CHAPTER 30

"WE MUST STOP THE INFORMATION about the fog," Ruvbain insisted. He was presiding over the Council of the People, which was now made up of his own handpicked advisors, as the "people" could no longer be trusted.

"We thought once Ran-dahl was removed, the problem would go away," Tasay added.

"But it didn't," Ebol confirmed. "It's only gotten worse." He was concerned about the group known as the Fog.

Ruvbain wondered if they understood the problem as he did—or at least, as he thought he did. "What do you make of the fog?" he asked.

"As I said, they are worrisome," Ebol replied.

"No, not the group. The fog, the real fog. The fog that lies off Ran-dahl's island."

His ministers looked at him, not understanding. Ruvbain wondered if he should go on. Should he explain the things he'd experienced? Were the others experiencing this as well?

"Have you noticed anything unusual?" Uncomprehending faces stared back at him. He pushed on. "Do you notice that things are just not right? That there is something wrong?"

"In what way?" Tasay asked.

"In any way." This was not going well. The ministers didn't seem to follow.

"We have noticed the fog is creating anxiety among the people, if that's what you mean," Tasay replied.

No, it was not what he meant—it was not even close to what he meant. But they would not, could not understand. They hadn't experienced what he had. The displacement of objects—that things did not seem to be where they were supposed to be. It was a slight displacement, he would admit, but noticeable nonetheless. It terrified him.

"Yes, that is what it is, Tasay. We must find a way to reduce the threat. So explain to me what has been done."

"We have infiltrated the Institute," said Kever, one of the newer representatives Ruvbain had appointed. His double chin was visible even through his slight beard. His substantial gut hung over the string that held up his pants. His body was slow moving, but he was quick of mind. He had studied at the Institute and had been one of the top students. But, as was common, once he'd left the Institute, the reality of buying food had set in. He'd been an easy candidate for Ruvbain to turn toward his will. "I have students who attend meetings and try to draw out the professors. We are making a list of potential Fog members."

"Potential members?" Ruvbain was concerned. "Haven't we infiltrated the actual members?"

Kever looked embarrassed. "Well, no. Not yet. They are very secretive and distrustful. But we will break into the organization, it's just a matter of time."

"I'm not so sure there is an organization as such," a skinny representative called Fite replied. Her short, slight frame was a contrast to Kever's bulk. Her bright eyes contrasted with her dark skin. She seemed almost insubstantial. But she was probably the brightest of his appointees.

"Go on," Ruvbain insisted.

Fite nodded. "I don't think they actually meet in person. They seem to have other ways of communicating with each other. As a result, following suspects won't work. We must become accepted and learn this new method they have for communication."

Ruvbain considered this. "Can this be done?" he asked.

"I'm not sure, but I have someone I think can do it." Then she added, "If anyone can."

"Then make it happen," Ruvbain said decisively, and dismissed the council.

CHAPTER 31

POM CLIMBED THE ROPE LADDER to the Community. Her arms and legs were heavy and her sight blurred with tears. There had been too much death—Yau was gone, and the leader of the thieves was gone as well. What bothered her more than the killing of the thief was that she felt relieved he was gone. Killing him had been wrong, but she didn't know what was right. He had reminded her of Gital, whom she missed.

She got to the opening in the cliff. The Wanderer had escorted her as far as the Community but refused to come with her any farther.

"Welcome" came the greeting from a tall, light-skinned man wearing the white robes of the Seekers. He looked oddly familiar. "I am Rogi," he said, like that was supposed to mean something to her. "I am—used to be—a wizard." The words stumbled out.

Pom should have realized this, she thought. He was light skinned, like the other wizards. But his companions were much darker. Four of them came forward.

"Tiox," said a tall, broad man.

"Theb," said a much shorter man with an ashen complexion.

"We are Contin and Arlin," said a woman in an earth-colored robe, her hand on the arm of an older man with dark eyes.

There was one other who greeted her, but he hung back.

From what Yau had told Pom, Contin and Arlin were from the Community; the others appeared to be guests.

"Pom," she said, and walked to the silent one and reached out her hand.

He looked at the offered hand and finally reached out his own. "Lefi."

His grip was weak and his hand sweaty. She didn't mind when he quickly let go.

Contin reached out her mind. *The Forty await you.*

"I don't want to go to them," Pom replied out loud. After her encounter with Malzus, she didn't want others interfering with her thoughts.

You are safe with them, Arlin countered. *There are things you need to understand before you go.*

Pom looked at the others and saw that they had heard as well.

"They helped me," Tiox said. "I don't think you have anything to fear from them."

Pom wasn't so sure. She wished the Wanderer had come so she could ask her guidance. But she hadn't—she had her own grief to deal with. Pom thought of Yau. These were her people. She looked into Arlin's dark-brown eyes and nodded. Arlin smiled slightly, and Pom followed him.

Pom ran her hands lightly on the cool stone as they made their way down the passage. "Did you know Yau?" she asked.

We all know each other. We are all part of the song, Arlin replied.

Pom closed her eyes and walked on, using her sense of touch to direct her. In her mind she saw the Forty waiting in their chamber. She needed to get better at reaching out, using her song rather than her words. Pom stumbled into Arlin and opened her eyes. They had stopped in front of the large metal doors that closed off the chamber of the Forty.

Go in. Arlin pulled on one of the massive doors, leaving enough space for Pom to squeeze through.

Aren't you coming with me? Pom reached out with her song.

Arlin smiled at her. *They want you. We will wait for you here.*

Pom looked once more at Arlin and hesitated. She was scared of the Forty and she wasn't sure why. She took a deep breath and slipped through the opening, which shut silently behind her. She felt alone in the gray light of the chamber.

As her eyes adjusted, she found herself in the center of a circle of brown-clad figures, each sitting in their own niche, the ceiling stretching up high above her.

Welcome. It was not one voice that reached out to her, or even forty. There were hundreds of voices. She was being welcomed by the entire Community. *We have heard much about you.*

From where? Pom asked.

Yau.

At the mention of her friend's name, Pom winced. Her death was still too raw.

You have been chosen to lead the quest to find Ran-dahl.

Why me? Pom asked. *I'm not as experienced as any of you. I'm too new to all this.* She spun around the room, trying to peer into the faces of the Forty, but they were all cowled in darkness.

Your song is pure. It is from your time with Asmar.

I don't understand. You also were with him.

But we rejected him. You did not. The Moment affected people differently. Those who were close to Asmar and were open to his message have more sensitivity than others. You and your companions have that sensitivity. We do not.

Pom wasn't sure if this was true. *Why did you want to meet me?*

To help you find your way. Open your mind to us and let us help.

Pom stood frozen. She didn't want to open up to anyone. It was too intimate. Yau had been that close, and she couldn't afford to let anyone else in.

We know you are reluctant. But just listen to the song.

Before Pom could answer, the music flowed into her. It was familiar, comforting. It was Yau. Pom fell to her knees and started to sob uncontrollably. Yau couldn't be alive, Pom knew this. But it was definitely her song.

Yau's song lives on in the Community. It is available to you whenever you need it.

Pom nodded in the darkness and let Yau's song wash over her. She reached out her own song and let it meld in harmony with Yau's. The two songs mixed and shared melodies. Pom said goodbye to her friend and slowly pulled away, letting Yau fade into the background.

Thank you, she said to the Forty.

Join with us to reach out to the one called Ran-dahl.

Pom let her mind relax and float in the midst of the Forty. She waited for them to go to Ran-dahl, but they did not. They were waiting for her. So she reached out, tentatively, not knowing which way to go. Previously she had followed others; now she was being asked to lead. Her mind wouldn't go, and she kept looking for others to show her the way, but still they waited. She was trying too hard, trying to force her mind to go rather than just letting it flow. The more she thought about it, the more difficult it became.

Finally, she rose from the center of the room. *I can't,* she admitted. She felt the disappointment of the Forty, but there was nothing to be done.

We know you can, they encouraged her, *but it may be too soon. Go, join the others, and remember Yau as we do.*

Pom was escorted back to her cell. She had no desire to see her companions. She needed to reach out and find the one called Ran-dahl. There was a reason the Community had called her—there had to be. Otherwise, Yau's death was meaningless.

Pom sat on her hard cot and listened to the silence. Her mind was trapped, and she couldn't let it go. She kept coming back to Yau's death—how Yau had tried to protect her, how it was her fault that her friend was dead. Tears poured out as Pom sobbed. She remembered how Yau had helped her free her mind. She needed to reach out—she couldn't disappoint her friend.

Pom calmed herself and her sobs subsided. She reached out her mind, but it was still no good.

Let me help. The song sounded like Yau's, but a little different.

Who are you? Pom asked.

I'm called the Founder came the reply.

You sound like Yau.

She is part of me.

I don't want to disappoint her, or you.

It's not about us, the Founder replied. *What do you want?*

Not to let everyone down. They all put so much hope in me.

That doesn't matter.

Then what does?

What do you want?

Nothing. Everything. Pom paused. What was it she wanted? *I want to be like Nomey. I want to help.*

Then picture those you want to help.

Pom let her mind drift. Nomey's face appeared, and Tiox's, and then Areana's and Bradoc's. But others as well. Gital's, and finally Yau's. The images of the people melded together and started drifting away. She followed them. The Founder joined her, and then the Forty. They gave her the power to travel farther.

She felt the freedom of leaving her body, of traveling over the oceans. She felt the mind of Ran-dahl reaching out. And then it stopped. Her mind crashed back into her body and she felt nauseated. Everything went dark. She felt people around her, a wet cloth on her head. Her vision cleared and she saw Arlin standing over her. A blanket was pulled up to her chin. Her body shivered.

"Thank the Golden Tree," Arlin said.

"What…" Pom found she could barely speak. "What happened?"

Arlin shook his head. "We don't know. We were all with you, and then… there was nothing. We were all affected, but you the most. You've been out for three days."

"Three days!" Pom said, and tried to sit up, only to collapse back on her pillow.

"Try this." Arlin put a silver cup to Pom's lips. The liquid was bitter, reminding her of the concoctions Nomey had put together. Pom forced down the drink and felt a little better.

"I need to try again," Pom said.

"Wait until you've recovered more. Your friends are anxious about you. Should I let them in?"

Pom shook her head. "Not just yet. I think I want a bit more rest."

"Then I'll leave you for now." Arlin left, gently closing the door behind him.

Once Arlin was gone, Pom propped herself up and breathed deeply. She knew the mistake she had made. There had been too many accompanying her on her journey. They had attracted the attention of someone who didn't want them to find Ran-dahl.

Slowly Pom reached out her mind, hiding from the others, hiding from the Forty. She was alone as she gently lifted out of her body and started traveling. Her mind was like a cloud, light and insubstantial. She traveled unseen toward the thoughts of Ran-dahl. Before she could reach her, she felt a barrier—the one that had stopped her the last time. But now she slid through it unnoticed.

You made it, Ran-dahl greeted her. *I need you to come to me.*

Why?

Ran-dahl connected her mind to Pom's, and then Pom understood. Gently she returned to her body and fell into a deep sleep.

The next day, Arlin came to check on Pom, who was out of bed and dressed in her robes. Arlin smiled. "We're glad you're better. Now come and show your friends."

Pom joined the others and told them she had connected with Ran-dahl. Then she asked, "What do we do now?"

"We go in search of Ran-dahl," Rogi said.

"But how do we do that?" Theb asked. "We'll need a ship to get to her."

"My people aren't sailors," Tiox said. "And I don't know the first thing about building a boat."

"Nor do I," Lefi admitted.

They looked at Pom, who shook her head.

"You forget," Rogi said, "that the wizards traveled here by ship. I may not have been the strongest wizard, but I was the one who captained the craft."

"You had a ship?" Pom realized this should have been obvious.

"It was called the *Elpida*," Rogi said. "In my language it means hope."

"Where is it now?" Pom asked.

"The ship is in Tuland," Rogi answered. "Or what's left of the *Elpida*. Our goal was to find the Golden Pulcher. We wanted no way to get back to our home in Insula, so we sunk it."

"So what good does that do us?" Tiox complained.

Rogi shook his head. "Maybe none. But it was made of bronze pulcher, so maybe it can be repaired. I suggest we travel to Tuland to find out."

Theb rose. "Let's go, then. Remer is in Tuland, maybe he can figure out what we need to do."

"Or maybe the Wanderer will help."

Rogi nodded. "Before we go to Tuland, we must return to Dolcere."

Pom's face paled—she didn't want to go back. "Why do we need to go there? That's where I came from. Yau told me to come here."

"But we need the white crystal that is in Dolcere to power the ship."

Pom knew the crystal, the one Malzus had worn. "But if I had known you needed to go back to Dolcere, I could have stayed there."

You were needed here came the voice of Yau.

"But if I had stayed, you'd be alive!" Pom sank to the floor.

The others stared at her in silence.

CHAPTER 32

"I NEED TO GO TO Nomey's village," Pom insisted as they set out from the Community.

Lefi shook his head. "I don't want to go back there."

"I promised Nomey I would deliver this." She took out the sheaf of papers.

"I don't want to go," Lefi repeated.

"But these are cures for illnesses they don't know about. People's lives are at stake. I must deliver them."

"We must go, then," Rogi replied. "We need not stay long."

Reluctantly, Lefi agreed.

When they arrived, the town was full of white-robed Seekers hovering around a central building. Pom stopped one of the Seekers.

"What is in that building?"

"It's the healing center," she said, and then limped off to join the others.

"The town has changed," Lefi said.

"You've been here before?" Pom asked.

Lefi nodded, looking nervously around. "The village now has paved roads and two inns. Those were not here before."

As they walked down the main street, they saw the white robes of the Seekers intermixed with a handful of the violet and indigo robes worn by the priests of Yahad. "We should change out of our white robes," Lefi said.

"Why do we need to do that?" Theb asked.

"The priests don't approve of the white robes. That's the color only for the High Priest of Yahad."

"Much has changed here since the Moment," Rogi explained. "Their god has become kinder."

"In what way?" Theb asked.

"Well, for one, they no longer practice rebirth," Rogi answered.

"What was that?" Theb asked.

"They killed those who didn't believe," Lefi said curtly, and walked ahead of the group.

Rogi turned to Theb. "Even though rebirth is rare, if you question their god, there is a chance that the priests will bring you before their courts."

"But to what end?" Tiox shifted his bulk defensively.

"If you are fortunate, you will be expelled from the Domare lands."

"And if you're not?" asked Theb.

"Rebirth is not a common practice, as I've said. But it is practiced."

The group walked down the cobbled main road of the small village toward the healing center. As they walked down the street, they were watched, not by the Seekers, but by the townspeople. A blue-robed woman, her head wrapped in a scarf of the same color, walked up to them and bowed deeply.

"Welcome to our humble town," she said, staring at Lefi.

Lefi shifted uncomfortably as the woman's eyes brightened. Her dark-brown eyes looked through him.

"It *is* you," she said. She looked toward the others in the colored robes and called out, "It's the Converted One."

Lefi started walking away.

"You can't go." The woman grabbed the hem of Lefi's robe.

Tiox pulled the robe out of her grasp and followed Lefi. "Why is she calling you that?"

"Asmar freed me from my life as a Saeren when he fought Malzus. Since that time I was called the Converted One."

"He is a holy man," said the woman, who was following them.

Lefi stopped and turned to the woman. A crowd started to form around them. "Why are you wearing a priest's robe?"

The woman smiled warmly. "Since the Moment, women are allowed into the priesthood."

"And Beldowien allows this?" Rogi asked.

The woman shook her head. "It is his wife, Halid, the High Priestess, who has allowed this. I am the first woman priest of Yahad." She looked at the travelers. "I am Dasis, and I was one of the first to greet Asmar when he came to our town."

Three men and one woman stepped forward from the crowd.

"I am Ey, of the town elders. And the others are Rov, Cyram, and"—he indicated the young woman—"our newest addition, Wen."

Pom took the papers Nomey had given her and handed them to Wen. "These are for you, from Nomey."

Wen studied the sheets and smiled. "This is very helpful. Thank you."

"Please follow me. We have rooms for you in the temple of Yahad," Ey said.

"That is unnecessary," Lefi replied.

Rov replied, "We could not show such disrespect for the Converted One."

Pom stepped forward. "Please show us where we can stay."

Rov showed them into the two-story building that was used as the house of worship for Yahad.

When they were settled, Cyram said, "After the Moment, it became clear that we had been focusing too much on the revengeful side of Yahad. Our High Priestess came to us and explained the other side of Yahad. This made more sense to us, particularly after the Moment. She called Asmar a prophet of the new Yahad and told us we needed to live with love. She immediately stopped the forced rebirths and pardoned the rebels."

"That was fortunate for me," Wen remarked. "I was one of the rebels and was scheduled for rebirth. Another couple of days and I probably wouldn't been able to benefit from the Moment."

"Except in your next life," corrected Rov. He went on, "Of course, the Converted One became a symbol of our rebirth. Tributes to him—" Rov looked at Lefi. "Tributes to you occur all over the Domare lands. You have saved many who otherwise would have been reborn."

"It was also decided that we would become more open to spreading the word of Yahad. We welcomed pilgrims to our villages and showed them the love of Yahad. That has turned out to be a much better way to get converts than the battles we used to fight." At that, Rov shook his head.

"As you might expect, our village has attracted more than our share of pilgrims, both for our healing center and as a place the Prophet visited. Our village has grown and we have had to make adjustments. One of which is to expand our healing center and house of worship. We now have rooms in both for distinguished visitors—of which you are the most distinguished," Rov concluded, and bowed to Lefi.

As they entered the house of Yahad, they saw a crystal-enclosed display case with a thick book inside. Rov explained, "This is *The Book of Healing*. We had to decide whether to keep it in the healing center or here, as it holds much for both houses. In the end it was decided that it contains the words of the Prophet, so it belongs here."

"Weren't there two books?" Tiox recalled.

"Well, yes—" Rov began.

Wen interrupted. "This is the second book. The first was destroyed before the Moment. Luckily, Coige—Nomey's mother—had another copy and safeguarded it until the High Priestess's influence manifested. These pages"—Wen raised the sheets that Pom had given her—"will be joined to the book once I have read and categorized them."

"I will show you to your rooms," Cyram said. "How long did you plan to stay?"

Tiox, hoping for a few days' rest until they could reprovision, started to reply.

"Tomorrow," Lefi cut in. "At first light. We cannot stay longer."

The disappointment on the faces of the elders was apparent. "If you could stay just a bit longer—" Ey implored.

"That is quite impossible," Lefi insisted. And to cut off further discussion, he said, "Please show us to our rooms. I am quite tired."

Ey sighed. "Very well." And he led the way up a set of stairs next to the hallway that led to the main area of worship.

"We have only a few rooms," Ey apologized as he showed them to a midsized room that could hold seven but was currently unoccupied.

"This is fine," Lefi said dismissively, and rushed the elders out of the chamber.

Once they were alone, Rogi turned to Lefi. "What is the trouble?"

Lefi waved his hand dismissively. "They have not learned."

"Learned what?" Theb asked.

"They have not progressed since the Moment. They have not learned from it."

"They seem to have progressed quite a bit," Tiox countered. "Think of all they have given up. They no longer do the forced rebirth, they allow pilgrims into their city, women are allowed to be priests. This is progress."

"Yes, it is," Lefi admitted. "But they have not learned. They still think the same as before—that it's their god that tells them to do something different. They never answered the question I asked Beldowien on my last day."

"And what was that question?" Tiox asked.

"It's not important right now. But I don't want to be part of this worship, I don't want to be another prophet. I will not allow them to use me instead—"

"Instead of what?" Theb asked.

"Instead of thinking for themselves."

"And the question you asked Beldowien was what?"

"Does Yahad exist?"

The four turned toward the door and saw Wen standing there, holding blankets and sheets for the beds. She was motionless, as if the question had paralyzed her. Finally, she looked deep into Lefi's eyes and calmly said, "No, she does not." She carefully placed the linens on the foot of one of the beds and turned and left the chamber, silently shutting the door behind her.

"What does all that mean?" Rogi asked. "How can you ask if a god exists? It seems a meaningless question."

"Why is that?" Lefi asked.

"Because the concept of God goes beyond logic, beyond proof."

"Why should God be exempt from the logic we apply elsewhere? Why should God be beyond proof?"

"Because of what he does. If you look at the Koan and the truths it contains, that is the proof of God."

Lefi shook his head. "The so-called truths you cite have caused misery to many. I know about the mind wars of the wizards and about the Saeren. I know too much about your god not to doubt."

Rogi wanted to protest, but he stifled the instinct. He wondered how he really felt. He had been so used to believing in the god of his people, to assuming the Koan was the word of their god. "I will think about what you have said."

"Well, whether gods are real or not, I'm starving," Theb broke in. He opened the door to the chamber and brought in the food that had been laid outside their door.

They rose early the next morning, before the sun had woken, and hastily packed for their departure. Tiox was used to being on the move at a moment's notice, an invaluable skill as a soldier. Rogi had little to take—as a wizard he had learned to do without. Lefi similarly had little to take with him.

Theb was still trying to cram some extra food into his pack. "I have more to take than you do." He seemed to need to justify himself. "And I have the crystal."

"Yes, I can see how that might take days to pack," Tiox joked.

"Well, I'm ready now. Let's go on to Dolcere," Pom said.

They tried to make their way from the town unobserved, but this turned out not to be possible. On exiting their lodging, they discovered hundreds camped outside in the streets, waiting quietly for some view of the holy man. Many held candles that gave the early premorning darkness a warm glow.

Wen approached. "They wanted to see you. You cannot blame them for that," she said to Lefi.

Almost imperceptibly, Lefi replied, "Yes, I can."

Wen seemed surprised at this. "I don't understand your objection. These people mean no harm. You are special to them. You represent freedom, a break from the past and a new life. What is wrong with that?"

Lefi was visibly uncomfortable. "There is much wrong with that, but it's not for me to judge or explain. I have nothing to teach them. I didn't do anything worthy of praise."

"It's not your actions they revere, but what you symbolize."

"And what do I symbolize?" Lefi's voice grew agitated. "Cruelty, because of what I did to my people? The helplessness of the individual? Lack of personal responsibility? These are the things I represent. What these people think of me is in their minds alone."

"It is their perception that makes these things true. Whether you believe them or not, it provides a symbol for them, something to strive for. It is all for the good, so I don't understand why you object so strongly." Wen kept her voice quiet, as some of the followers were becoming uncomfortable. "They would like you to say a few words before you leave. You owe them that, at least," she implored.

"I owe them nothing, and they owe me even less. Believing in me is their problem."

Wen made a short bow. "As you wish." She stood aside to let him pass. Similarly, the assembled stood aside, and the troop was allowed to pass freely from the town.

CHAPTER 33

ROGI LED THE GROUP ALONG the old road through the forest to the edge of the desert. Traders had come back to the towns, and the ancient road was being repaired. Before going into the desert, Rogi had them exchange their white Seeker's robes for more practical sand-colored talizes.

The monotonous routine of walking through the desert was just what they needed after the time with the Community. Each was alone in their thoughts, except for Tiox and Theb, who talked incessantly about the crystal. They camped each night before the winds started, lighting a fire to stay warm and keep the wolves away.

When they got to Dolcere, Rogi would have to go to Malzus for the white crystal. It wasn't something he relished doing. Would Malzus give him the crystal? And even if he did, was it possible to resurrect the *Elpida*? Using the ship again had never been contemplated. Their mission was to find the Golden Tree, even if it took a lifetime. They were not supposed to return. But he was not returning—he was going forward.

Rogi thought about the voyage to Bracat from Insula. It had taken all his skill to keep the ship afloat. He remembered the waves crashing over the deck night after night, and barely being able to see in front of the ship. Maybe one day in nine it was clear enough to see the stars and get a reading of their position. Then he'd had to hurry to correct his route before the winds and rains started up again. If the ship hadn't been fashioned from bronze pulcher, they would never have survived.

They entered Dolcere unnoticed and made their way to the Tower of the Wizards. The tower glowed golden in the afternoon light. As they approached the massive gates, a guard blocked their way.

"No one is allowed in the tower without the permission of the Keepers."

"Do you know who I am?" Rogi asked, drawing himself up to his full height.

The guard seemed unimpressed. "No one is allowed in the tower. Those are my orders."

Rogi had hoped he wouldn't have to touch the guard's mind, but he had no choice. Reaching out his mind to the guard, he sent the vision of a blue-clad wizard with a silver staff. The guard blinked and then stepped aside, allowing Rogi and his companions to enter.

Their steps echoed as they walked up the winding stairs of the tower toward the room he had once occupied.

"We will stay in the tower for now," he said.

Pom looked particularly nervous as she gazed around. "I don't want to be here," she said. "They're calling to me. He's calling to me."

Rogi closed his eyes and felt the presence of the Keepers. But it wasn't them Pom was afraid of. Malzus was calling to her.

Rogi reached out to his fellow wizard. *Leave her.*

Malzus ignored him and pressed Pom. *Come to me. I need you. I knew you'd come back.*

Rogi tried to block Malzus, but he wasn't strong enough.

Pom responded, *I am not back for you.*

But still Malzus pressed her. *I need you. You are my only hope.*

More voices entered. *Leave her be.* It was Areana. The three Keepers joined with Pom to resist.

But Malzus pressed through. Rogi watched Pom sink to the cold stone floor of the tower. This was wrong. He couldn't let Malzus do this, not again. He hurried to where Pom rested and put his hands on her shoulders. Closing his eyes, he reached out, joining the Keepers and Pom. A flash of light went through his mind, and then they were free. Malzus was gone from Pom's mind; the Keepers were gone as well. Rogi sank down beside Pom.

"Thank you," she said quietly. "I don't want to stay here." Pom rested her head on Rogi's shoulder. Her cheek felt wet and her breath was warm. "I'll go to the hostel for the Seekers. It'll be safer there."

"I'll go with her," Theb offered, clutching tightly onto his crystal.

Rogi looked around. "Where's Lefi?" Panic surged in Rogi. Had Lefi gone to Malzus, his former torturer? Quickly Rogi reached out his mind, and then relaxed. Lefi was safe. He had never followed them into the tower—he wouldn't go near Malzus.

"I'll stay with you," Tiox said.

Rogi shook his head. "Help protect your companions. I need to deal with Malzus on my own." Why he felt Malzus was his problem, he wasn't sure. They were both wizards, but that gave them little in common. Rogi debated whether to go to Malzus right away, to get it over with, to ask for the crystal and be gone as soon as he could. But he was too tired, from the travel and from fighting off his fellow wizard, so he went up to his cell to rest. Tomorrow would be time enough to face him.

His cell was just as he had left it, empty except for a neatly made-up cot in one corner, a small table with a clay pitcher, and a small writing desk under a slit of a window. In the corner were his blue wizard's robes and his silver pulcher staff. Rogi wondered who had brought them all the way from Tellurium. Was it Preadus's way of telling him he was still a wizard, still one of the nine? Rogi went to the staff and gently touched the warm wood. He picked it up and felt the healing warmth move up his arm. The fatigue he felt from his encounter with Malzus slowly drained away, and he collapsed onto his hard bed and fell into a deep sleep.

The light filtering through his window woke him the next morning. He went over to the pitcher to pour out some water, but it was dry. He rubbed his eyes and sat on the edge of the bed. He knew what he had to do, but he dreaded the need to go up into the tower to confront Malzus. He looked at the blue robes neatly piled in the corner. Should he put these on? Should he take the staff? Rogi took a deep breath. He would go as he was, with neither the blue robes nor the silver staff.

Rogi rubbed his hand through his hair. It had grown out over the past months. He had stopped cutting it short in the style of the wizards. He wasn't sure why, but he felt more himself. Rogi closed his eyes and reached out to Malzus. *I am coming,* he said. He waited for a reply, but none came.

He walked slowly up the stairs. It had been years since he had last seen Malzus, although their minds had touched more frequently. He was going to meet the one who had been called the Dark Wizard, in the tower where Vetus had died. It was the day Malzus had tried to take over the minds of the council and had almost succeeded. If it hadn't been for Preadus, Rogi and the others would have been turned into the hated Saeren. He reached the top step and pushed the door open, not knowing what to expect.

Malzus sat on a low stool, his hair cropped short in the manner of the wizards, but with a black robe, rather than the wizard's blue. He smiled as Rogi entered, and a chill ran up Rogi's back.

It's good to see you, Malzus greeted him.

Rogi didn't answer.

I assume you don't feel the same, Malzus concluded.

I wouldn't be here if I didn't need something from you. Rogi tried not to show his unease. Malzus tried to push into his mind, but Rogi blocked him. *You'll never be able to enter my thoughts again,* he warned.

We'll see, Malzus replied. *Then you need to tell me why you came here.*

I need the white crystal.

Malzus reached for the crystal that hung from his neck and shook his head. *This is the crystal that was given to me at my wedding. I can't part with it.*

Rogi let out a low laugh. *Your wedding, and poor Asmira, meant nothing to you. You should want to get rid of the reminder of what you did to her.*

Malzus rose. Rogi had forgotten how tall he was.

Why do you want it?

That is not something you need to know.

There are other crystals that are just as strong, Malzus said.

Rogi met Malzus's gaze. *I am going with the others to find the Tree.*

You believe that woman, that Ran-dahl, has the secret to the Tree?

Rogi nodded. *I do. And this is the only crystal that fits our ship.*

He was afraid of what would come next. Would Malzus insist on going with them?

Slowly, Malzus lifted the chain from around his neck and held the white crystal in his hand. Rogi wanted to reach for it and grab it, but he waited for it to be offered.

I'll give you the crystal if you send Pom to me. Malzus closed his hand around the crystal.

Rogi felt the connection between the two, one that benefited Malzus but injured Pom. If he sent Pom, would he be able to protect her? Rogi realized he had been hunching over since he came into Malzus's presence. He stood straight—still half a head shorter than the other—and in his most commanding voice answered, "No!"

To his surprise, Malzus laughed. Not a short laugh, but a deep and enduring laugh, as if Rogi had said something funny. And then he tossed the crystal to Rogi, who, in his surprise, almost dropped it.

You're right, of course, Malzus said, once his laughter subsided. *I shouldn't be left alone with Pom. Take the crystal and find the Tree. That is, if you survive the voyage.*

As Rogi turned to leave, Malzus said, *One more question. How are you planning to raise the Elpida from the bottom of the sea?*

Rogi stopped and looked at Malzus. *I have no idea.*

He made his way back to his cell, white crystal warm in his hand. As he fell onto his hard bed, Rogi let out his breath—he hadn't realized he'd been holding it in. He had the crystal to power the ship, but Malzus was right. How were they to get it from the bottom? One step at a time. He looked at the cell where he had spent so many years of his life, now almost deserted. He didn't want to stay there by himself. He wanted to be with his friends. He rose from the bed and considered his few possessions, the blue robes and the silver pulcher staff. The robes would stay, they were his past. He moved closer to the staff. It had been handed down to him by his mentor in Insula, as he lay dying. It brought back memories of lost times, of roads not taken. The staff was also part of his past. Leaving it where it stood, he left the small cell to join his companions.

Rogi walked from the wizards' tower, thinking it would be the last time he would ever see it. His life had changed. Ever since he had been accepted as a wizard, that had been his identity. Now he was something else, but what? He walked out of the center of town to the hostel for the Seekers. The doors were open and nobody seemed to notice him. A large group was huddled together in the main meeting area, and as Rogi approached, he heard familiar voices. Pom was telling the others what had happened to Yau. They listened in silence.

Pom looked up and noticed Rogi. She turned back to the group. "This is the wizard I told you about. The one who is going to take us to . . ." she hesitated. "I'm not sure where he will take us."

Rogi realized that he didn't know, either, where he was taking them.

That evening the companions met, and Rogi showed them the white crystal. Theb examined it and marveled at its quality. "How is this going to help us?" he asked.

"The ship's engine needs the power of the crystal to run," Rogi explained. "That's how we were able to make it here. Other ships used sails, and with the constantly shifting winds and storms, they couldn't go very far before being overwhelmed. Since we didn't need sails, we designed the ship to be totally sealed against the weather. That way, even large waves would just wash over the *Elpida* rather than sink it."

"But the ship sank," Tiox said.

Rogi shook his head. "Not exactly. We cut a large hole in its side and let the water flow in. That's why the ship sank. In order to raise it, we need to repair the hole and put the crystal back in its place."

"How do we get the water out?" Pom asked.

"The crystal will do that. There are pumps in the ship to push the water out. But they don't have any power. Once the crystal is back in place, the pumps should be able to empty the *Elpida* of the water, and then it will float once again."

"That seems pretty easy," Theb said.

"Except that we need to get below the water and fix the hole, and then get inside the ship and fit the crystal in place," Lefi said, looking at the others. "Have any of you ever done that before?"

The group was silent.

"We need a way of going underwater that will give us the flexibility to work," Rogi finally said.

"There is someone who could help figure out a way," Tiox said. The others looked at him. "Remer. If anyone knows a way to do that, it would be him."

"Then let's go ask Remer. From what the Keepers' guard told me, he's in Tuland," Pom said.

The troop left the next day for Tuland. Rogi turned back to look at the city that had been his home for most of his life. Oddly, he was not sorry to leave. For the first time in a long time, he felt free. All the rituals and restrictions of the wizards no longer bound him. He was free to explore. To think for himself.

CHAPTER 34

THEY TRUDGED THROUGH THE DESERT, Rogi in the lead and Pom walking with Lefi.

"You didn't speak with the Seekers," Pom said to Lefi.

Lefi shook his head. "All anyone wants to know is what it was like being a Saeren. I don't want to think about that anymore."

Pom also wanted to know what it had been like, especially after her encounters with Malzus, but wouldn't ask. "I don't think Malzus is as repentant as others think," she said. "When I used to visit him, he wanted to use me to know more about the woman Ran-dahl." She paused. "He still wants to find the Tree, but he knows he needs to change."

"He can't!" yelled Lefi. "He can't change, and I can't change."

Pom shook her head. "It's not the same. He forced you to do things. It wasn't your fault."

Lefi let out a short laugh. "Of course it was my fault. I wasn't strong enough to fight him. Others were. Why wasn't I?" He strode forward to walk with Rogi.

Theb came up to her. "Believe it or not, Lefi is getting better."

"He still has a long way to go," Pom replied. "I think we all do."

Theb nodded. "The voyage through the seas will take a while, if that's what you mean. But when we get there"—he unconsciously touched his pack containing the gem—"you'll understand."

"What exactly do you think will happen with your gem when we find that woman?" Pom asked.

"I think . . ." Theb looked into the distance, as if he had forgotten Pom was there.

"What do you think?" Pom prompted, trying to bring him back.

"About what?" Theb replied.

"About the gem. What will happen with the gem once we find Ran-dahl?"

Theb shrugged. "Don't know," he said, and trudged silently next to her for the rest of the day.

They made camp, and for the first time that day, all five of them gathered around the evening fire. As the sands blew against their makeshift shelter, Pom closed her eyes and reached out her mind. Without the others she couldn't find Ran-dahl, but she sensed another presence nearby. As the winds died down, Pom rose and started walking out into the desert. She heard the howls of the wolves, but they were far off. She heard Rogi behind her saying something, but she kept walking. The cool desert wind carried the smell of sand. She squinted, trying to see in the darkness.

"I know you're there," she called into the emptiness.

Rogi came up next to Pom. "We should get back to the camp," he said, and gently took her arm.

She pulled away. "I know you're there," she repeated.

"We are" came the response.

Pom heard footsteps making their way through the sand, but she felt no threat. Tiox had joined her, as had Theb and Lefi.

Out of the darkness emerged a figure in a white talize, eyes obscured by the cowl drawn up tightly around his head. "You're not Aris," he stated.

"Why does that matter?" Tiox stepped forward, shielding Pom with his bulk.

"Some of the Aris take objection to us," the stranger said.

"And why do they do that?" Rogi asked.

"That is a good question," he replied. "I suppose it's because we're a threat."

Ten more white-clad figures approached. They carried no weapons and made no hostile movements.

"You don't look like a threat." Tiox still stood blocking Pom.

"I guess it depends who you are," the man responded.

"And who are you?" Pom stepped from behind Tiox. She didn't need or want his protection. She felt a warmth coming from the stranger.

"I am Orien. And the others are ones who believe as I do."

"And what way is that?" Theb had stepped forward, the pack containing his gem slung protectively on his back.

"We believe in the Moment."

"And don't the other Aris also believe?" Pom asked.

"Some," Orien answered.

One of the other white-clad figures stepped forward. "We are not all Aris. I am Vogos. I was a Sitire before the Moment. But we believe there are no distinctions between Sitire and Aris, or even Cautes or Breccians. We are all one."

"And there are those who believe otherwise?"

"The new leader of the Aris, Adomas, did not participate in the Moment."

"I knew Olmar had died, but why didn't Areana succeed her father?" Rogi asked.

"It would have been good if she had done so," Orien answered. "But she has remained in Dolcere as one of the Keepers. We are traveling there to try to convince her to come back to Arane, although it might be too late."

Vogos looked at Orien. "He is our leader. He stood up for the Sitire when Adomas tried to cast us out of Arane."

"We have just come from Dolcere," Rogi replied. "And Malzus resides there along with the Keepers."

Orien nodded. "We will be careful. But this is our best hope."

"No, it's not," Pom interrupted. She had been listening to Orien, and she knew that his hopes for Areana would be fruitless. "Your best hope is to lose the names of Sitire and Aris and just be one."

"That is not so easy to do," Orien said.

"No, it's not," Pom admitted. "But that is your best hope."

"Perhaps," Orien responded. "But for now, we go on to Dolcere and you travel south."

"Why do you travel at night?" Lefi asked.

"Adomas is searching for us. It is safer if we travel in the darkness and hide during the day." Orien took a deep breath. "We must keep going."

Rogi put a hand on Orien's shoulder. "We wish you safe travels." He watched as the white-clad travelers receded back into the dark.

CHAPTER 35

RUVBAIN DIDN'T TRUST HIS MINISTERS to discover what Ran-dahl was up to. None of her plotters would dare meet. Instead they used their thoughts to communicate. It had been over five years since Ruvbain had practiced the technique, when he had been forced to leave the Valki Institute and take over from his father. It had taken him another year to understand why the Institute was so dangerous. But he was afraid of the fog, and he had received reports that it was growing. So far, the fog had not enveloped any of the islands or towns of Ognita, but it was only a matter of time. He was torn. He needed to keep his people calm and unafraid of the encroaching fog. But he also had to know what it was to stop it's advancing. For that he needed Ran-dahl, but she must be kept isolated and alone.

Ruvbain went down into the depths of his castle to find a small room where sound couldn't penetrate and he wouldn't be disturbed. In the light of the small crystal he'd brought with him, not bright enough to see clearly but enough to find his way, the room was a pale gray. He sat on a soft cushion and tried to get comfortable. He shifted and stiffened his back to keep his body aligned. It had been so long since he had practiced. He closed his eyes, but the gray didn't disappear. When he was finally comfortable on the cushion, he tried to let his mind go and reach out. But thoughts kept creeping into his head. He tried the deep-breathing exercise he had been taught. The external thoughts drifted away. He used to be good at this, but now it was a struggle. Half the day had passed, and he'd accomplished nothing. He rose and picked up the crystal to guide him back into the light.

Suddenly he felt a light touch in his mind. *Ran-dahl*, he said. *You are still there.*

What is it you want?

What is happening with the fog?

You would know if you hadn't arrested all my friends.

They were my friends as well, Ruvbain replied. *Can you control the fog?*

No.

What will happen?

Eventually, the fog will envelop us all.

Isn't there anything you can do? Ruvbain waited, but the connection had been cut. He was alone again, and he had no answers. What was he to do?

CHAPTER 36

AS THE TRAVELERS APPROACHED TULAND, Rogi kept thinking about the ship he had sailed from Insula and the gaping hole they had cut in the side. He remembered feeling trapped as he watched it slowly sink into the ocean. He would need to locate the ship before they could even tackle the problem of raising it.

The sand started to firm as they passed a large rock that marked the end of the desert and the beginning of the Tuland delta. Soon the scenery would change and there would be farms and trees along the road. It had been so long since he had visited Tuland, and he was looking forward to seeing Remer again.

As they approached the center of Tuland, they saw groups of white-clad Seekers walking about.

Pom came up to Rogi. "I don't think we should tell them who we are."

"Why not?" Rogi asked, knowing that with his pale skin, some would figure out he was a wizard, even though he wore none of the accoutrements.

"Because we'll never be free of them. We'll be caught up in their endless religious arguments."

Rogi nodded as they passed through the white robes and made their way into the town. Rogi had not expected everything to be so crowded. He had thought they would just enter Tuland, find Remer, and figure out a way to resurrect the ship. Now everything was going to be more complicated.

"How will we find where Remer lives?" Theb asked Rogi.

"I don't think that will be very difficult." Rogi pointed to a small two-story house with hundreds of white-robed Seekers crowded around it. In the street, vendors had set up stalls and were selling everything from foods to small souvenirs such as cheaply painted images of a golden pulcher.

Tiox pushed ahead, using his bulk to create space so that the others could follow in his wake. Still, they had to navigate through the maze of white robes before making it to the small wooden door. Once there, Rogi gently rapped on the weathered wood. Nothing. He struck again, this time a little harder. Either Remer wasn't there or he was deliberately ignoring their knocking. Rogi couldn't blame him. He considered knocking even harder but knew it would do no good.

Instead, he closed his eyes and reached out his mind. His mind wandered through the first floor, and he felt the warmth of the cooking stove. There was a faint smell of fresh bread, probably made a couple of days ago. He traveled up the stairs and felt the presence of three people, none of them Remer. One was familiar, someone he had met before. Shara. Gently he touched her mind, and she looked around. Finally she understood and came downstairs. Slowly the door creaked open and the hundreds of Seekers grew quiet. A small hand beckoned to them, and the four travelers quickly made their way into the house.

"I'm sorry," Shara apologized. Her dark hair was pulled back into a bun. She rubbed her hands together. "But with all those people out there, we never answer the door."

"I understand." Rogi was sympathetic.

"I don't know what they want from us. They just sit there all day. At night the elders make them go away, but they keep coming back. It's driving me crazy."

"Do you want me to do something?" Tiox stared out through the window. "I could try to make them leave." He unconsciously put a fist against his palm.

"No, but thank you. They keep Remer away all day. He only comes back once they leave."

"What do they want from him?" Pom had moved next to Shara and had an arm around her shoulder.

"They want him to say something, anything. I think they want him to explain Asmar. But of course he can't. He has enough problems explaining himself."

Rogi looked around the small but tidy home. There were books neatly stacked on almost every surface and papers piled on the one wooden desk in the corner. Sitting in the chair was a dark haired girl of around three, trying to stay hidden behind the papers.

Shara followed Rogi's gaze. "They all see you, Asmera, so you might as well come out and say hello."

The girl slid off the chair and neatened up her yellow dress dotted with pink flowers. She walked edged out from behind her desk and cautiously looked up at the travelers.

"These are friends of your father," Shara said, and the girl nodded.

Rogi got down on one knee and extended his hand. "Very nice to meet you, Asmera." He sensed behind the shy exterior a curious mind. "Have you been reading your father's books?"

Asmera nodded. "I remember them all."

Rogi looked at Shara, who sighed. "She has her father's gift—or curse. Depends, I guess, on how you use it."

Tiox lowered his bulk next to Asmera, who reached up and put her arms around his neck. "You're too big!" She giggled, and Tiox laughed.

She walked over to Lefi, who had been standing quietly just inside the door. "Why are you so sad?" she asked, and Shara hurried toward her.

"Lupa!" Shara called out, and a woman with graying hair and flour smeared on her face stepped out from the kitchen. "Could you take her with you?" she implored, and Lupa reached out a hand.

"Come along, Asmera. You can help me make the pastries."

"The pink ones with the cream filling?" she asked excitedly.

"What else?" Lupa replied.

As Asmera lost interest in her guests and followed her grandmother, Shara showed the others into her living room and indicated that they should sit. "Remer isn't here," she repeated. "He goes to the library and stays there all day. If you want to wait, he'll be back by nightfall. In the meantime, I hear there will be some pastries ready soon."

"I wouldn't mind a rest," Pom said as she let herself fall into one of the padded chairs. Tiox and Rogi sat on a large sofa. Lefi stood at the window, peering out into the growing darkness.

The aroma from the kitchen wafted out into the sitting area and, despite all his training as a wizard and his ability to do without, Rogi realized he was hungry. When Asmera carried the pastries out, balanced carefully on a ceramic plate, Rogi was the first to take one—or the second, by the look of the powdered sugar on Asmera's lips.

"Why isn't Remer in Dolcere with the others?" Pom asked.

"He wanted to be left alone with his studies." Shara let out a stifled laugh. "But here he still is not left alone. That's why he hides in the library." She paused. "That's not really fair. He's working there. Ever since Vellum passed, he has taken on the role of librarian. Also, he's writing."

At this, Lefi turned away from the window. "What is he writing?"

Shara shook her head. "About his cousin."

Lefi drew closer to the others. "Is he writing about Asmar's beliefs?"

Shara flushed. "No, he's writing about his own." She glanced at the stack of papers on the desk. "His mind wanders, so sometimes it's difficult to understand him."

There was a click and the creak of a door opening. They all looked up at the front door, but it was still closed. As the footsteps came closer, Shara jumped to her feet and a smile crossed her face. Then Remer walked in.

"I see we have guests," he said as he hugged Shara and picked up Asmera, who now had cream all over her face and clothes. Even Lupa made an appearance from the kitchen. Remer stood rooted to the spot at the entrance to the room. "This is an odd group to travel together." He stepped forward. "A wizard! I never expected a wizard would come to my home since the time Preadus came here. And Tiox, it's been so long since I've seen you. And the same for you, Theb. I see the two of you have become good friends. Who would have thought?" Remer walked over to Pom. "And the last time we met, if I remember correctly, you were deciding if I was to live or die."

Pom rose from her seat and shifted uncomfortably. "I did let you live."

"Yes, you did, and Shara is very grateful." He turned to Shara, who nodded her head slightly.

"And this is the former Saeren." Remer took a tentative step toward Lefi, who took a step back. "You seem to be doing better than the other ex-Saeren."

"It depends what you mean by doing better. Most of them are dead."

"So you are doing better," Remer replied.

Lefi shrugged.

"Forgive me for being late, but I had no idea we had company until one of the Seekers found me at the library and said a group of people had been let in to my home. It always takes me a while to sneak in with all of those . . . people out front."

"They just want to see where Asmar lived," Theb said. "It's all part of their religion."

Remer rubbed the back of his neck. "Why do they have to make everything into a religion?" He sat himself on the arm of Shara's chair. "But you didn't come this way just to hear me complain. What is it you want?"

"We need your help to find a ship," Rogi answered.

"You don't mean just any ship, do you?" Remer asked.

Rogi shook his head. "We need the ship the wizards used to come here from Insula."

"I thought that had been wrecked," Shara said.

"I thought that too," Remer answered. "But I think scuttled is a better word for it. The wizards sank the ship but didn't destroy it."

Rogi nodded. "How did you know?"

"It didn't make sense that the ship happened to be destroyed just as you arrived on the shores of the place you wanted to go. It made more sense that you made it here and wanted to discourage anyone from going back."

"And now we need the ship again," Rogi said.

"To find that woman . . ." Remer closed his eyes. "Ran-dahl?"

Lefi's eyes opened wide. "You've heard her too?"

"Will you come with us to find her?" Theb asked.

Shara's eyes opened wide, and Remer put a hand on her arm. "It's a tempting offer, but I think my place is here." Shara's shoulders relaxed.

"But what do you want from me?"

"We have to find and repair the ship. We scuttled it up the coast a way. I think I could find the place, even after all these years, but the currents might have moved it."

"Even if we could find it, we would need a source of power." Remer was leaning forward, his hand on his chin.

"I have that." Rogi reached into a pocket and pulled out the white crystal.

"That was Malzus's." Remer stared at the brilliant light coming from the crystal.

"No!" Rogi replied sharply. "It never belonged to Malzus, it belonged to the council. I took it back."

"How are you going to get that crystal into the ship? And for that matter, how are you going to repair the ship in the first place?" Remer asked.

"We were hoping you could help with that." Tiox looked expectantly at him.

Remer sat in silence, eyes slightly turned upward.

Pom broke the silence. "Can you?"

Remer's head began to nod. "Possibly," he replied.

CHAPTER 37

"THEY ARE MARCHING ON THE castle." Agata tried to control his anxiety. "We need to do something, fast."

"If we do something, it will just rile them up more," replied Trastevere.

Ruvbain listened to his cousin and brother, trying to understand the risks. He turned to one of his other ministers, one who was not related to him, one who was calmer. "Spada, tell me what is going on."

"Your Excellency"—he bowed reflexively—"it is Vanqa. She is leading thousands of her followers toward the castle."

"But why? We gave her what she wanted the last time. I closed the Valki Institute. What else does she want?"

"She wants a crackdown on the scientists from the Institute. Even with Valki shut, the remaining scientists still research the fog in secret. She wants that stopped," Spada explained. "But what I think she really wants is for you to step down."

"And if I do that, who will take over? My son? He's only three years old!"

Harrach stepped forward. "She would be fine with your son taking over if she was appointed regent until he became of age." Harrach looked at his feet, not daring to meet Ruvbain's eyes.

"This is outrageous!" Ruvbain shouted. "I'll not let her get away with this!"

"Of course not," Harrach replied. "But she is marching on the castle and has enough people to overrun us if we do nothing."

"We could send the army out against them," Agata said.

"That would look good, having the army attack our own people. All that would do is turn the rest of the country against us," Trastevere replied.

"Bring the army inside the gates and then shut the gates against Vanqa's horde," Ruvbain said. "But have her brought to me. Maybe she will negotiate."

Harrach nodded and hurried out of the room.

"The people will think we're hiding from her," said Eusebio, another of his advisors.

"We *are* hiding from her!" Ruvbain snapped. "What else are we to do?"

"We could do what she asked. Hunt down the Valki scientists," Eusebio countered.

"Get out! All of you, get out of my sight!"

The ministers looked at each other, confused and frozen for just a moment. Then, bumping into each other, they retreated toward the massive gold doors that marked their exit.

Once they were safely gone, Ruvbain collapsed onto his padded throne and put his head in his hands. *The fools!* he thought. *All of them are fools, but especially my cousin. They don't understand.*

He rose from the throne and marched out of the room and straight into his living quarters, looking for the only person who would understand—K'ren, his wife. He found her in their son Nipio's room. Ruvbain looked at the two playing and imagined Nipio on the throne if Vanqa got her way.

K'ren saw him and signaled to the nurse to take over. She led him out the door. "You're upset," she said softly, closing the door to their son's room.

"It's Vanqa. She's causing trouble again."

"I've heard. You're not going to give in to her?"

"What choice do I have?"

"What does she want now?"

"She wants me to hunt down all the Valki scientists."

K'ren fell quiet and stared at her husband. Then she said, "Does that include me?"

"Of course not. I don't think Vanqa knows you were a member."

"As were you."

"None of that matters. I need to put her off, so I'll have to arrest more of the scientists."

"You'll never find them. They've gone into hiding and only communicate through their minds."

"I know. I tried reaching out to find them, but it's been too long. I've lost the technique."

Ruvbain looked at his wife. He knew from the change in her expression, from concern to confusion and finally anger, that she understood what he was asking.

"No!" she yelled, and then quickly lowered her voice. "I won't do it. They were my friends. I won't help you destroy them."

"I'm not destroying them. If Vanqa finds them first, she'll kill them. If I do, I'll only imprison them."

"And how many have already died in your prisons?"

Ruvbain shook his head. He didn't want to argue. "This has to be done. The science must be eliminated. The people think the fog is a symbol from God, and there is nothing we can do to alter that."

"But you don't believe that. You know there is an answer to the fog. What caused it, how to protect ourselves from it. The scientists are our only hope."

"They give us no hope if the people don't believe them. I need to hold the kingdom together, and that means no science—at least, not right now. I've done all I can do to protect Ran-dahl. She is on her island and nobody bothers her. If she can figure out the fog, great, but there has to be a kingdom left after that happens. You *must* help me."

"And if I don't?"

"You'll leave me no choice."

K'ren slapped her husband hard across the face and turned to go back to Nipio, but Ruvbain grabbed her arm.

"I said, you leave me no choice." He called for the guards and had his wife dragged down to the dungeon, where, he hoped, she would change her mind. Now he had to deal with Vanqa.

Ruvbain peered out a high window. The gates had been closed and the army sequestered inside the thick walls, but all the stone couldn't prevent the spread of ideas. And Vanqa's ideas were seeping in everywhere. He strode to his throne, his steps echoing, and wrapped his purple satin robe around him—these trappings were important if he was to have the upper hand in the negotiations.

A guard pounded on the solid wood door, and it slowly creaked open. Leading the procession was his brother, Trastevere, followed by his cousin, Agata, and the other ministers. At the rear was Vanqa. She had come alone. She was tall, taller than Ruvbain. He needed to remember this when it came time to sit. He couldn't let her overshadow him. For now she would stand, and he would tower over her on his throne.

As the ministers passed in front of the throne, they bowed slightly to him. When it was Vanqa's turn, she merely stood unbowed and stared directly at him. One of the guards placed a heavy hand on her shoulder to force her to obey, but Ruvbain waved him away. He stood slowly, trying to appear as regal as he could.

"Why have you attacked the castle?" He wanted to put her on the defensive.

"I've just brought thousands of your loyal subjects to the castle to see you." A slight smile crossed her face.

"And what do these loyal subjects want?"

"Why, they want me." Her hand went to her hips as she stood defiantly.

"Then not as loyal as you make out." Ruvbain said, trying to control his anger. He had a mind to have her thrown into the prison with his wife, but he was unsure what the thousands outside would do.

"They want you as well." Vanqa looked around at the others in the throne room. "Perhaps we can find a place to talk . . . alone."

The impudence of the woman infuriated Ruvbain. He had no desire to speak with her alone, but he had no choice. He rose and gestured for her to follow. He led the mob leader to a small private room behind the throne. There was a small table in the room, and Ruvbain made sure to sit at the head.

"How dare you threaten me!" he accused as the door closed.

Vanqa didn't answer. She didn't sit either.

"I heard you arrested your own wife. Have things gotten so bad you can't control her?"

"That's a private matter and none of your business," Ruvbain shot back, wondering how she'd known so quickly. "What do you and your mob want?"

"My mob!" Vanqa laughed. "My mob, as you call it, is scared. The fog is creeping closer, and you and all your friends at the Valki Institute can't stop it."

"They're not my friends. I've already arrested most of them."

"Most of the teachers. But the students have gone free. And that one—Ran-dahl—is still free."

"I can't arrest the students. Their parents are the nobility—they own the land, they pay the taxes. If I were to arrest them, everything would fall apart, and you know it."

"Everything *is* falling apart. The more you study the fog the bigger it gets and the more the real people of this land will suffer."

"That's ridiculous!" Ruvbain could barely control his temper. "Without someone studying the fog, we have no chance to stop it. That's why I let Ran-dahl alone. But she's by herself, isolated from all her students and the remaining teachers."

Vanqa paced. "You really believe that." She shook her head. "Do you want to know what my followers believe?" She paused, but Ruvbain stayed silent. "They believe this is a test from God. We need to stop the infidels. We need to stop the defamation of our holy books. We need to stop teaching your fake science and get back to the principles of the holy books."

Ruvbain knew there was no reasoning with Vanqa, but there had to be a compromise. Otherwise, her mob would have attacked rather than wait outside his walls. "What do you want?"

"I want you to step down and have me replace you." Vanqa said firmly.

Ruvbain stifled a surprised laugh. "That's not going to happen. The nobles would never accept you. The army would never accept you."

"I have my own army," Vanqa said, then paused. "But I have no wish to throw the country into a civil war—at least, not yet." She sat at the opposite end of the table and leaned forward. "Until then, I want you to name me as your top minister. I want to be the head of the religious arm of government. All the priests will report to me, they will take their orders from me!" She banged her fist and the table shook.

Ruvbain stood and yelled back, "You're crazy if you think I'd do something like that. I'd have to depose my own brother to make you the leader of the religion." He tried to sound convincing but there were thousands outside the castle, thousands who would storm the castle on Vanqa's orders—or if they didn't hear from her. He knew he had no choice. He slumped back into his chair.

Vanqa smiled. "I'm glad we have an understanding."

CHAPTER 38

REMER HAD EXPECTED ROGI AND the others to show up in Tuland eventually. He had listened to the song of Ran-dahl and felt the tug of her call. The others needed to reach Ran-dahl, and that meant traveling over the oceans to her rocky island. The only way to do that was to take the wizards' ship. He was pretty sure he could find it once Rogi told them where it had been scuttled. The other problems—well, he'd just have to deal with them as they came along.

"Tomorrow I'll take you to the library and we can develop a plan. For now, you need some food and a chance to rest. Unfortunately, we have only a small home, so the best I can offer you is the floor. The library has some rooms you can use for the rest of your stay."

"The floor will be fine. After camping out on the sands and in the open, it will be welcome," Tiox replied.

Remer made his way up to bed late that night. He had been in deep conversation with Rogi and the others, but by the end, none of them could keep their eyes open. Shara had put Asmera to sleep and retired herself a long time before. Remer slipped into bed, trying not to wake her, and lay in the darkness.

"You want to go." Shara's soft voice broke the stillness. Her gentle hand touched his back.

Remer turned to face her. "I want to go, but not as much as I want to stay."

"I don't want to keep you against your will. This is your second chance to find the Tree. You may not get another."

Remer thought back on his last parting with Asmar. His cousin had asked him to come find the Silver Forest, but Remer had refused. That time, it had also been for Shara. "Not everyone is meant to find the Tree. I think I'm in that category."

"Why do you say that? You're as smart and dedicated as any of the others."

Remer smiled in the dark. He liked that Shara thought of him as smart. "That has nothing to do with it. You must be willing to put the world behind you, give up everything. Think about who's found the Tree. Asmar had me, but otherwise he was alone. Rogi has the other wizards, but he has become more of an outcast. Lefi certainly has nothing to hold him here. Whereas I have you and Asmera and my research. I have too much to give up."

"I just don't want to be the one who stops you from pursuing your dreams."

Remer reached out and drew Shara close. "You are my dream," he said softly. He heard a slight sniffle from Shara, and the two lay in bed in each other's arms and fell asleep.

The next morning, Remer gently slipped out of bed, not wanting to wake Shara. He smelled cooking coming from downstairs—Lupa was up early. He slipped into his over-sized blue shirt and tan pants and went down to meet the others. The makeshift camp in his living room had been cleared, and the five of them were sitting at the table with large piles of food in front of them.

Theb had his plate stacked with Lupa's pancakes and was reaching for more. "These are great!" he said with his mouth full.

Tiox laughed. "You act as if you haven't eaten for days!"

"I haven't," Theb replied. "At least, not like this."

Remer helped himself to the food, but his plate was half the size of the others. "When we finish, I'll take you to the library and get you settled. We can also talk about our strategy to find the ship."

The others finished quickly and shouldered their packs. They made their way to the front door, but Remer stopped them.

"I don't go out that way."

Lefi was looking out the window. "It's crowded with Seekers again," he said.

Remer sighed. "If we go out the front, I'll be mobbed by Seekers grabbing at me and yelling. I have another way out. Follow me."

He led them to the back door, but instead of going out, he knelt down and pulled up a door in the floor. "I made this after I got back to Tuland, before the Seekers got to be such an annoyance." Remer climbed down a ladder. Pom was the first to follow.

Remer touched the wall, and a series of crystals illuminated a narrow passage. "The crystals are thanks to Melis," Remer explained.

Theb, who had just made his way into the hallway, shuddered. "He's barely spoken to me since I carved the Peace Crystal."

Remer nodded. It was unfortunate that Melis still held a grudge against his best student. They were all in the passage, even Tiox, who's bulk made it a tight fit. They followed Remer down the long, straight corridor and stopped next to a short wooden ladder. "We need to be careful that nobody sees us when we come out," Remer said, and began to climb. When he reached the top, he pushed open a trap door and quietly climbed out into the fresh air, emerging in a small copse of trees.

Hurrying the others along, Remer led them down a short path that led to the back of a one-story wooden building. As they went down a short flight of steps, he said, "This is the back entrance to the library. Nobody really knows it's here. Well, I do," he corrected himself, "and a few others. But hardly anyone."

Tiox cut him off. "Let's go."

Remer nodded, opened the door, and led them through. As soon as they set foot in the subterranean floor of the library, crystals burst to life and illuminated the large room.

"What is all this?" Pom was practically spinning around the room.

Remer smiled. "This is my workshop. I don't usually show it to anyone—they wouldn't understand—but some of what I do here might come in handy."

"What is this?" Theb was leafing through drawings that lay strewn across Remer's workbench.

"It's drawings of the images I see through this magnifying tube." Remer reflexively put his hand on a small metal object that had a barrel with two lenses attached. "It was a present from the Wanderer."

"Does she still come here?" Lefi asked, moving closer to the group.

"Sometimes. Much of what's here is hers. Although I haven't seen her since . . ." Remer trailed off.

"Her brother died," Pom filled in.

Remer nodded and moved quickly to another table, where a map of the Tuland coast was laid out. "First thing we're going to have to do is find the ship." He turned to Rogi. "Do you remember where you left it?"

Rogi reached out a finger and tapped the map. "It was here, right here. I'm sure of it."

The spot where Rogi had pointed was just up the coast, but that wasn't the problem. Remer frowned. "The water's pretty deep there."

"That's why we sank the ship there. We didn't want to make it easy to raise."

Remer sighed. "This is going to be difficult." He started flipping through different drawings he had scattered about. After throwing a dozen papers on the floor, he pulled out one and held it up. "This is it."

Rogi examined the document Remer held. "What is it?"

"Something the Wanderer designed. It's a suit that allows the wearer to go underwater."

"That's just what we need!" Theb exclaimed. "Where is it?"

Remer laid the paper on a wooden worktable. "Nowhere, I'm afraid. These are just designs. Nobody has ever built one."

"Then how do we know it'll work?" Tiox stared at the design.

"We don't," Remer admitted.

"It will work." Lefi traced the lines on the paper with a finger. "If the Wanderer designed it, then it will work."

"But the problem is still making it. You see the helmet is made from glass, and it needs to be fit into a metal collar that must be part of the suit, which needs to be sealed tight."

"But you have ideas on how to do all that?" Tiox squinted at the plans, then looked at Remer.

"Of course. But I'll need the Aris and Cautes to do the helmet and fittings. The suit itself we can do here in Tuland, and we'll use boiled seaweed to make everything watertight. And that's just for the suit. We also need to build the hose that goes to the suit, and the pump to make sure enough air gets to the diver." Remer paused, making sure that his guests understood the complexity of what they were trying to do. "None of this is tested, so it will be dangerous for whoever decides to attempt this."

Rogi stepped forward. "I'll attempt the dive," he said simply. "I know the ship, I know where the crystal goes."

Remer nodded. "I thought it would be you," he replied. "So now we need to get the different craftsmen together.

Theb, you can work on the metal fittings. I'll give you the specs of what we need. There is an Aris craftsman in Tuland who can fashion the helmet, and Shara has agreed to do the suit. It's all very complicated and exciting."

"But none of this is any help unless we find the ship," Tiox stated.

Remer nodded. "We could use the help of the Wanderer."

"And we have no idea where she is," Tiox added.

"Maybe we do." It was Lefi's soft voice.

Rogi went over to him. "You know where she is?"

Lefi shook his head. "No, but I can reach out. She'll hear me."

"But will she come?" Pom asked.

"I'm not sure, but I'll try."

"Well, I guess that's it, then. One more thing." Remer motioned for them to follow. "This is going to take a while for everything to come together, so you'll need a place to stay." He pushed open a door that led to a small room. There was a high window that let in rays of light, revealing a bed and desk. "I stay here sometimes when I'm working late. I think we can fit in a couple more beds." He turned to Pom. "You can stay here if you want, or Shara would be happy if you wanted to stay with us."

Pom looked at the others and smiled. "I'll stay with you."

CHAPTER 39

ROGI WANDERED THE STREETS OF Tuland to clear his mind. He thought about his journey from Insula and how the ship had been nearly destroyed by the crashing waves and the fierce storms. The others didn't understand the risks they were taking. The bay of Tuland was protected by a seawall, but once you went beyond that, the waves grew larger and more dangerous. Farther out at sea, where you couldn't see the land, the waves would crash down on the ship. Rogi remembered that when a storm hit, it felt like the ship would be cut in two. The wizards had had no choice but to lock themselves in the belly of the ship and just hope they would survive. The pumps had worked full time, ridding the vessel of the water that constantly seeped through any cracks in the bronze pulcher. Rogi had curled up in the prow of the ship, his eyes shut tight, reciting passages from the Koan and wondering what it would be like to drown. Should they undertake the journey? he wondered as these thoughts raced through his mind. Should he even tell them he knew how to find the ship?

Rogi walked down to the bay and breathed in the salty air. He looked out to the horizon, at the deceptively calm waters. He would be going out to ocean again. He watched as the sun set and turned the sky crimson. The breeze coming off the water made him shudder.

"You're cold," said a soft voice from behind him, one Rogi knew well. The Wanderer.

Rogi turned. "You came."

The Wanderer was his height and wore a tan cloak with a cowl pulled over her head. She let the cowl fall away.

"What else could I do?" Her eyes looked sad and her voice was soft, soothing.

"I don't want to go back out there," Rogi said. He remembered when the wizards first had learned of the Wanderer and thought her a threat to their rule. They had been right, she was a threat—but their rule needed to be threatened.

"Then don't," the Wanderer replied.

Rogi sighed. "If it were only that simple. I need to find the Tree. That's what I have lived for."

"But if it's not what you want to do . . ." The Wanderer trailed off.

Rogi was silent for a few moments, head bowed. Then he looked into the sad eyes of the Wanderer. "I do want to do it," he admitted.

The Wanderer nodded.

"But there is so much that needs to be done, much that has never been done before. We need to raise the ship, and before that we need to find it."

"We can do both," the Wanderer replied. "It will take time, but the task is not impossible. I have a plan for finding the ship, but I'll need the crystal that you took from Dolcere."

"What do you plan to do with it?"

"I plan on attaching it to a very thin wire made from the bronze pulcher. Since the gem was made to fit into the receptor in the ship, if we get close enough to it, there should be an attraction between the two. All we need is to follow the pull of the crystal, and it will lead us to the ship."

The idea was brilliant. He should have expected that from the Wanderer. "And the wire is made of the bronze pulcher for the same reason." Rogi smiled as he understood the full plan. "The woods attract each other, so that will add to the pull."

The Wanderer nodded. "But finding the ship is only the start. What happens when you find Ran-dahl?"

"She will lead us to the Tree. At least, that's the plan," Rogi replied.

The Wanderer turned away and gazed out over the water. "That's still a long way off." She sighed heavily.

Rogi remembered what Lefi had told him, and he put a hand on the Wanderer's shoulder. "You lost your brother." He didn't know what else to say. Her brother, the Old Man, had killed Yau, so Rogi wasn't exactly sorry he had died. But he saw the pain it caused the Wanderer.

She turned from the water, a tear running down her cheek. This surprised Rogi; he had always thought the Wanderer had no emotions, or at least kept them deeply hidden.

"He was not a good man," the Wanderer said simply. "But he was good to me."

"The Old Man?" Rogi used the only name for him he had ever heard.

"He hated that name," the Wanderer replied. "But he refused to use his given name, the one our parents gave him."

"What was his name?" Rogi asked.

"Prostatis."

Rogi nodded and then realized the Wanderer had a name as well, one she had never shared with anyone, not even Remer or Asmar. "And do you also refuse your given name?"

A slight smile crossed her face. "No one has ever been that interested."

"I am. What's your name?"

"My parents called me Alitheia."

"I like that name." Rogi looked at the Wanderer—Alitheia—as if he were seeing her for the first time. She must be at least his age, but in a way she was timeless. It seemed she had spent so much of her life alone. Or maybe he was projecting. It was he who felt alone. "Are you going to the library?"

"Later, maybe. For now, I have a place where I stay when I come here. It probably is in terrible shape as it's been so long since my last visit."

"Oh, then I won't keep you," Rogi said, but made no attempt to move.

Alitheia reached out her hand to him. "Why don't you come with me? I also have been alone too long."

Rogi took the offered hand and followed Alitheia down the coastline to a small cabin with white wood planks and a window overlooking the water. When they entered, Rogi was expecting the small room to be crammed with books and papers, but it was the opposite. "You don't work here."

Alitheia laughed. Rogi had never heard her laugh before.

"I do most of my work here—when I'm in Tuland, that is."

"But . . ." Rogi pointed to the emptiness.

"Thinking is most of my work. I like to sit here and look out over the water. I come up with some of my best ideas here. Then I'll go to the library, or somewhere else, and see if it works."

"Is that what you've been doing to raise the ship?"

"Let's not talk about that now. Today is for looking out over the water and thinking of possibilities."

Rogi wanted to ask what possibilities, but when he saw the faraway look in Alitheia's eyes, he just turned and looked out the window and rested his hand on hers. She moved closer to him, put her arm around his waist, and rested her head on his shoulder. Rogi put his arm around her waist, too. Alitheia gently kissed his ear. It tickled. She led him toward the bed, and her sweet floral scent enveloped him.

The next morning, Rogi was awakened by the smell of breakfast. He wasn't used to breakfast being something you could actually smell. In Dolcere, breakfast, if there was anything, had been cold and tasteless. The aroma made him hungry. He rubbed his eyes and thought about the night. Suddenly he blushed. Not at what they had done, but at what it meant.

"What happened last night . . ." he started hesitantly.

Alitheia turned to him. "You're not going to become all wizardly on me, are you?"

"I don't know what you mean."

"Yes, you do. As a wizard you took a vow of celibacy, and now you're not sure if you're a wizard. And what about breakfast? This would be too much of an indulgence for a wizard."

"Well, yes."

Alitheia waved her hand. "The vow of celibacy is ridiculous. How can you understand life without experiencing it? And as for breakfast, I'm not that good a cook."

Rogi laughed. "Compared to what I was used to eating as a wizard, this is a feast. You're the best chef in the world." He sat at the small table in front of the window and filled a plate with food. He stared into Alitheia's eyes. "I just don't know what I am anymore. Am I a wizard? And if not, what then?"

"Is that so important?"

Rogi shrugged. "I used to think it was."

When they had finished, Alitheia said, "We should go. There is plenty of work to do if we're going to make your ship seaworthy." She draped her tan cloak over her shoulders.

Rogi remained seated. "What of us?"

Alitheia turned. "You're not the possessive type?"

"I . . . I don't know."

"I lost my brother and you lost . . . you lost your way. Maybe we helped each other. Let's not think further than that."

Slowly, Rogi rose and nodded. He put on his robe and followed Alitheia out the door.

CHAPTER 40

THEY'RE AFTER ME!

The intrusion woke K'ren, cutting through the musty smell of her cell. The mind was familiar.

You have to help me!

K'ren felt the desperation in the cry. She shook her head. *Eot?* Yes, it was Eot, one of the other students from Valki. She was in trouble. What was happening?

Ruvbain had thrown K'ren into prison, ripped her away from their own child. He was scared of the fog, but also of his own people. Vanqa and her followers believed the fog was a judgment from God and it was sacrilege to study it. But he couldn't give in to her. Understanding the fog was the only way to defeat it. And if they were to have any chance of doing that, they needed Ran-dahl and Eot.

But there was little K'ren could do while she was locked up. At least her husband had assigned her one of the better cells. It was musty but had a window that let in fresh air and afforded her some sunlight. That had to mean he would come to her soon and, if she was contrite enough, even let her free.

K'ren concentrated. She was out of practice with linking minds. *Hide for now. There is nothing I can do. When it gets light, I hope I can help more.*

When it's light they'll find me!

Try to stay hidden. Go down to the waterfront and I'll try to do something.

You need to help now! came Eot's plea.

Do as I say. Now we have to sever our link, or they may find us, K'ren concluded, and broke the contact with Eot.

She lay on the hard plank bed, thinking about how she could help her fellow student. There was only one place she could hide safely, and that was on Ran-dahl's island. But how to get her there?

K'ren closed her eyes again to think, but in her tiredness she drifted off to sleep, her mind going back to her days at the Valki Institute. She had been happy there; Ruvbain had been happy there. He had changed so much since he'd taken over from his father. He had become . . . crueler. But she could still see the inquisitive boy he had been, although now she needed to look deeper to find him.

The rattling of the door woke her. It was her husband. She quickly rose from the bed and smoothed her skirt. K'ren kept her gaze on the cold stone floor, trying to seem repentant.

"I had no choice," her husband began. "If you only knew the pressures I'm under. I had to negotiate with that disgusting rebel, Vanqa!" He pounded a fist into his hand.

K'ren could tell he'd made a deal with her, a deal he didn't like. "I'm sure you did what was needed." Her husband wouldn't believe her if she expressed too much repentance. If she wanted to free herself, she had to strike a balance. "What do you need from me?"

Ruvbain shook his head. "Nothing. I only need you to renounce the Valki Institute, to have nothing more to do with them."

K'ren nodded. "I just want to be back with Nipio. He'll miss me if I'm away too long." She stole a look at her husband. He was giving in, he was going to let her out!

"If you communicate at all with the Institute, you'll leave me no choice but to lock you up, and the next time it won't be in the better cells."

"I understand," K'ren replied. She was thinking of how she could help Eot and still keep her actions from her husband.

"Very well. You may go." Ruvbain turned from her cell.

K'ren followed close behind. "I'm tired," she said. "I need to lie down and rest." She paused, then asked, "What deal did you have to make with Vanqa?"

Ruvbain clasped his hands behind his back and cleared his throat. "She is to become my religious advisor."

K'ren couldn't stop herself from letting out a small gasp. "Have you told Trastevere?"

Ruvbain shook his head. "I will let my brother know in good time," he said, and turned his back and walked away.

K'ren headed into her room. She needed to act quickly. Once Vanqa was in the castle, there would be very little she could do. She sat at her desk and wrote a note, one that would seem to say nothing if intercepted, and called her maid, a woman she knew she could trust with her life—which was what she was doing now.

"Go down to the docks and give this note to the captain of the ship *Sortria*. And hurry!"

As soon as her maid left, K'ren sat on her bed and reached out her mind to Eot. *Find the captain of the ship Sortria. He will take you away. That's all I can do for you. You mustn't contact me again.*

K'ren hoped she had done enough.

CHAPTER 41

THEY FELT THE TUG ALONG the thin bronze pulcher thread as it pulled their small craft through the water. It had been almost forty days since they had started going out in the boat, but Rogi felt that today was the day. He had been staying with Alitheia since that first night. Neither of them spoke of it, but at the end of the day, he just followed her back to her hut—and she didn't refuse. In the mornings they put the crystal in the water, secured by the pulcher line. At first the crystal just floated under the surface of the water, and the two of them would sit, sometimes talking but many times in a comfortable silence, as they floated calmly in the bay.

But today was different. There was a tug on the line and their small craft picked up speed. Rogi slowly let the line of bronze pulcher out as Alitheia rowed to keep up with the receding line.

"I think this is it," she said, not able to stifle a laugh. "I didn't think it would really work."

Salt water splashed Rogi's face as the small boat raced ahead. His pulse beat quickly. This was what he had been hoping for. But it was only a start—they would have to raise the *Elpida* and make sure it was seaworthy. Then they would need to figure out how to find Ran-dahl. But one step at a time.

The boat slowed and then stopped. Rogi let out a bit more thread. He felt a thud, and the rope went limp in his hands. "It's here." He looked at Alitheia, who nodded back.

"We need to mark the spot," she said.

He reached for a small buoy they had brought with them and let it slide into the water, and they pulled up the white crystal and headed for the shore.

"Next time we bring out the diving suit," Alitheia said.

As they came to the shore, Tiox strode out into the water and pulled the rowboat onto the sandy beach. The others fell silent, waiting expectantly.

"Well?" Theb demanded, breaking the silence.

"We found it!" Rogi replied.

There was a brief pause before the others started yelling; even Lefi seemed excited.

"Tomorrow we'll bring the diving suit and go down and assess the damage. Then we'll figure a plan to bring the ship to the surface. So tonight I recommend we all get a good night's sleep," Alitheia said.

That night, Rogi and Alitheia lay awake for hours, despite knowing they needed to be well-rested rest for tomorrow. "I'm nervous about using the diving suit," Rogi admitted.

"I'll be close by if anything happens," Alitheia reassured him.

He reached out and took her hand, and they gently drifted off to sleep.

The next day when they went down to the beach, Remer was busy with a small machine. He fitted a crystal into its center and stepped back as it came to life. He was explaining to Theb, "It pushes air down through the tube and into the helmet of the diving suit. That way the diver will be able to breathe."

"But won't that just fill the entire suit with air and make it blow up?" Theb asked.

Remer nodded. "It would, except that as the diver breathes out, the air goes into the water, keeping the suit from expanding."

"But—" Theb began again.

Remer sighed. "It works, okay? At least, the books say it works, and that's all we have to go on." He stood and walked over to Rogi and Alitheia. "We're ready to go anytime you are."

"Let me put on the suit," Rogi said. He went to the shoreline, where the diving suit had been laid out, and slipped it on, except for the helmet. He stepped in the boat with Remer and Alitheia by his side, and they rowed out to the buoy.

"The ship is pretty far down," Remer said. "But the tube should be long enough that you can get there."

"I'll try to assess the damage to the *Elpida*," Rogi replied. "And if I can, I'll put the crystal where it belongs to see if I can restore power."

When they reached the buoy, Rogi put the crystal in a pouch in the suit and tightened his helmet, then dove off the boat. The feeling of weightlessness hit him as he gently floated down under the surface. At first he struggled to breathe through the tube that fed into his helmet, but he forced himself to relax and the breathing became easier. He peered down into the murky waters for the ship that had carried the nine wizards from their home in Insula to the new land of Bracat. He had forgotten so much about Insula that it was hard for him to think about a time before he had arrived. Rogi twisted a small crystal embedded in his helmet, and a soft light shone out into the water ahead of him. It was hard to see very far, but he stayed close to the chain that held the buoy in place. Slowly he made his way down. His heart beat quickly as his anticipation grew.

When his diving boots landed on the bottom, he looked up, but all he saw was darkness. He was alone. He was reminded of his training, when he had been put in the chamber of no sensation. But now he was a wizard and could control his panic. He walked forward. The ship had to be here. He took out the white crystal and held it in front of him. It gave off a stronger light than the small crystal in his helmet. What was more, he could feel it pulling him forward, toward the place it was supposed to be. Toward the ship.

At first he didn't recognize it. There was just a mass of seaweed cascading down its sides. But the crystal drew him closer and the light reflected back a glint of bronze.

This was it—the ship he had sailed all those years ago. He worked hard to control his breathing; too fast and he wouldn't get enough air. He reached out, grabbed a handful of the seaweed, and pulled. It drifted down slowly, revealing the bow of the ship, with the name—*Elpida*—burned in white.

Rogi gently touched the wood and felt it vibrate through his gloves. He stared at the structure, trying not to get caught in all the memories it contained; of their tumultuous voyage from their homeland, and of all the people he'd left behind. It was time to think about the future and where the *Elpida* could take them.

He walked around the exterior of the ship, inspecting it for damage. He went to the spot where they had cut into the wood, letting the ocean water rush in. The wood was scarred, but the hole was gone—the living pulcher had drawn together and healed itself after all these years. The ship was whole. All he needed to do was put the crystal in its place and see if the pumps could start ridding the ship of the water that held it down.

He found the hatch leading inside, but the pressure of the water prevented him from pulling it open. He finally gave up and tried to think of another way in. He could cut into the pulcher wood at the side of the ship, just enough to let him enter. Then he could swim inside and plant the crystal in its rightful place. But he didn't have the tools for it. He tugged the rope that connected him to the small boat above; he felt an answering tug, and he was hoisted away from the *Elpida*.

"It's there!" Rogi said once his helmet was off. A rush of emotions filled him as he described the *Elpida*. "We can make it run again. I know it." He felt like a young boy again.

"We'll need to figure out how to get air into the cabin." Remer was catching Rogi's enthusiasm. "Once the pumps start working and pump out the water, we'll need air to replace it. That way, the ship can be floated to the surface."

"Of course," Rogi replied. "We can get it ready to sail in less than twenty days. This is better than I thought."

Alitheia had been slowly rowing them to shore, where the others were waiting expectantly. As the boat came closer, the others ran into the surf to pull it in. Rogi told them of what he had found.

They spent the next few days preparing for Rogi's next dive. Remer figured out how to hook up another hose to the air machine he'd developed and provided Rogi with the tools he would need to cut through the bronze pulcher. After seven days, they were ready to go out again.

They rowed to the buoy, and Rogi donned his suit and slipped into the water. When he touched down on the sandy bottom, he removed the tools in the murky light. It had been many years since he had cut the pulcher, and he had never been an expert, not like Malzus had been. He knew the basics, but still, this was going to be a very rough cut.

He took out a sharp blade and gently inserted it into the wood. He felt the revulsion of the pulcher to the cold metal as it flowed away from the honed tip, leaving a small hole. Rogi inserted the metal tip farther, and the wood fled from its touch. Slowly he worked the knife and then inserted metal bars to prevent the wood from flowing back together. Gradually a space began to appear, large enough for him to fit through. He took a deep breath and entered the ship he had abandoned over eighty years ago.

Rogi navigated past the layer of seaweed that caked the sides of the ship and made his way toward its stern. He removed the white crystal from its pouch and walked slowly to the aft of the ship, where the crystal belonged. His hands shook as he settled the crystal in its place. Nothing happened. His heart sank. They had no other plan—this had to work.

He removed the crystal and inspected the seat where he had placed it. It had become encrusted, so he used the blade to scrape off as much as he could. When it was clean, he placed the white crystal carefully back in place. The ship came alive!

Crystals embedded in the sides of the ship illuminated the eerie scene. The inside of the ship was caked in a white scum, but nothing was alive. The ship had been sealed against light and closed to the rest of the ocean. If they were ever going to get it to float, the most important thing to see to was the pumps. There were two in the bow of the ship, two in the midsection, and two aft. He wondered if they would be able to pump out so much water.

He started with the bow and found the two pumps. They were jammed with the white precipitate from the ocean water. He took the knife and chipped away, trying to free the mechanism. He felt short of breath; his exertion was causing him the breathe too quickly. He calmed his mind and slowed the intake of air, then got back to work on the pump. Large chunks of the white substance came away and the pump sprang to life. He moved on to the other pumps and managed to get four of the six to work.

But there was one more thing he needed to do. There had to be air coming in to displace the water. He made his way back to the opening he had cut. It was still there—the metal spacers he had used were holding. He slipped through, took the extra hose Remer had given him, and placed it in the opening. Then he removed the metal barriers and watched as the bronze pulcher slowly closed on the hose. He had done all he could. Now they would have to wait to see if it worked. He tugged his line and let himself be pulled back up.

CHAPTER 42

THE PRIEST STOOD WITH HIS arms raised, facing the image of the Golden Tree. K'ren listened as the music rose up and filled the space of the great kirk. She had come here for sanctuary, to escape from everything going on in the castle.

Vanqa had managed to arrest most of her husband's advisors and put her own people in their place. It was only Trastevere, Ruvbain's brother, and Agata, his cousin, whom she couldn't get rid of—not yet. But K'ren knew it was only a matter of time. Her time would come, as well, and then her son would not be safe. Finally, even her husband would be replaced. How could he have been so stupid?

There was one hope: Ran-dahl. If she could explain the fog—no, that wouldn't be enough. She would have to stop the fog. Until that happened, Vanqa would keep gaining support.

K'ren closed her eyes and let the music wash over her. She had come here because the priest had been a friend—but now her friend was gone, replaced by a priest in the red robes of Vanqa's cult. It wasn't safe here, she knew that. But she had sent a message to Eot to meet her here. K'ren rose slowly, trying not to look suspicious but needing to get out and warn Eot before she entered.

The priest eyed her as K'ren stood in the aisle and bowed on one knee to the Golden Tree. She wanted to flee the place that had once been her sanctuary, but she controlled herself. She pushed open the heavy doors of the chapel and emerged into the clean, fresh air. She steadied herself against the cold stone of the building and looked around. Which way? Eot was still on the *Sortria* down at the wharf, so that's where K'ren would go. As she walked through the town, she kept looking over her shoulder. Was she being followed? That was silly, of course she was. There was no way Vanqa would let her have her freedom.

She made her way to the market, which was crowded and would afford her some cover. She walked through the outdoor stalls, stopping occasionally to look at some fabric or a silver bauble. She could see the man following her. His head would turn every time she looked over. K'ren almost laughed. He was too tall to go unnoticed. K'ren knew the market and could lose her pursuer at any time, but if it seemed deliberate, she would be reported to Vanqa.

K'ren drew closer to the docks and looked over her shoulder. Her pursuer was still there. When she broke free, she would have only a short time to contact the captain of the *Sortria*. She had to time things perfectly.

A young woman walked by, and the tall man couldn't help but follow her with his eyes. This was her chance. As soon as he looked away, K'ren turned a corner and was out of sight. She imagined the tall man's panic when he found her gone. Quickly she walked to the piers and went directly to the *Sortria*.

When the captain saw her coming, he hurried down the gangplank and pulled K'ren into a small alley. "You shouldn't have come here. You could be watched."

"I am being watched," K'ren replied.

The captain looked over his shoulder.

"He's not here. But I only have a moment before he suspects something. Is the woman safe?"

The captain nodded. "She is, but she's not happy. She doesn't like the cramped quarters of the ship and only being able to go out once it's dark."

"She'd like the cramped quarters of a cell even less."

The captain shrugged. "I can't keep her there forever."

"I know. Tell her not to go to the kirk, it's not safe."

The captain nodded.

"Be ready to sail. They are closing in on me and I will have to leave quickly."

"I've already laid in supplies. Where will you want to go?"

"To Ran-dahl."

The captain's eyes opened wide. "How will we navigate that? The waters are too rough."

"That's the only place that will be safe."

The captain didn't argue.

"I need to go," K'ren said. "Be ready."

She left the alley and turned back up toward the market. She saw the tall man desperately searching through the crowd. He wasn't looking her way, so she stopped at a fabric seller and said loudly, "How can you charge that much!" The seller looked surprised, but as K'ren walked away, the tall man finally saw her. She started back to the castle.

The castle was bustling with red-clad men and women walking deliberately from place to place. These were Vanqa's people, and they were taking over. They hadn't been there when she left, but now they seemed to be in every corner. She needed to make sure Nipio was safe. She ran up the wide staircase and made her way to the nursery, where the nanny was standing in front of the crib as two red-clad women came forward.

"We will take care of the baby," one of the women said as she reached out.

"I can't. Not unless my mistress says it's okay," replied the nanny, lifting Nipio and holding him protectively. She saw K'ren and ran over to her. "They want the baby," she said, tears streaming down her face.

K'ren took Nipio from the nanny. "Who approved this? Who said you could take my child?"

"It is on Lord Vanqa's order," said the other woman.

"Lord Vanqa now, is it? At least it's not Queen Vanqa."

"Not yet," replied the other.

"Well, until it is, the baby stays with me." K'ren turned her back on the two women. She could feel their gazes burning into her back.

"Very well—for now," said one.

"But we'll be back," finished the other.

K'ren looked out the door to make sure Vanqa's people were gone.

"We need to get out of here," she said to the nanny.

"I know a place I can hide with the baby," the nanny replied. She looked around to make sure they were alone. "I hate those people!"

"Not as much as I do," K'ren replied in a hushed voice. Do you think you can sneak out on your own? I would go with you, but they're following me."

The nanny nodded. "I have relatives—" she began, but K'ren cut her off.

"Don't tell me. The fewer people who know, the better. When all this is over, bring Nipio back."

"How will I know when it's over?" the nanny asked.

"When that awful Vanqa is gone."

"I will leave tonight."

K'ren carefully handed her baby back to the nanny. Her eyes moistened as she wondered when she would see her child again. But she knew it was the right choice. If Nipio stayed with her, Vanqa would use him as leverage against her and her husband. K'ren took one more look and turned away from the nursery.

Everything was coming to a head. Her husband was not strong enough to fight Vanqa. K'ren was on her own. There was only one other who could help her. She needed to reach out to Ran-dahl; she would know what to do.

She walked the halls of the castle, looking for a secluded space where Vanqa's minions wouldn't see her, where she would have time to reach out and connect with Ran-dahl's mind. As she passed down a narrow corridor, she came across a small, closed door. She stopped and tried it, and found it unlocked. It was a closet, crowded with mops and other cleaning supplies. She laughed at the idea of using a small closet as her meditation room, but it would be somewhere nobody would look for her. After a quick look down the corridor, K'ren slipped into the closet and wedged the handle of a mop against the door. She rearranged the buckets to provide a somewhat comfortable seat and then settled in and closed her eyes.

She started breathing deeply to clear her mind, but she kept on coming back to images of Vanqa's two women and Nipio. She pushed down the anger—she needed to stop thinking about Vanqa if she was to reach Ran-dahl. She stood up and shook her hands and then sat back down. Ran-dahl had told her to use a special word if she had difficulty clearing her mind, a word that she could concentrate on, rather than letting in the outside world. She breathed in and let her mind surround the word *kan*; when she exhaled, the word in her mind was *anu*. Again she breathed in with *kan* and out with *anu*. She wasn't sure what they meant, but it didn't matter; it was something to concentrate on. Slowly her mind relaxed and her thoughts freed. She reached out farther, looking for her mentor, her friend, alone on her island. She needed her help, her guidance. As her mind traveled farther out over the water, she could feel the rising and crashing of the waves. It wasn't safe, and the closer she got to the island, the more treacherous it became. In addition to the roiling waters, rocks guarded the island, rocks that could destroy even the sturdiest boat. Suddenly she couldn't go any farther. It was as if a barrier had been stretched across the island. But by whom? Had it been constructed by Ran-dahl or Vanqa? If Vanqa had the power to build this barrier, then they were all in trouble—she was stronger than they had given her credit for. But it made sense; why else would so many follow her? She had to be able to get into their thoughts and twist them. K'ren's panic rose. Would Vanqa know she had reached out? Would she be able to find K'ren?

Suddenly K'ren felt a tug, like a strong hand grabbing her by the arm and forcing her through the barrier. There was a bright light, and then it dimmed. K'ren opened her eyes, and standing before her was Ran-dahl.

I'm glad it's you! K'ren reached out to the image of her friend, but it was not solid.

You are lucky I sensed you. Otherwise, it might have been Vanqa standing before you.

I didn't think she was capable of that.

She's very strong. You will need to be careful and block your thoughts. It might be better if you don't go back to the castle, Ran-dahl replied.

But what about my son? K'ren didn't like the idea of being separated from Nipio. When she'd given him to the nurse, she'd thought they would be apart for only a short time. But if Vanqa was so strong, it could be a very long time.

He will be safer without you, at least for now. But there are more important things we need to discuss.

K'ren couldn't think of anything more important than her son, but Ran-dahl didn't give her time.

The fog is growing.

K'ren was silent for a while. Then she said, *How close is it?*

It is still a way from my island, but we need to determine why it is growing.

Could it have something to do with Vanqa?

Possibly, Ran-dahl replied.

But as the fog grows bigger, she gains power.

True. But we must be careful about our assumptions. We have no proof of a causal link. That had been one of the first lessons Ran-dahl had learned at the Valki Institute: any hypothesis must be supported by fact, and what she had now was just intuition. *There are others coming,* she continued.

To help? K'ren asked.

Yes. They are bringing the tools I need to pierce to fog.

K'ren let out a gasp. *Nobody has been able to pierce the fog. It's foolish, it's . . . suicide!*

I think not. But it must be tried, in any event. If the fog keeps growing, it will take over everything. Ran-dahl's voice was calm.

That was not at all how K'ren felt. *What do you need from me?* she asked.

Those who are coming may need protection from Vanqa. You may be their best hope.

But what am I supposed to do?

For now, stay hidden and stay with Eot. When the time comes, I will contact you.

Ran-dahl's image began to fade. K'ren rose and hit her head on the mop barring the door. She opened the door slowly. There was no one there, so she slipped out and made her way to the docks to find Eot.

CHAPTER 43

AFTER FOURTEEN DAYS, ROGI COULD see the tip of the main mast peeking through the water. It wouldn't be long now until the ship broke the surface. Then it would need to be fully cleaned of all the sediment and seaweed and all the mechanisms checked, but it was only a matter of time. They had started gathering food and supplies, including sails in case the crystal failed them. Clean water would be supplied by the desalination machine on board.

"How will we know which way to sail?" Theb asked.

"Your crystal will have to be our guide."

"But how?" Tiox asked. "How will Theb's crystal be able to tell us the direction?"

"It will get stronger the closer we get to Ran-dahl." Lefi's voice was soft but firm. "It will pull us to where it wants to be."

That night, Rogi sat on the shore as the stars appeared. This was what he wanted—this was his purpose. He was going to get the chance to find the Tree. But Alitheia would not be coming. Or had she already been there? She was an enigma to him. So much of her was still hidden. He stared up at the darkening sky, the vast emptiness. There was so much yet unknown. He wasn't sure what he expected from the voyage to Ran-dahl.

The days passed with much activity, but to Rogi they seemed to go so slowly. The ship broke the surface, and they enlisted many of the townspeople to drag it up onto the beach, where it could be repaired and cleaned. Rogi was amazed at just how little damage there was, given the years it had been at the bottom of the water. There still remained a dampness that had made its way deep into the wood, but, Rogi knew, even that would dry quickly.

Every night he would go back with Alitheia and they would talk about the journey, about what it had been like for him to brave the ocean to get to Bracat. He was the only experienced sailor, and he hoped he could manage to get them safely to Ran-dahl.

But this wasn't what troubled him most. What concerned him even more was leaving Alitheia. This was the first time since he'd arrived in Bracat that he felt he didn't want to leave. But he had a chance to find the Tree. He tried to talk to her about his feelings, but she kept putting him off. Finally, as the ship was just about ready to sail, he knew he couldn't wait any longer. He walked the beach, looking up at the stars, and then made his way to Alitheia's cottage.

I don't want to go. He used the more intimate mind-to-mind communication.

"But you know you must," she said back.

This surprised him—she was pushing him away.

"If you don't go, you will always wonder what you missed. You are using me as an excuse to stay, to not try."

Rogi realized she was right. He wasn't sure. In any event, he didn't argue.

The days passed uneventfully. The *Elpida* was outfitted, and he tried out his new crew on its deck, rigging, sails, but that was just a precaution. The crystal would power the ship and he would steer it. But the practice kept everyone busy and took their focus away from the dangers that lay ahead.

After ninety days had passed, Rogi couldn't put it off any longer. The boat was ready, the crew was as ready as they could be. They stowed the provisions and had one last meal with those who were being left behind. Remer and Shara prepared a lavish feast, but Rogi could barely taste it.

"What's it like out on the waters?" Theb asked Remer, drawing on his total recall.

"From what I've been able to discern from my books, not only are the waters rough with storms, but there are whirlpools that can suck a ship down to the bottom. And there are large ocean creatures that can ram a ship and send it to the bottom."

Tiox hadn't taken his eyes off Rogi. "Did any of this happen to you?"

Rogi wished he could lie and tell them it had been an easy passage from Insula. But they needed to know. "All of that happened. Except being sent to the bottom of the waters. We managed to avoid that part."

"How?" Pom asked.

"Sometimes by skillful sailing and other times by luck. I hope we'll have both on our journey."

The dinner seemed to go on forever. All he wanted to do was go back to the cottage and spend his last night with Alitheia.

"Did you ever find the Tree?" Rogi asked, once he and Alitheia were alone.

They lay in bed together, her head resting on his shoulder. He felt her nod.

"Then why are you here? Why didn't you stay with the Tree in the Silver Forest?"

"It's not right for everyone."

Rogi shook his head. "How could it not be right?"

"How can it be right for everyone? Do you even know what it is?"

"The key to understanding," Rogi replied.

"Understanding what?"

Rogi paused. He had always felt that finding the Tree was the answer, but he'd never really thought about what the question was. "I was taught it gave you the key to understanding the nature of the world. That all the questions you had would be answered by the Tree."

Alitheia laughed. "Then you will be disappointed. Well, maybe not disappointed, but it's never what you expect."

"What should I expect?"

"I don't know. It's different for different people."

"What was it like for you?" Rogi stroked Alitheia's gray hair.

She lay silently for a while. Then her voice seemed to come from far away. "It made me realize I needed to come back. That I had work still to do here."

"Have you been back to the forest since the first time?"

"Yes."

"Could you take me there?"

Alitheia let out a sigh. "If I tried to take you, I wouldn't be able to find it. You need to go on your own journey."

Rogi fell asleep dreaming of the Silver Forest.

They woke early the next morning. Rogi wasn't hungry but ate anyway. The sun was just rising as they made it to the beach. The others were there as well. Pom and Theb were already climbing the rope ladder to the deck while Tiox and Lefi held the flimsy ladder taut.

They would need to push the boat out into the harbor as soon as the tide came in. Remer had organized the Tulanders who would be needed to slide the ship back into the water. Shara sat with little Asmera, who was making a castle with the damp sand.

"It's time for you to join the others," Alitheia said quietly.

Rogi nodded and went to embrace her, but she stepped away.

"What we had is over now," she said. "We must both move on."

Rogi held her gaze a little longer, and then nodded. His stomach knotted up, and he felt dampness on his cheek. Was she pushing him away so he would go on the journey, or was it really over? It didn't matter—he had to go. The tide wouldn't wait.

Rogi reached out his mind. *Thank you.* What he'd said felt weak, but she understood.

He started to walk down to the water and heard, *Maybe we will meet again in the forest.* Alitheia's touch was light and Rogi almost didn't hear. He turned, but she had already started walking away.

Tiox and Lefi were holding the rope ladder. "The two of you go next." Before either of them could argue, Rogi grabbed the ladder and looked away, toward the beach. But Alitheia was gone. Once Tiox and Lefi had gone up, he knew he couldn't put it off any longer.

Remer came to his side and steadied the rope ladder. "If you see Asmar, tell him . . ." He didn't finish.

"I'll tell him you miss him," Rogi filled in, and Remer nodded.

Rogi made his way up the ladder and made one last check to make sure they were ready. He watched as the tide came in. It wouldn't be long now. He wanted to stay on the deck as long as possible. Once they were out on the ocean, days when it would be safe to be on deck would be rare. He had told the others that, but they hadn't yet experienced the crashing waves and the high winds. They would learn.

Theb came up to Rogi, carrying the pouch with the crystal hidden inside. "How are we supposed to use the crystal to find our way?"

"The crystal will enable us to hear Ran-dahl, and she will direct us," Rogi said, hoping he was right. The others still saw him as the one with the answers because he was—or had been—a wizard. The truth was, he had little more understanding of what was happening than they did. But it made them feel better to think he knew more.

He felt the lurch as the tide finally rose high enough to lift the boat off the soft sands of the beach. They floated free, and Rogi's heart leapt in his chest. There was no turning back. He was heading for the Tree, and away from Alitheia.

Rogi steered the ship out from the protected waters of Tuland's bay. They now needed a direction. He called them all together and had them open their minds, and they reached into the crystal for guidance. Nothing happened. Rogi tried himself to reach out to Ran-dahl, but all he encountered was emptiness.

"I thought you said the crystal would lead us," Theb said.

"It will," Rogi replied, but wasn't sure this was true. He thought of just selecting a direction but knew that would be pointless.

He rose to stretch his legs and the others followed. All except Pom—she sat with her eyes closed, unmoving. Rogi was about to reach out to her, to let her know it was okay to stop trying and they would attempt this another time, when the crystal began to glow. Then it quickly went back to its ordinary appearance. Rogi's mind connected to Pom's, and he knew which way to go.

CHAPTER 44

AS THE DAYS PASSED, ROGI drilled the others in the ship's operations. What they'd found easy on land became more difficult in the tossing boat. The rolling motion made Tiox sick, and he spent much of the day below deck until the medicine Rogi gave him took effect.

For the first ten days the weather was similar to what they had experienced as they left Tuland, only the waves were bigger and rocked the boat more. But on the tenth day of the journey, Rogi saw what he had feared—the first test for the crew. Storm clouds appeared in the distance, heading right for them. The wind picked up, and he told the others to go below and secure whatever was not already tied down. Once that had been done, Rogi closed the hatches and sealed them in against the water. He took his position at the front of the ship and opened a portal covered in crystal that would allow him to see the approaching waves and steer the ship, yet keep the water out.

When the first wave struck, Rogi managed to steer into it, but still the front of the boat went almost vertical until it came crashing back down.

He looked at the others. This was their first real experience with what the seas could do. Pom had rolled to the stern of the ship and fallen onto Theb. Rogi had looped his arm through a strap and had stayed at his post.

"You had best tie yourselves in." Rogi indicated the straps secured to the hull. "This is going to get worse for a while."

While the ship sat momentarily still, the others hurried to secure themselves so that when the next wave hit, nobody was thrown back.

The storm lasted three days and ended with only minor bruises.

"Is this what we can expect for the entire trip?" Tiox asked.

"That was a relatively minor storm," Rogi answered. "I told you the waters were rough."

That was a lot more than rough," Theb complained. "Do you think the ship will hold up to the beating?"

"It will have to," Rogi replied. But he wasn't sure if it could. "Until the next storm hits, you might want to get some air on deck."

Rogi climbed the short ladder and threw open the hatch. Some of the railing had broken and the mast was gone. They would have to rely on the white crystal. The ship rocked from side to side as they cleared up the damage on the deck.

Far from being a clear day, more storm clouds loomed on the horizon. Flashes of lightning came down from the clouds. When the storm got to them, that same lightning could hit their ship and cause all sorts of damage.

Theb looked around at the ocean and at the cloudy sky. "Where are we?"

"I can't tell unless we get a clear day to see the sun or a clear night to read the stars. At least we're far enough from land that we don't have to worry about running aground."

But how do we know we're headed in the right direction?"

Rogi shook his head. "Right now, we don't. But we should try to connect again with the crystal."

They all went below deck, and Theb unwrapped his crystal. It was in its dormant phase and appeared as a rock. "I don't think this is going to do us much good," he said to Rogi.

"We'll see."

When they all were safely stowed below deck, Rogi held Theb's crystal. Pom came over and touched the crystal, and it glowed briefly.

"I believe the crystal only responds to your song," Rogi said to Pom. "We need you to guide us."

Pom nodded and sat with the crystal in her lap. The ship began to sway gently as she pulled the others into her song. The storm reached them and the rocking became more severe. As they grabbed ahold of the straps, Pom connected their minds, their strength adding to hers. Lefi was the last to join.

Through Pom, Rogi felt the crystal glowing. He followed Pom's song as the ship lurched in the storm. Their minds flew across the waters to the small island that held Ran-dahl.

They are coming for me. You must hurry, Ran-dahl said.

The ship lurched again, and a wave of water washed over Rogi. He lost his connection and looked up to see a hole the size of two fists opened in the side of the ship. Water was pouring in. Rogi reached out to the others for help, and slowly they realized what was happening.

We must plug the hole. The sound of the storm made it necessary to communicate mind to mind. The water was up to his ankles and rising. Rogi trudged to the stern of the ship and managed to open one of the covered boxes. In it were watertight cloth they could use temporarily to patch the hole. Tiox had made his way to the leak and put his massive hands over it to slow the flood.

Rogi rushed over with the cloth, and Theb picked up a covered bucket with a sticky tar and a brush. The shipped lurched again, and Theb fell into the rising water. Rogi grabbed the bucket from his outstretched hands and painted around the hole as another wave of water drove its way in. Then he covered the hole with the cloth and held it in place until the seal was strong enough. He could relax, at least for a moment. The boat rolled and seemed to ride lower with the excess water, but the pumps would take care of that—assuming there were no more leaks.

Rogi looked around to inspect the damage and saw Pom still seated, her eyes closed, holding the now-glowing crystal.

She opened her eyes. "We are off course," she said. "What happened?"

CHAPTER 45

RUVBAIN SAT ALONE IN HIS rooms. K'ren and Nipio since had disappeared, and Ruvbain hoped they were safe from Vanqa.

He wanted his country back. He had done what was needed. He'd gone against the Valki Institute, he'd embraced religion. But it still was not enough. Vanqa was a true believer and, therefore, dangerous. He had to get rid of her.

All of his allies had been replaced, except for his brother, Trastevere, and cousin, Agata, but they were being closely watched. He needed to get word to them, to rally those who were still faithful to him. Ruvbain had one advantage—he knew the maze of secret corridors in the castle and could sneak out without being seen. He would wait until it was dark and enter Trastevere's rooms. Together, he and his brother would formulate a plan.

When it was dark, Ruvbain took a small crystal from his bedside table and uncovered it. It gave off a warm golden glow. He went to the tall bookshelf in the corner of the room and gently pushed one of the books, and the bookshelf quietly swung open. Ruvbain walked through and turned a knob on the interior wall, and the opening closed behind him. He held the crystal to guide him through the maze. Inside the hidden corridors he felt safe; the damp, musty smell reminded him of his childhood. He even thought of staying there to protect himself from Vanqa. But she would eventually find him. He didn't know why or how, but she was good at discovering secrets.

He reached his brother's room and touched the hidden knob. Slowly, cautiously, Ruvbain opened the door and peeked through. His brother was alone, lying in his bed. Ruvbain walked silently toward him and, placing his hand over his brother's mouth, gently shook him until he woke with a start. Once Trastevere had recognized him and calmed down, Ruvbain removed his hand and stepped back.

Trastevere jumped out of bed and looked around furtively to see if there was anyone else in the room. "What are you doing here?"

"We need to talk. We need a plan."

"A plan for what?" Trastevere asked.

"To retake Ognita from Vanqa."

Trastevere gazed silently at his brother. Then he said, "Why would we do that?"

Ruvbain stared at the man standing in front of him. This couldn't be his brother. His brother wouldn't ask such a question.

"Are you following her now?"

Trastevere looked down. "You have to understand."

"Understand what? That you are complicit in the downfall of Ognita? That you no longer care about the truth?"

To his surprise, his brother laughed. "That's rich, coming from you. You turned on the Valki Institute. You turned your back on the truth a long time ago."

"That was different," Ruvbain replied, but he knew it wasn't. "If I hadn't done that, the fog would have panicked the entire country. Once we learn how to turn back the fog, we can let learning start again."

"And what makes you think you'll be able to turn it back?"

Ruvbain had no answer to that.

His brother went on, "We have to start thinking about living with the fog. Once it encroaches on Ognita, what will we do? You have no answer to this—but Vanqa does."

"What's her answer?"

"To pray."

"That's it? We just pray? And if we do that, what's supposed to happen?"

Trastevere shook his head. "What will happen if we don't pray?"

"You haven't fallen for this, have you?"

"I am Lord Vanqa's minister now. I must believe this."

"So that's what happened. You were given power in exchange for loyalty."

"It's not like that. When you're with her, she makes you see what can be done with prayer."

"So you are a true believer, then?"

His brother nodded.

"What of cousin Agata?"

"He is my deputy."

Ruvbain shook his head. "Then I'm alone."

Trastevere didn't respond.

"Will you turn me in?"

Trastevere sighed and shook his head. "Not this time."

"I guess I should thank you."

"But next time I'll have no choice."

Ruvbain went back to the secret entrance and then turned back to his brother. "There is always a choice."

When he made it back to his own rooms, Ruvbain was shaking. He wasn't sure if it was from anger or fear. His own brother had turned on him. His wife and son were gone. He had nowhere to go now. He needed a way forward. He could reach out to any of the Valki Institute scientists who were left and plead with them to take him back, but he doubted that would work. He might try reaching out to Ran-dahl, but she wouldn't trust him either. His only hope was to be accepted by Vanqa.

Ruvbain couldn't sleep that night—he kept thinking of a strategy to approach Vanqa. Did she still need him, or had she already wrested enough control to make him useless?

The next morning he dressed in his most majestic clothes, hoping to impress Vanqa. He arrived early for an audience, but he was made to wait until well after lunchtime. By then he was worried she was done with him. When he finally entered the large throne room—his throne room—he was surprised to see that she was sitting at the elevated dais but not on his throne. This was his opportunity. He would have an audience with Vanqa, but he would be king and she the supplicant. He started toward the throne, but as he neared it, Vanqa rose and blocked his way, a slight smile on her face.

"I'm glad you came to see me." She offered Ruvbain a plain wooden chair on the floor, lower than hers.

Ruvbain didn't know how to react. Should he bow to her? What should he call her? He knew she had taken the title of "lord," but he couldn't call her "my lord"—he was still the king and superior to her.

"Lord Vanqa"—he finally settled on the title—"I wish to be of service to you."

"Your brother suggested you might."

So his brother wasn't as discreet as he had claimed. "He speaks the truth. He has made me see the error of my resistance."

"There is only one thing I need from you." Vanqa rose and stared down at him.

"Anything," he responded.

"I want you to abdicate."

Now Ruvbain rose. "But that makes no sense. My son is just a child. He can't rule." What was she after? Did she want to become regent until Nipio was old enough to rule?

"Your son will not take over. When you abdicate, you will designate me as the new ruler."

"No!" came automatically from Ruvbain's lips. He regretted it immediately. "I mean, that's not how it's done. The title gets passed down from parent to child. The people won't accept this." He couldn't do what Vanqa demanded. Once he'd made her queen, there would be no reason for her to keep him around. He would be signing his own death warrant.

"Let me worry about the people," she spat back, and turned and strode from the room.

CHAPTER 46

LEFI HATED THE CLOSED DAMPNESS of the ship. It reminded him of his time as a Saeren, when his world had been dark and he'd been trapped in his own mind. Going up on deck—during the brief periods when there wasn't a storm—helped. That, and their meditation sessions. Rogi helped him calm his mind.

Theb's crystal started to get brighter. Rogi marked off the forty-fifth day at sea. None of them knew how much longer they would be.

The weather had been good for the last three days, if you considered damp and overcast good. Rogi had been able to see some stars and check their position. He also took soundings of the water to judge its depth and temperature.

"We need to be careful," he told them after his latest testing. "The waters are warming up."

"What does that mean?" Pom asked.

"It means we're getting closer to land, but it also increases the risk of whirlpools."

"Is there a way to avoid them?" Tiox stared ahead, as if trying to see the troubles to come.

"No. We will have to ride through them. It will be rough going, but the ship has been able to handle things so far." Rogi paused.

"What else?" Theb asked.

"The kraka," Rogi replied.

"What are kraka?" Theb asked.

"Large ocean creatures with tentacles that have been known to break ships in two."

Lefi listened to all the dangers Rogi detailed. What would it be like to drown? he wondered. He took a deep breath and thought of water rushing into his lungs. How much different would that feel from air? He almost welcomed the sensation.

"We still have some time until the next storm hits, if anyone wants to go on deck."

They all nodded and made their way topside. Lefi breathed in the dampness and felt the hazy sun shining on his face. The air was cold, but he welcomed it. He looked out at the waters and saw the white tops of waves getting larger and the sky darkening in the distance. He had become all too familiar with the signs of the next storm and was getting better at gauging when they would come. They had nothing to fear from the oncoming storm for a while.

As the evening fell, the haze turned from gray to black. They sat on the deck and joined their minds as the wind rose. This was the hardest part of the day for Lefi. Could he learn to trust again? Could he allow the others to see into the darkness that made up his thoughts?

Rogi opened his mind and gathered the others. First Pom joined and then Theb. Tiox was next. Reluctantly Lefi let down his guard, and Rogi gently joined him with the others. Once together, they reached out toward Ran-dahl. It was getting harder—something was blocking them. Rogi reached back, looking for Alitheia, but she was too far away. Rogi led them to push harder into the barrier. They followed Pom's song and were finally able to break through. Ran-dahl greeted them.

You need to hurry, she implored. *What you felt was from Vanqa. She wants to stop you.*

I believe we are near, Rogi replied. *But we still need to get past the whirlpools and the mating grounds for the falan.*

Impatience emanated from Ran-dahl. *There will be others to guide you once you get closer.*

Water lapped onto the deck and broke their concentration. Rogi looked out at the seas once again. "We need to get below deck. The storm is about to hit."

Reluctantly, they followed Rogi and prepared for another storm, getting cloths ready to patch any holes. After Lefi, the last to follow, made it down into the cabin, Rogi closed the hatch, sealing them in from the storm, and they clung tightly to their straps.

The waves swelled and the ship began to rock from side to side. Lefi closed his eyes and let the motion relax his mind. Slowly his thoughts went out toward Ran-dahl, but she wasn't there. Instead he felt another presence. He knew it didn't sense him, but it sent a chill up his back; his hands became icy and his breath short. It felt like Malzus, but it couldn't be—Malzus was back in Bracat.

The ship lurched, but Lefi held the connection. The presence became aware of him and tried to enter his mind. The pain in Lefi's head grew. He couldn't let this happen, not again—he wouldn't survive another intrusion. He fought back and let out a silent yell, a plea for help. The ship rocked side to side again, and then the stern of the ship lifted and crashed back down. He heard yelling as icy water flowed past him. He pushed harder and freed his mind. Cold water splashed his face and he opened his eyes.

The others were rushing to different parts of the ship, trying to cover leaks in the hull. He needed to help. His mind cleared, and he grabbed the cloth and tar and ran to the largest breach. As Tiox covered the hole with a cloth, Lefi reached into the tar with his hand to seal it shut. They went on to the next hole and kept going until all the holes were sealed. The water began to recede as the internal pumps cleared the water.

Lefi was exhausted and collapsed into the pool of water. When he woke, Rogi was standing over him.

"What did you see?" he asked.

"I saw evil," Lefi replied.

"That must have been the one Ran-dahl called Vanqa," Theb said.

"I suggest we all try to get some more rest now. I think the storms are over for us, but we will face other challenges soon. Not to mention confronting Vanqa."

The next few days were calm, and they were able to go on deck to recover. There was even a bit of sun that shone through the clouds from time to time. Lefi enjoyed the warmth of the rays on his skin. It reminded him of summertime in Adular, before Malzus had ruined it all. They had skipped their evening sessions of linking their minds. Lefi, still raw from the link with Vanqa, was glad of this. He noticed Rogi standing at the helm of the ship and staring out over the waters.

"What are you looking for?" Lefi asked.

"Maybe nothing," Rogi replied.

"But maybe something?" Lefi asked.

Rogi nodded. "The falan or the whirlpools."

"Which would be worse?"

Rogi shook his head.

With five more days gone and no further storms, Lefi was surprised when Rogi suddenly yelled, "Everyone below deck, *now*!"

No one argued. When they were all down and secured, Rogi went to the stern of the ship and stared out his viewport.

"We're approaching the whirlpools," he explained. "Nobody speak to me until this is over. It will be some delicate maneuvering before we are free."

They all held on tight as the ship began to rock side to side. The motion was less severe than the violent movements of the storms, and Lefi and the others began to relax—all except Rogi, who stared intently forward. The slow rocking motion quickened and intensified, flinging them left to right, over and over. Then, suddenly, the ship turned fully around. Rogi fought with the controls, but the ship kept spinning, slowly at first, then more quickly.

Holding tightly to his straps, Lefi managed to look over at the others. They all were perfectly still, but he could tell they were frightened. He reached out his mind, something he had been loath to do. Pom was the first to join him, and then Theb and Tiox. They found strength in their union.

Rogi was still struggling to control the ship. Now the bow of the ship was pointing down and they were under the waterline. The wooden planks creaked as more pressure pushed against the sides. Sweat broke out on Rogi's brow as he seemed to lose control of the ship. Even though they had been instructed not to interfere, Lefi reached out his mind. He felt Rogi's panic—something none of them had expected. The three of them broke through to the wizard and Rogi's panic was pushed back, his hands moving more assuredly over the controls. The spinning stopped and the ship crested the water. The creaking went silent. The ship still spun from side to side, but now Rogi seemed in control. Finally, the lurching ceased, and Rogi slumped by the controls.

"We're free." He sighed. "You can go up on deck and see what we just went through."

Slowly, they unwound from their supports and made their way on deck, all except Rogi, who stayed behind. Lefi was the first on deck. He turned to the aft of the ship and saw the swirling waters and the downward funnel that stretched as far as he could see. What a masterful job Rogi had done! He had steered them between the funnels—given how tightly spaced they were, that had been no easy feat. As the others came on deck, they also recognized Rogi's skill. They slumped down over the railing and just stared behind them.

When they went below deck, they found Rogi still slumped over his controls. They gently lifted him and laid him down. The day wore on and the ship sailed smoothly as Rogi slept. The others took turns looking out the portal and making sure they stayed on course. When it was Lefi's turn, he thought he saw a dark shape pass in front. Then there was a loud crash into their side. The impact echoed, and Rogi sat up with a start.

"How could you let me sleep!" he yelled, and dashed back to the controls. "A kraka!" He started to steer the ship away from the creatures. They felt another bump, but gentler this time. Rogi stared ahead, then closed his eyes and reached out.

He gave a sigh. "It is just a falan. You might want to go on deck and see them."

"But they attacked us," Theb protested.

Rogi shook his head. "They were just saying hello. They were just trying to get our attention."

"They certainly got mine," Pom said.

"They think we're one of them. Go on up and look."

Lefi emerged on deck and heard waves breaking and loud splashes. When his eyes adjusted to the bright sunshine, he looked out to see more than twenty giant creatures, the smaller ones the size of their ship and the larger two to three times its length. They breached the waters with giant spouts of water emanating from the holes on their backs. Two of these giants swam over to the ship and softly nudged it. Lefi reached out to them and felt the gentleness of these great animals. Then the two let out a huge stream of water, soaking them all, before diving under the surface.

Rogi joined them on the deck. "They are amazing, aren't they?"

They all nodded, unable to find words to respond.

"We were lucky to find them," Rogi went on. "They tend to scare away the kraka."

Theb asked, "Will we see them at some point?"

"I hope not. I'm going to follow the falan as far as I can toward Ran-dahl. By then, the waters will be too shallow for the kraka and we should be safe."

Lefi was pleased that they would be escorted by these gentle, giant creatures. He sat on the deck, his back to the unused mast, and breathed in the mustiness of the falan.

CHAPTER 47

IT IS TIME TO GO. Ran-dahl reached out to K'ren. *They will be here soon.*

I'm on the ship, K'ren replied. *Captain Naftis doesn't seem that eager to go.*

Convince him. If he doesn't set sail soon, Vanqa will come and arrest him.

I will try, K'ren replied. And the connection with Ran-dahl was broken.

K'ren looked over to Eot. "It begins now. We go to Ran-dahl." She stood and banged her head on the low ceiling and let out a muffled yell. "I'll never get used to this," she said.

She made her way to the deck, looking around carefully to make sure none of Vanqa's soldiers were around. "Captain," K'ren called in a hushed voice. "Captain Naftis."

"Get below!" he ordered.

K'ren nodded but motioned for him to follow. When they were all safely below, she said, "It is time. Ran-dahl has called us."

Naftis sighed. "We must wait for the tide" was his only reply, and he started stowing whatever couldn't be battened down.

The tide came in as the sun was setting. Naftis went below and told K'ren and Eot to be prepared for a rough journey. When the boat had passed outside the harbor and the risk of being spotted by Vanqa's followers was gone, the two emerged from below.

Eot took in a deep breath. "It's nice to be out."

"Enjoy it now," K'ren responded. "The waters will start to get rough pretty soon."

"We need to reach out to Ran-dahl. She said others were coming to help," Eot said.

The two sat at the stern of the ship, where it was smoother. K'ren breathed in the salty air and opened her mind, and Eot joined her. As their thoughts connected, K'ren felt Eot's relief at being out and able to do something to help. Together they reached out toward Ran-dahl.

K'ren felt the interference—as she had feared, Vanqa was trying to intercept their thoughts. As they tried to push through—Eot, the stronger of the two, taking the lead—an icy wind washed over them. K'ren wasn't sure if the chill was from the waters or from Vanqa. Eot was struggling, and K'ren tried to lend her strength. Together they made some progress; the chill lessened and the resistance faded away. Eot slumped against the side of the ship and let out a deep sigh. K'ren fought to keep their connection.

The fog is almost here, Ran-dahl communicated to K'ren. *The others are near. You must find them and guide them— make sure they arrive here safely. We need the crystal before the fog reaches here.*

Eot was puzzled. *What crystal?*

A crystal that exists both in our world and in alternative worlds. It can guide us into the fog.

I don't understand, Eot replied.

You do not need to. You just need to guide them.

We will, K'ren promised.

Ran-dahl sent them a vision of where the other ship was. They were about to enter the swirling waters. If they could navigate that successfully, Eot and K'ren could guide them to the shore of Ran-dahl's island.

We need to hurry. Vanqa is mobilizing her followers. I will not be able to break her barriers after this. You must succeed. Those were Ran-dahl's last words before the connection broke.

K'ren went on deck to inform Captain Naftis of their plans. He wasn't happy to be going into the rough seas, but, K'ren realized, he was never happy.

After three days of relatively mild seas, the water became choppier. Naftis ordered Eot and K'ren below, so only Naftis and the two crew remained on deck. The ship began rocking from side to side as they entered the currents that caused the churning waters. Water leaked through any small space between the timbers of the boat and started accumulating. The one lone pump worked hard to keep the water from rising. As the day passed, the rocking became worse and the bow rose and came crashing down. The timbers creaked but held strong. K'ren was worried for the sailors on deck but had to hope they knew what they were doing. Eot sat in the corner, the swaying and the lurching of the ship making her sick. K'ren reached out her mind to try to calm Eot, with limited success.

As one large wave lifted the ship up high and sent it crashing back down, one of the timbers in the stern cracked and water started gushing in. K'ren leapt up, grabbed the patches, and laid one over the impacted area. It held, but water still leaked in. She knew the patch would not last long.

Another day, and the more severe waves stopped. Naftis opened the hatch and let fresh air in. He and one of the sailors came down to inspect the damage. K'ren and Eot went on deck, but the other sailor was not there. They went below again, where Naftis was repairing the hole in the planking. When he looked up, there were tears in his eyes.

"You should look out to port," Naftis said as he worked. "I think you'll find what you were looking for."

Eot and K'ren scrambled back on deck and peered off to the port side. In the dim light they could make out a ship, three times the size of their small craft. It seemed to glow in the grayness of the day.

K'ren closed her eyes, and she and Eot joined minds. They reached out.

We have found you! came the reply from the other ship.

CHAPTER 48

"THERE'S A SHIP!" THEB YELLED as he stared into the murkiness.

The others stared ahead, too, and then looked at Rogi.

"Is it a friend?" Tiox asked.

"I think so."

Theb wasn't convinced. "Is there any way to tell?"

"We could reach out to them," Pom said.

Rogi nodded, and they all sat on the deck and joined their minds. *Who are you?* they asked.

We were sent by Ran-dahl to make sure you arrive safely came the reply, from someone called K'ren.

It took half the day for the two ships to reach each other. When they did, the ones called K'ren and Eot transferred over to the *Elpida*.

Once they were safely aboard, K'ren said, "We are being followed."

"We felt a coldness the last time we reached out to Randahl," Rogi replied.

Eot nodded. "It's Vanqa. She wants to stop us."

Captain Naftis came aboard and spoke with Rogi. Then he turned to K'ren. "I'm heading back. I wish you luck."

"Thank you, Captain. It was a brave thing you did," K'ren replied.

"Make it count," he said, and returned to his ship.

"Naftis gave me the information I need to navigate to the island," Rogi announced.

Once they were below deck, Theb said to K'ren and Eot, "I can show you the crystal, if you want."

They both nodded. Theb took out the box and felt a warmth emanating from it. Gently, he removed the crystal and unwrapped it. As the covering fell away, the beauty of the gem revealed itself. It let off a warming, golden light.

"It's never done that before," Theb admitted.

"It's beautiful!" Eot put her hands on the stone and closed her eyes. "I can feel its power."

Theb looked at Tiox. "I told you it was special."

Tiox smiled. "You were right, as usual."

"Waters are going to get rough soon," Rogi warned, "so everyone hold on."

Theb showed Eot and K'ren where the straps were, and they all grabbed tightly in preparation.

"I hate this," Eot said. "If I never see the water again, it will be too soon."

Theb couldn't argue with that. Still, he thought, it had been quite a trip, and he was glad to be here.

Rogi guided the ship toward Ran-dahl. Soon the water became choppy and larger swells tossed them from side to side. Eot lost her grip and was flung to the stern. Theb crawled toward her, grabbed her around the waist, and held on tight. Blood dripped from her forehead and she seemed disoriented.

"You'll be alright," Theb whispered, hoping he was right.

The swells died down, and K'ren, managing to keep her footing, came over to examine Eot. "She'll be okay." She retrieved some bandages and cleaned up the cut on Eot's head. "She might be a bit wobbly from the bump. Can you look after her?"

Theb nodded, looking relieved.

Rogi and K'ren opened the port leading to the deck, and a rush of fresh, cool air came in. The two went on deck and then quickly reappeared.

"We're being chased!" K'ren cried.

"Vanqa?" Eot's speech was slightly slurred.

"We are faster than they are, and we have a lead. So we will arrive at the island before them."

"There's something else." Rogi looked over at Pom.

"You might want to look for yourself." Pom went onto the deck and the others followed. The sky was gray and the water the exact same shade. Nothing was visible past that wall.

"The island is almost completely enveloped in the fog." she said.

Theb stared at the massive wall of . . . of what? He couldn't describe it. "That's the fog?"

K'ren nodded.

"And people have tried to get through it?"

"Yes," K'ren replied.

"And?" Theb felt K'ren holding back.

"And we don't know. None of them came back," Eot filled in.

Theb tried to control his panic. "So they could have made it through. They could be inside the fog."

"Or on the other side of it," Pom added.

"There is no other side. Ran-dahl has made measurements, sent in unoccupied ships with sensing equipment, with ropes to pull them back. When she pulls them back—well, they don't come back."

"So you don't know what's inside the fog," Tiox said.

K'ren shook her head and repeated, "We don't know."

"The Tree!" Theb shouted.

Just then, a wave crashed over them and water flowed into the still-open hatch. Rogi hurried them back below deck and quickly closed the hatch. He yelled, "I'm going to try to ram the ship into the island. It's going to be rough."

They all grabbed their straps and held tight as Rogi steered the ship. Waves pushed the boat from side to side, and even the bronze pulcher planks creaked under the power of the waves.

One large wave lifted the ship high and then brought it crashing down. A rock jutted out from the bow of the ship—even the strength of the bronze pulcher hadn't been enough to protect them. Water gushed in.

"Abandon ship!" Rogi yelled. He opened the hatch and helped each one up the ladder.

Theb grabbed his stone and followed Pom up. A wave washed over the deck and blinded him. When his vision cleared, he saw the ship was embedded on the rocks that led to the shore. Rogi had destroyed the ship—but he'd gotten them to where they needed to be.

Theb felt the strong hands of Tiox directing him toward the island. They climbed up the boulders that lay along the coast. Theb slipped, struggling to hold onto the crystal, and Tiox caught him.

There was one more rock to climb before they reached the shore. When they got to the top, Theb looked out. "The other ships are almost here!"

"Move faster," K'ren called.

Tiox had gone ahead, carrying Eot. "Over there!" he yelled, and pointed at a small figure on the shore.

"That's Ran-dahl," shouted K'ren. "She's come out to meet us."

CHAPTER 49

A WAVE SPLASHED OVER RAN-DAHL as she helped K'ren onto the shore. Eot was deposited by the one she knew as Tiox. She concentrated on the one carrying the crystal—Theb.

It was hard to speak over the sound of the crashing waves, so Ran-dahl reached out with her mind. *Vanqa is close. Bring the crystal,* she said to Theb.

Theb ran up to Ran-dahl and handed his treasure to her.

Ran-dahl clambered up the slope and found a spot where the waves couldn't reach them.

Please, sit, she said, and they all gathered in a circle.

Theb looked at the grayness that was closing in on them. "Is that the fog?" he asked.

Ran-dahl nodded. *We don't have much time. Vanqa is on the island and the fog is closing in quickly.*

When they were ready, Ran-dahl gently joined their minds. She first drew power from Eot and K'ren. Then she reached out to Rogi and Tiox. Ran-dahl felt a chill—the fog almost upon their circle. She heard footsteps running up the hill. Theb's mind was joined to theirs, but still the fog encroached. Pom and Lefi joined the circle, and Ran-dahl tried to push back the fog, but it kept coming. Then Vanqa appeared and yelled orders to her soldiers. There was nothing more Ran-dahl could do. She had failed.

Then a song, purer than she had ever heard before, joined them. She recognized the song, but before it had been far away. Now, so close, she was struck by its beauty. A warmth spread out from the crystal as Pom joined them. It glowed with a brilliant golden light, providing a haven from the grayness of the fog that enveloped them.

Ran-dahl led the others toward the fog. Shapes appeared out of the grayness, but they were insubstantial and quickly dissolved. Rogi tried to help her give the shapes more substance, but none of them lasted. Vanqa and her soldiers were getting closer. There was only one way to escape—into the fog.

Ran-dahl tried again to create something substantial from the fog. She understood what had happened to the others who had entered. They had all been absorbed by the fog—they had all become part of the grayness. She wouldn't let this happen to them. The fog had to be conquered. She sent her song out into the fog again, and the others joined. They pushed it back temporarily, but to avoid Vanqa, they needed to go into the fog.

The song joined them again—not strong, but pure—and the crystal began to glow even stronger than before. The song grew as it drew strength from the crystal. The crystal brightened, the fog ebbed. Shapes formed and didn't dissolve. Then the fog was gone, and so was Vanqa.

Ran-dahl rose and looked at Pom. *You have brought us to the other side of the fog.*

They all rose from their circle and took in their surroundings. The landscape was barren, but it didn't go away.

"Did you see that?" Eot pointed.

Ran-dahl looked but saw nothing.

"Over there!" Eot called again. "It's gone."

"How could something hide out there?" Tiox asked. "There's nothing there."

"It's as if it was there and then vanished. I don't understand."

"This is all very strange," Theb commented, and picked up his crystal.

"You think the Golden Tree is out there?" Rogi asked.

"I do," Ran-dahl replied.

"Over there!" Eot called again.

This time they all saw it. A tree. Its bark was dark, almost as if it had been burned, and it had no leaves. It was silhouetted against the sky.

"Where do we go from here?" Eot asked.

"Toward the tree," Ran-dahl replied.

They walked toward the silhouetted tree, but it didn't appear to get any closer.

"Stop," Ran-dahl said. "We are approaching this the wrong way. We are treating this like we would if we were on the other side of the fog." Then, finally realizing, she added, "We need the crystal."

Theb, placed the crystal down, and the eight gathered in a circle once again.

"Pom," Ran-dahl said, "you must lead us."

"Why me?" she asked.

"The crystal responds to your song."

Pom shook her head but said, "I'll try."

She started linking the others' minds. As they followed her song, the grayness began to fade. Leaves budded on the tree, and more trees appeared. The first were bronze; then trees with silver bark appeared. The light and warmth from the Silver Forest gave them all strength. It was the most beautiful sight any of them had seen. There was a hum in the air, as if the trees were transferring their power to the burnt tree. The charcoal bark began to shine and give off a golden light.

Ran-dahl opened her eyes to take in the wonders. She rose and started toward the Golden Tree. But when the others followed, the forest disappeared. The silver trees were gone, the bronze trees were gone. Only the one scraggly tree was left.

"It felt so real." Theb let out a sigh.

"It was real," Ran-dahl replied. "It *is* real," she corrected.

CHAPTER 50

ROGI'S HEART RACED. HE HAD seen the Silver Forest and the Golden Tree. The Golden Pulcher had been there, and then . . . it was gone. How could that be? Could the gods be so cruel as to let him see what he couldn't have? This land was so strange. It had nothing to do with the Koan or Talum.

He thought back to what Alitheia had said: The Golden Pulcher would be nothing like he expected. She was right. This strange place was not what he'd expected.

"Let's keep walking." Ran-dahl's voice echoed in the emptiness.

"We'll never get there." Theb's frustration was evident.

Rogi studied the others. Tiox walked slowly ahead, constantly looking around. K'ren and Eot followed close to Ran-dahl. Pom and Theb walked together, staring into the emptiness.

Lefi walked alone, staring straight ahead at the lone tree.

Rogi went up to him. "There is nothing here."

Lefi shook his head. "What we saw was real. I know it."

"How could you know that? Look around you."

"I can feel something. For the first time since . . ." He paused. "For the first time in a long time, I feel at peace."

Rogi kept thinking of the teachings of the Koan and the Talum. It was the Talum that focused on finding the Tree. The Koan gave lessons on how to behave in society. Over the years the wizards had equated the two—to find the Tree, to obtain enlightenment, you needed to bring harmony. That's what the wizards thought, that's what drove them. But what if that wasn't true? What if there was no need for the Tree?

He stopped as the others walked on. To find the Golden Tree was not the path he needed. He was not like Asmar, who could use the power of the Tree to connect the minds of people and get them to see things differently.

Ran-dahl came back to Rogi. "What's wrong?"

"I'm not going with you. If I stay with you, the Golden Tree will never reveal itself."

"But you came all this way to find it."

Rogi shook his head. "I came all this way to find enlightenment—and I have. For me, that was not the Tree."

Are you sure? Ran-dahl touched him mind to mind.

You know I'm right, Rogi replied.

Ran-dahl placed her hands on his shoulders and nodded.

"I'm going to stay with Rogi," Tiox said. "I've known for a while that I'll never find the Tree. I'm not ready for that. I still have other things to do."

Theb walked up to Ran-dahl. "I'm glad we were able to rescue you from your island and help clear the fog, but this is as far as I can go as well." He reached into his pack and pulled out the crystal. "This is yours. It always has been." He gently handed the wrapped package to Ran-dahl and went to stand by Tiox.

Eot and K'ren opened their minds to all of the travelers. *We will also stay behind. Eot will restart the Valki Institute, with my help, and I will take over from my husband and banish Vanqa.* She paused. *And I will see Nipio again.*

Lefi looked at Tiox and then Rogi. *I will go with Ran-dahl. It is the only place I can find peace.*

They all turned to Pom. It had been her song that had brought them through the fog.

"I . . ." She put her hands to her head. "I can . . ." she tried again, and sunk to her knees.

Rogi rushed over to her. He sensed another presence, a familiar one, and reached out to Pom. *Join with my mind. I can help.* As Pom desperately tried to open her mind to him, he found a gap and entered. He felt the coldness of Malzus.

You must go with them to the Tree, Malzus commanded Pom.

I can't. You will destroy it, Pom pushed back.

Leave her be. Rogi joined his mind with Pom.

You can't stop me. Malzus tried to push Rogi away.

No! Rogi fought back. He didn't know if he was strong enough, but he had to try.

<hr>

Pom reached out again and tried to soothe Malzus with her song, but it didn't work. They were losing. Malzus was trying to take over Pom's mind and, through her, be delivered to the Golden Tree.

Suddenly, a burst of swirling golden light broke through. Malzus let out a scream, trying desperately to keep a hold on Pom. His grip slipped away, but he fought back and regained control.

Another voice entered the fight. *You promised to look after her.* There was a softness to the touch—Alitheia.

But I'm so close, Malzus replied.

You said you cared about others.

But . . . The intrusion slipped away. Malzus had let go.

CHAPTER 51

RAN-DAHL AND LEFI WALKED TOWARD the Tree. Ran-dhal reached out to Pom. *You can join us.*

I know, Pom answered. *But I will stay here. There are things I still need to do, people I can help with my song.*

The others sat and watched, their minds reaching out to their two friends. The bronze trees started to reappear, and then the silver. Rogi closed, then opened his eyes. This time, the Silver Forest remained.

It's real, he communicated to the others as they also stared ahead.

But if we try to follow them, it will disappear, Eot said. *We were not meant to find the Tree.*

We each have other things to do, Pom replied.

As Lefi and Ran-dahl went into the forest, the others continued to watch them, letting their minds follow.

They walked through the silver trees, expecting to see the Golden Pulcher, but it was nowhere.

Suddenly, Ran-dahl and Lefi stopped at the burned-out, skeletal tree that had first appeared to them. Ran-dahl took the crystal from its wrapping and reverently placed it in a niche at the base of the tree. Then both she and Lefi laid their hands on the darkened trunk, and the tree began to grow and change, from the shadow it once had been into the Golden Pulcher.

Their minds raced through the fog and expanded to Vanqa's soldiers and then beyond. Minds throughout Ognita were connected—it was the Moment once again. The scientists of the Valki Institute, the ones who formed the Fog, came out of hiding. Ruvbain's despair dissipated.

Pom felt the song of Yau and was at peace. She didn't need to enter the Silver Forest. She wanted to get back to her friends.

Suddenly, the vision was gone and the connection broke. Only a warm afterglow remained. The six looked around to discover the Silver Forest was gone. The Golden Tree was gone. Ran-dahl and Lefi were gone.

As they stood staring into the emptiness, the wind started to blow. It grew in strength, until they had to huddle together to keep from being blown away from each other. Once anchored, K'ren felt the song the wind carried—even at its fiercest, there was a gentleness to the wind. Her mind flew with the wind toward Ognita. She saw her husband, alone in the castle. Nipio was safe in the countryside, Ntan playing with him. The other scientists from the Valki Institute reached out to her. Eot joined, as did the newcomers. They felt the connection between themselves and the people of Ognita. Some hid from this connection, but others welcomed it.

The wind blew for a full day before it died down to a gentle breeze. K'ren's mind rejoined her body. When the wind finally stopped, she looked around. The forest was gone, but so was the grayness. There was brilliant sunshine and green grass, as well as a grove of bronze pulchers.

"The fog is gone!" Eot yelled in excitement.

"The fog is gone," K'ren repeated. "Now our work begins."

They rose and started back to where they had beached the ship. K'ren had no idea how they would get off the island. She went to Rogi. "Do you know where you will go now?"

He shook his head. "I am just glad I was able to experience the Moment this time. I am happy here, for now. Neither Bracat nor my home in Insula hold anything for me anymore." He thought of the last words Alitheia had said to him. Had he been wrong not to go into the Silver Forest? But Alitheia wasn't there. Maybe he would go. But not now.

"We could use your help to put things right again."

Rogi nodded.

K'ren went over to Pom. "You could have entered the Silver Forest with Ran-dahl and Lefi."

Pom shook her head. "I'm not ready to give up my friends back home. Besides, as long as Malzus can enter my mind, the forest is not for me."

K'ren nodded and breathed in the salty air. She needed to see Nipio again.

"Over there!" Theb yelled. "There are people coming toward us."

"Vanqa," K'ren said under her breath.

"What do you want us to do?" Rogi asked.

K'ren said. "I will deal with this." She walked ahead of the others.

Vanqa was leading a troop of about a hundred soldiers, who seemed confused. K'ren realized they were looking for the fog.

K'ren strode up to Vanqa, who turned to the soldier next to her. "Arrest her!" she yelled, pointing an accusing finger at K'ren.

The soldier approached, and K'ren recognized him. "Stratios, it's good to see you."

The soldier bowed his head slightly. "And you," he replied.

"The fog is gone," K'ren went on. "There's no need to listen to that fraud anymore."

K'ren felt Vanqa reach out and try to enter the mind of Stratios.

"I saw the Tree," Stratios said, and he pushed Vanqa from his mind. "I'll no longer follow you."

Stratios turned to his soldiers and pointed to two of them. "Arrest her!"

The two soldiers grabbed Vanqa's arms and started marching her back to their ships. The Tree had freed them from Vanqa's influence—they could make their own decisions now.

Stratios turned back to K'ren and repeated, "The fog is gone."

"Vanqa has no more power over you or anyone else. She will find no one will listen to her anymore," K'ren said.

It's time you returned to the castle and saw your son again." Stratios replied.

ABOUT THE WANDERER SERIES

"Engrossing, spiritual, thought-provoking and unique."
— Patrick J. LoBrutto, World Fantasy Award–winning editor

ASMAR, A YOUNG AND NAÏVE WIZARD, is sent on an impossible quest—to stop the renegade wizard, Malzus, from finding the tree of wisdom.

The Great Council of wizards, desperate to find the Golden Pulcher tree, the source of all knowledge, sends nine wizards over the impassable seas to the faraway land of Bracat—only to face years of frustration and failure.

Until one of their own turns against them.

Armed with a golden staff to amplify his power, the rogue wizard, Malzus, flees the wizards' city of Dolcere and begins a ruthless hunt for the Tree.

Meanwhile, Asmar, a misfit who has grown up in the small, protected village of Tuland, is suddenly called to Dolcere. There, he learns that he is to become a wizard, tasked with stopping the death and destruction caused by Malzus.

The Great Council tasks Asmar with not only defeating Malzus but returning the golden staff to them. But Asmar doesn't trust the wizards and their influence over him. Can he break the cycle of violence and selfishness and determine his own destiny?

The Silver Forest is a two-book literary fantasy adventure exploring magic, morality, and self-determination. Read on for an excerpt of Book One.

CHAPTER 1

SEVENTY YEARS. SEVENTY LONG YEARS wasted, searching for the golden pulcher tree, hoping to find it and tap its knowledge, to make things right. It was so long ago that he and the other eight wizards had left Insula to come to this backward land of Bracat. The Great Council in Insula, sensing the tree was here, had sent the holy number of nine wizards to this land, but when they arrived, they found nothing.

These thoughts echoed in Malzus's mind as he left the wedding hall. He had just been married. It was the only way to save the Nine now that Vetus was so sick. If Vetus died—Malzus shook his head—*when* Vetus died, there would only be eight wizards, and that was not enough to find the golden pulcher tree, the tree of knowledge, at least according to the Koan. The children of the other wizards, the children they had before they took their vows, were back in Insula. And the wizards were so old now that, even if they were given a waiver of their celibacy vow, as they had done for him, it was doubtful they could sire a child. So it was up to him, assuming he had a boy. If not . . . well, they'd have to deal with that later.

His wife waited for him; he was excited. He wondered what sex was like, but he was also scared. Celibacy focused his mind. If he gave that up, would he be strong enough to find the tree?

This shouldn't have been needed; he shouldn't have had to make the choice. It was his father's fault. The Great Wizard Preadus! His father had failed to bring peace and prosperity to Bracat, which is what the Koan said was needed before the golden pulcher tree would reveal itself. And even after this failure they still followed him, and he followed the teachings of the long-dead wizard Heil. But Heil's teachings were so passive, just like his father. They didn't allow the wizards to use their true powers, to control the minds of others, to bring prosperity to the land and have the tree reveal itself. As a result, the wizards had accomplished nothing in the seventy years since the Great Council of Insula sent them here. Not a sign of the golden pulcher tree. He felt there had to be another way to accomplish what the Koan demanded. Malzus had searched for years, studying the books they had brought with them from Insula and those in the dungeon library of Dolcere.

Then, two years ago, he found a book. It wasn't one of the local books; his father had brought it from Insula and hidden it among the dusty shelves of the cavernous Dolcere library. Malzus recognized the name, *The Book of Shammai*. Shammai was once as great a wizard as Heil, but his teachings were banned after the First Mind War that Shammai was said to have caused. As Malzus studied Shammai's teachings, he understood why the Nine had failed so far and what was needed. Unlike Heil, Shammai advocated using the full power of the wizards to take over minds of others and use their power to bend them to one's will. If he could take over the council and use the minds of the other wizards, he would have enough power to bring about the changes needed to have the tree reveal itself. He knew what he had to do, and the key was making sure his father didn't find out.

Go to your bride. His father's voice echoed in his mind. Malzus looked up at the Great Wizard standing in front of him, holding the staff of golden pulcher. That was the key; the golden staff would give him the power he needed to take over the Nine and draw on their power. Malzus shielded this thought from his father. *The council will meet later,* his father finished.

Malzus stood frozen, staring down the hall that led to his new bedchamber. He needed to concentrate on the council meeting; that's when he would act. Until then, he needed to pretend everything was normal. Malzus sighed. There was no more delaying, and he started toward his bride. His steps echoed in the emptiness.

Malzus paused at the entrance to the room that was to be his new home. Taking a deep breath, he pushed the door open.

"I was waiting for your arrival, my . . . my husband," said his bride, Asmeera. The words sounded awkward and hesitant as she spoke them for the first time. Malzus found the sound of her voice vaguely irritating. His new wife sat alone on the thin mattress of their wedding bed that occupied the far side of the room. The bed, Malzus noted, was larger than any he had ever slept in as a wizard. Asmeera had placed flowers beside it and had also chosen a collection of small orange and yellow lamp crystals to light the room with a warming, golden glow.

Asmeera rose. She wore a silvery gown that clung to her body, revealing the curves of her form in the soft light, the gown falling away carelessly to reveal her naked shoulders, her dark skin glowing in the golden light. He wanted to go to her, he wanted to hold her and possess her . . . but he stood on the other side of the room, holding himself back.

He walked forward hesitantly and sat down on the bed next to her.

"They don't understand." He wasn't sure why he said that, why he wanted to confess his plan, his years of frustration.

She placed her hand gently on his shoulder. "There is no need to explain. Here, with me, is where you can be at peace."

Her voice was soothing and her touch was electric. He realized in that instant how much he wanted to trust someone. To trust her.

He tried to resist, but desire overtook him. Grabbing her shoulders, he pushed her hard down onto the bed. She pushed back, instinctively.

"Not like that." Her words washed over him and he stopped, his hands shaking as he sat up, not sure of what to do. Asmeera smiled and took his hands, kissing them, then placing them gently on her breasts. Malzus felt her mind reach out to him, soothing and calming him.

How could that be? She wasn't a wizard. She wasn't trained. These thoughts drifted within him as Asmeera caressed him and gently lay him down on the bed.

Slowly she directed him, and Malzus felt her passion along with his own. He felt their connection, not just in body but in their minds. The golden pulcher ring he had given her at their wedding ceremony caught the light as she kissed him. That had to be what made her so strong and connected them; their wedding rings were linked, their minds were linked. He suddenly felt hope that he would not be alone anymore.

After they made love, Asmeera put her head on his shoulder and lay next to him, gently stroking his chest. In the quiet and stillness, his mind wandered. He was jolted out of his trance. What had he done? He had been distracted. He was being weak; he couldn't let himself be taken in by this woman.

"What's wrong?" Asmeera asked, putting a calming hand on his shoulder.

"Nothing," said Malzus hastily, getting up and brushing her hand away. Standing naked at the foot of the bed, he looked down at her. Part of him wanted to get back into bed with her—to make love to her again and forget all of the plans he had made. He shook his head, trying to clear everything from his thoughts, but couldn't. Was Asmeera somehow part of his father's plan to weaken him? Was she meant to make him more compliant and forget all of his hopes? Did his father know what he was about to do?

"Please, come back to bed, Malzus," Asmeera said, reaching a hand out toward him, the covers falling from her body.

Malzus stood, frozen. He thought he had felt a connection to her. He stared back at Asmeera. He should go back to bed with her; that's what he wanted. He came to her and wrapped his arms around her. He let himself bask in her warmth, her scent. But suddenly a piercing voice disrupted his thoughts: it was his father's summons, *Come to the council.*

How could they do this to him?! He wouldn't go. He wanted to stay with his bride. But he had to go. This was his opportunity to set things right, to take control of the council. Malzus grabbed the white crystal he had been given by his father as a wedding present and put its silver chain around his neck. Then he threw on the blue robe of the wizards and grabbed his silver pulcher staff. He rushed from the room, not looking back.

Malzus entered the council room, where he took his place among the Nine. *This is a joyous day for you,* Preadus proclaimed, reaching his mind out to Malzus and the others. Each wizard held their silver pulcher staffs as they turned to look at him. His father stood at the head of the council table, his silver hair tinged gold from the light of the golden pulcher staff he held. Malzus nodded, even though the day was anything but joyous to him. He kept this thought hidden from the others.

Let's begin by joining our minds in meditation, Preadus conveyed, beginning the meeting as all council meetings began. This was what Malzus was waiting for—the chance to enter the minds of the others unhindered, to be able to draw power from them and turn them. The Nine started to reach out to each other, sensing each other's frustrations and joys. Malzus felt all of them: Rogi's embarrassment at indulging in pastries on one of his fast days, Vetus's fear of his disease, and Dragorn's insecurity at being one of the weaker wizards. He even sensed Karal and Mentaire, who always held back, not wanting to share all of their thoughts with the others. Finally, the two strongest of the wizards, Thurmore and Wellum, opened their minds to the council, holding back even more than Karal and Mentaire. When his father joined, Malzus created the appearance of sharing his inner self, but he knew his father well enough to feel the secret barriers.

Now the others were waiting for him to join and open his mind.

That's when Malzus began his attack, reaching quickly for Vetus before the others realized what was happening. He twisted into Vetus's mind and dove deep into his thoughts, stealing the wizard's strength.

Malzus moved next to Dragorn, sending an icy touch into the wizard's mind that bored deeply into his thoughts and quickly drained him of strength. Vetus and Dragorn slumped over in their chairs.

With the power of the two wizards, Malzus moved swiftly on the others. Rogi fell quickly to his assault, but Karal and Mentaire held out against his onslaught. He had expected this, so rather than trying to overcome them, Malzus filled their minds with false visions of himself holding Preadus's golden staff, the symbol of leadership over the Nine.

My father has ceded control of the Nine to me, Malzus proclaimed, confusing Mentaire first, who then quickly fell under his control. This gave Malzus another surge of power, and he used it to quickly sweep away Karal's hesitation. Things were going exactly as he had planned. Only his father, Thurmore, and Wellum eluded him. He communicated to them all:

How we've searched for the golden tree will now change. The Koan decrees we must be worthy, but the tree is still hidden. We have been judged unworthy. I will find it. I will bring prosperity to this land. I will bring peace.

Malzus felt his father's horror. Power swept out from the Great Wizard, strengthened by the golden staff. Malzus resisted his father's onslaught, bringing his hand to the crystal at his neck. Locking eyes with his father, he grasped his silver staff tightly and drew more power from the wizards he controlled. His plan was working—power was surging into him. He focused this strength on Wellum and Thurmore.

We will follow the teachings of Shammai, Malzus continued, sending them visions of the land at peace and the golden tree glowing in the moonlight. *Open your minds to me so that we can be as one, and I promise the tree will be revealed!*

Rogi and Dragorn started to let down the final barriers that protected their innermost selves, the barriers that no wizard would let another cross, which were violated during the Mind Wars so many, many generations ago. As these barriers gave way, Malzus started to push their minds farther down, sapping more of their strength. Thurmore and Wellum still resisted, while Malzus blocked another powerful attack from his father. The room pulsed with energy.

Vetus's mind stirred and the old wizard found the strength to pull his mind away. *He should not be able to do this,* Malzus thought, and he shifted his attention back to Vetus and worked to calm him with another round of energy as their minds joined. Vetus's struggles faded as Malzus pulled him further and further down into the stronghold of his own mind.

Malzus had never felt such power. He went after Thurmore with renewed determination. Next to his father, Thurmore was the strongest wizard on the council. Malzus increased his effort and felt barrier after barrier give way.

Suddenly there was a flash of gold, followed instantly by a blinding, immobilizing light. A figure appeared in his mind, surrounded by a golden halo that blocked all his thoughts and sight. Emerging from the center of that halo was his father, his blue robes radiating a brilliant incandescence. He was holding the golden staff high over his head. Immediately behind him was Wellum, who joined his strength to the Great Wizard's. Malzus's hold on Dragorn and Rogi faltered, then crumbled away. Vetus pulled away as well.

"No! No! No!" Malzus screamed, feeling energy pour out of him, draining him of power. Then everything went completely dark.

When he regained consciousness, there was a profound silence. Malzus felt a gaping emptiness; everything was black. His sight was gone, the other wizards were gone, and he was utterly alone. His mind throbbed.

He lay groaning as the light trickled back and his vision slowly returned. His father towered over him, knuckles white as he grasped the golden staff, and he stared down at Malzus, his blue eyes like ice.

Malzus tried to reach out—to his father first, and then to the others—but his father had isolated his mind. He knew there was nothing he could do. His father had won, for now.

"You have found the book of Shammai!" His father's voice sounded so odd and cold, uttered out loud in the physical space of the chamber. "You tried to take away our minds so you could use our power to find the tree and leave us as mindless"—his father froze, the words stuck in his throat—"as Saeren."

"What have you done?" Dragorn groaned aloud, grasping his head, his face wretched with shock and anguish.

"How could you?!" bellowed Rogi, rising to join the others, who were surrounding Malzus.

Malzus stood up in defiance, but his father firmly reached into Malzus's mind and smashed Malzus into his seat. His father physically slapped him across the face with a force so hard it blurred his vision. Malzus's head didn't move. He stared at his father but was met by a crushing pressure coming from Thurmore. Malzus tried pushing back, but he was too drained and empty.

"YOU—you were willing to make us all your slaves!" Thurmore's words were slow and deliberate, his voice revealing the outrage and hate he felt for Malzus. "There is only one punishment fitting for you."

Malzus knew he meant death, but this wasn't going to happen. They couldn't kill him, not if they still wanted to find the tree. They needed him to complete the Nine. They had no one to replace him, unless they used a Bracion. No, Malzus reassured himself. Only those from Insula had the ability to become a wizard.

He needed to save himself, and he knew he had only one chance. If he could get the golden staff from his father, he would have the strength to escape. "Father." Malzus's voice was quiet.

"Please," he continued out loud, being blocked from the minds of the others, "I beg you to hear me. I am at your mercy." He paused, then went on, "You are right." Malzus walked cautiously toward his father.

"I didn't realize what I was doing." When Malzus was next to his father, he reached out and put his hand on the Great Wizard's shoulder. He felt his father relax. Now was the time.

With the hand that wore the golden ring, he grabbed the golden staff. The ring and staff melded together. Malzus saw the look of horror cross his father's face. The staff connected their minds. Now it was more even; now they both drew power from the staff. Malzus pressed down into his father's thoughts and tried to draw power from him, power he could use to subdue the others. But his father pushed back, joined by Thurmore and Wellum. Malzus needed more power. He attacked Vetus once again, but the old wizard was tired and weak from his illness. Malzus felt Vetus's strength waning. That couldn't happen; he needed to draw more power from the old wizard. Malzus pressed more. Vetus was slipping away; there was nothing Malzus could do. Malzus yelled and ripped away Vetus's memories, the thoughts of the other wizards that had come before him that were buried in a wizard's consciousness.

Malzus sank to one knee and held the staff tightly; his father looked over to Vetus and it distracted him, just for a moment. Malzus wrenched the golden staff from his father. Thurmore and Dragorn knelt by Vetus as Malzus pushed passed them. Rogi tried to block his way but Malzus raised the golden staff and struck him across the head. Rogi collapsed on the cold floor of the council room, alive but in no condition to pursue him.

Malzus ran out the door and onto the streets of Dolcere. The other wizards were slow but came after him. Malzus concentrated his mind. He felt the new strength the golden staff gave him. He reached out and clouded the thoughts of the others, creating a fog in their minds that protected him. He was free.

As he ran, he felt a mind reach out to him. It couldn't be a wizard—they were hidden in the fog he had created. He tried to concentrate. The mind called him again. It was Asmeera.

Where have you gone? Please come back to me.

Malzus clutched the golden staff tightly. He opened his mind to her.

You're hurt, she began, before adding quickly, *Malzus, what have you done?*

Malzus could feel her recoiling from him.

Come with me, Malzus pleaded, reaching out. *Together we can grow stronger, and together we can rule!*

No! came Asmeera's response. Her mind was floating away from him.

Malzus couldn't let her go. He tried forcing his way into her mind, but she pushed back, resisting his intrusion. He pushed in more forcefully. The more she resisted, the angrier he became. She had to come with him. He didn't want to be alone. He needed her; he must change her mind.

Malzus remembered the white wedding crystal around his neck and touched it, feeling the rush of power. He then gripped the golden staff tighter and an immense new rush of strength flowed into him.

He broke down the barrier she had created and was now inside Asmeera's mind. There was only silence; her resistance had stopped. At first Malzus thought he had finally reached her, that she had agreed to come with him. He spoke to her, but nothing was there. His hands started to sweat, and tears rolled down his face as he searched for her. He had gone too far. Her mind was now pushed so far back and down that she wasn't there.

He had destroyed her—the only one who had truly cared about him.

Malzus let out an anguished scream and then fled as fast as he could into the darkness.

ABOUT
THE AUTHOR

JODY "J.D." RASCH is a writer, artist, social activist, and author. His debut fantasy series, The Wanderer, incorporates social issues including politics, religion, and how we are influenced in our lives.

Jody is also a painter whose art explores the mysteries of our world. He worked in finance for many years but managed to use it for good by helping banks that give loans to the poor. Jody currently serves on not-for-profit boards that seek to make the world a better place.

A native New Yorker who was forced to move to the burbs, Jody now lives just outside New York City.

Connect with Jody
Instagram | JDRasch.com

www.ingramcontent.com/pod-product-compliance
Lightning Source LLC
Chambersburg PA
CBHW061116310726
48974CB00002B/558